12 Deaths of

Christmas

Paul Sating

ISBN-13: 978-1-7322617-1-6

Cover Art By: Kessi Riliniki

To Nikki & Alex, thank you for teaching me what
unconditional love means.

Rudolph

"Oh, come on Rudy," Jennica stomped her foot. "It'll be fun."

She gripped his hand and tugged him down Fifth Avenue. He was determined to maintain his current plodding. The snow, ever-relentless, pelted his face. Rudolph tucked his chin as far into his jacket as he could, but it didn't help. Icy chunks assaulted every part of his exposed and blotchy skin.

Jennica huffed. "If you're going to pout can you at least hold the umbrella so I'm not frozen by the time we get there?"

'There' was an upscale clothing store Jennica wanted to check out. Rudolph hated the idea, but Jennica insisted. That was easy for her, she wasn't the one funding this excursion. Insistence was simple when it wasn't you who was cracking open your wallet to buy overpriced shit you didn't need. He'd heard about the store from some friends who served on the Board of Directors with him. Rumor had it that it was expensive and weird, a better fit for Portland than New York City. Rudolph let her know as much, but it was Christmas and he still hadn't bought her any gifts. In fact, he hadn't even thought about what he could get her and there were only two shopping days left. This excursion might satiate her so she wouldn't throw some damn tantrum. Again.

Work was hectic and he was behind on a couple of projects, the type he didn't want to be behind on. Projects that paid enough to afford a wife and girlfriend, he reminded himself. Shopping for exorbitant gifts wasn't a priority when a shit load of money was on the line.

"Fine," he huffed. "Let's go."

Jennica bounced on the balls of her feet, clapping. "Yay! Thank you!"

"You're welcome," he said, faking enthusiasm.

Jennica was decent enough as a girlfriend—fifteen years his younger and a spitfire in bed, doing all those things his wife refused to do. But she could also be juvenile at the best of times and idiotic at others. Jennica was a test of his temperament and a fulfillment of his fantasies all wrapped in one incredible body. But that was part of the balance, the price he paid for world-class blow jobs on weekend trips and the occasional midweek extended lunch. The types of blow jobs that made Rudolph sometimes wish he'd married Jennica instead of Rhonda. At least until she opened her mouth to do anything but suck his cock.

Jennica tugged his hand, urging him to walk faster. "You're so slow!"

"That's because I don't want to bust my ass on icy sidewalks."

"You wouldn't have to worry about tripping if you weren't drunk again," Jennica reasoned.

Fuck her. He was a grown ass man and had every right to drink when he wanted to. She wasn't going to start complaining like Rhonda did. Rhonda bitched about everything and he didn't need Jennica following that lead. It was the holidays, the time for joy and cheer, and a little booze in the middle of the day never hurt. Hell, it was expected.

Jennica danced on her feet, pulling on his sleeve. How funny would it be to see her fall on her ass?

"We're so close." Jennica skipped around slower commuters, tourists, and the random homeless person.

The store's flamboyant amethyst-colored awning jutted out over the sidewalk. Two attendants manned the front door, decked out in immaculate red uniforms, gold trim everywhere there was a seam, like the uniforms were trying too hard to be tasteful. Both young men were handsome with almost identical square chins and perfect complexions. Jennica stared. She was always transfixed by finery and these men were objectively fine, even to straight men like Rudolph. The doormen examined Jennica and Rudolph in turn. Rudolph stood a little straighter. Who were they? He made more money in a day than they made in a month. Jennica tugged him as one of the petty assholes held the door open.

"Welcome to The Repertory," his plastic smile looked eternally etched on his face.

"Thank you," Jennica beamed.

The Repertory was renowned for elegance most people couldn't afford. Before the Internet, the store served as a bastion of snobbery and pretentiousness, even refusing certain types of people from shopping. That selectivity only enhanced its attractiveness to those who could. Even with his relative wealth, Rudolph had no need to spend money on things that didn't earn money back. His wife, Rhonda, did that plenty for the both of them. This assault on decency did little to appeal to him.

The same couldn't be said of Jennica. She pirouetted, taking everything in with a look of wonderment on her face.

Ambient music played at a low level from speakers hidden somewhere amongst the rows of hanging clothes. Walnut cabinets set three deep on each side of the main aisle displayed expensive suits and dresses. The cabinets ran the full length of the store, terminating in high walls filled with the best of the best. Men's clothing to the left, women's to the right. Hats, gloves, dresses, and suits. Shoes so fine they should never actually touch a human foot. Even the strategically placed mannequins donned expensive suits and dresses.

In contrast to the lavish merchandise, the air was stale, almost dusty. Rudolph grimaced, thinking how he'd probably hack up crap for days after this. Everything served as a sign to remind him why he had never shopped here before.

It wasn't any wonder why the store was empty. This was a dead retail space. A shame, really. Not a single customer, in the middle of a day at the tail-end of the holiday shopping season. The only thing that took human form here were the twenty or so mannequins atop pedestals, standing in poses of cultivation.

"Doesn't look like it's too popular of a place," he said.

"What you mean?" Jennica looked hurt.

6

Rudolph indicated the empty store. "Do you see anyone else? We're the only ones here."

Understanding dawned on Jennica's face. "Well, most people can't shop here."

"You sure that's the reason?"

Jennica's expression soured. "Don't ruin this. I asked you to bring me here forever ago and I want to enjoy it."

She was going to keep pouting if he argued. All he had to do was wait her out. One or two things from this store and Christmas shopping would be finished. He was already thinking about the post-shopping sex; it would be phenomenal. It always was. Just like when she unabashedly displayed her voracious appetite during a surprise cruise he took her on a few years ago. They spent most of their time naked inside the cabin. Rhonda thought he was at a convention in Europe. It was a fair trade-off.

An urbane accent caught his attention. "Can I help you?"

An older man appeared from somewhere between the walnut cabinets. Rudolph hadn't spotted him coming, or he would have found a way to avoid the man. He hated dealing with salespeople, ironic considering that he made his fortune selling things to people that they didn't need. The man was short, maybe five-and-a-half-feet on a good day, and dressed in a Brownell Cucinelli suit that was such a dark blue it looked black. The suit outlined him perfectly, making the vendor look like he achieved a level of fitness that men his age should have failed to maintain decades ago. The few strands of white hair horseshoeing around the old man's head were greased back. He might as well be bald. The man's hook nose projected from his face as if it wasn't the one he was born with but one he chose as a surgical supplement. His smile made Rudolph wish he were home with Rhonda. And her mother.

Jennica stepped to the man, offering her hand and bubbly personality. "Hi, I'm Jennica and this," she said turning toward Rudolph, "is my boyfriend, Rudy." She glanced at him and plastered that fake smile he'd seen her give to thousands of people he paraded her in front of at parties. "I mean, Rudolph. He doesn't like other people calling him Rudy."

The old man took her hand and wrapped it in his. His liver-spotted skin stretched over the bone; there was no form, no robustness in those skeleton claws. No matter how fit the old man was, age had beaten his efforts to hide it, at least on those grotesque hands. The old man's eyes traveled the length of her body before falling on Rudolph. Somewhere deep in his amygdala, Rudolph's instincts screamed for him to run. He suppressed the reaction. There wasn't a man or mission in the world he would run from.

Besides, he looks like he could run me down if I tried.

"So very nice to meet you," the old man said, bobbing Jennica's hand up and down in a smooth rhythm. When he pulled away Jennica's arm hung in midair as if she'd lost a lifetime lover.

When Rudolph shook the vendor's hand the sudden urge to walk off the edge of the world burned through him.

"I'm Neville. Neville Saviore. So very nice to meet the two of you, and welcome to The Repertory. Is this your first visit?"

"It is!" Jennica clapped.

"Yes," Rudolph nodded.

"Very well then," Neville smiled. "Are you looking for anything in particular or merely browsing?"

Neville directed his question to Rudolph as if Jennica weren't there at all.

"She's doing the shopping," Rudolph answered with a nod to his girlfriend.

"And you?"

"I've got everything I need."

Neville raised an eyebrow. "Do you now?" The question hung in the air like a challenge. Eternity passed, life rotted and was reborn. Stars fell from the sky. Finally, Neville laughed. It was the buoyant laugh of a man half his age. "Well, friend, then you are one of the fortunate ones. All should be so lucky."

Luck had nothing to do with it. The rewards of life were his because he worked his ass off and then, on those days he

8

wanted to rest, he worked twice as hard. Ball busting brought opportunities, not luck. Rudolph imagined someone with an asset like The Repertory, for real estate if nothing else, would understand that. But he wasn't interested in having that philosophical debate with Neville. He wanted Jennica to buy her damn Christmas gifts so they could go for dinner and a few drinks and get back to the hotel room for a prurient round of fucking.

"Yeah, I guess so," Rudolph said instead.

Neville wrapped Jennica's hand in his and stepped down the main aisle, deeper into the store. "Well, let me take you to women's wear. I'm sure you'll adore it. Rudolph," he said over his shoulder, "if you'll walk with us, please, I'll show you where you can sit while your lady and I prepare to dazzle you. I've some fine wines and cigars I'm sure you'll enjoy."

Rudolph wasn't interested in entertaining a marathon shopping session, but if The Repertory had complimentary wine, even if it was only half decent, this might turn out to be an enjoyable afternoon. Getting drunker while she shopped was a much more attractive option than walking around the city in the snowstorm.

As they walked deeper into the store, the daylight gave way to dead overhead lights that somehow projected more gloom than brightness. The plastic mannequins formed an honor guard down the middle aisle. Their eyes seemed to track the three as they walked through the store. Neville must have spent tens of thousands to achieve such realism. Rudolph shook his head. Bad lighting. Extravagant expenditures that didn't move merchandise. These weren't his problems to contemplate. If Neville wanted to put himself out of business, that was his albatross. Rudolph wasn't going to don it for the old man.

"Rudolph," Neville gestured, "at the end of that hallway you'll see a set of double doors. Walk through them to our smoking room. Enjoy any of the cigars you wish to try. You'll find the wine stock there too. I want you to enjoy your experience at The Repertory." And without another word, Neville walked off with Jennica on his arm. She gave Rudolph a flirtatious wave over her shoulder and then skipped toward the women's clothing area.

No old man should move that easily, Rudolph observed as the pair moved away. He was reminded of his own aches and pains from working too many eighty-hour weeks. The shitty diet wasn't helping either.

The room at the end of the hall was a buffer where the world couldn't touch him. It wasn't large, but it was big enough to store a few hundred bottles of wine. The racks formed a U-shape around a pair of overstuffed red leather chairs seated in the middle of the Turkish rug. Rudolph stood in the center of the room and soaked in the exquisite sight. This was living. No nagging wife, no snot-nosed kids, no co-dependent girlfriend. Just a man and the wealth of options of the world.

Rudolph spent the next 15 minutes searching Neville's inventory before finally selecting a 2008 Palmer Red. Finding the perfect cigar to pair it with was the most satisfying decision he'd made in years. Rudolph wrapped his fingers around a Gurkha Black Dragon.

Rudolph reclined in the chair. The leather stretched under his weight with just enough give to help his joints release. He could spend eternity here. After a few glasses of wine and the cigar, Rudolph fell asleep.

"Rudolph." A gentle voice floated in the ether between reality and dream. Rudolph blinked, not wanting to rejoin the world.

"Rudolph." This time the voice was firmer, more determined. "It's time to wake. Come on, good man. I think you'll enjoy what you see. I know I do."

Rudolph's eyes fluttered open. Neville stood, erect, beaming a rich smile and offering an extended hand.

"Wait until you see her. She's exquisite." His perfect teeth gleamed.

How long had he been out? How much money had she spent? How much of his money? "What-what time is it?"

Neville turned to leave the room. "Time is irrelevant. Useless," he answered. "What is time beyond the actual moment you're experiencing? And some experiences should last forever, should they not?"

Rudolph had absolutely no idea what this elderly dealer was peddling, and he didn't care to explore it. The wine and cigar made the world fuzzy and he would much rather explore the possibilities of a day-long nap. The world swayed when he stood.

Neville was there beside him in an instant. "Steady there, good man. You've chosen a fine vintage but perhaps had a little too much of it. I hope the experience was enjoyable."

Rudolph held his head, blinking away the swirling urge to vomit. "It was fine. Thank you."

Neville steadied Rudolph with a beefy grip. His smooth hands hid an underlying strength Rudolph envied. Too many years of office life had made Rudolph soft, he knew that. The only reason a woman like Jennica spread her legs for him was because of the size of his wallet, irrespective of the size of his gut.

"Let me assist you," Neville said. "I can hand you off to your lovely lady once you're reunited."

"Thanks." He would rather have stayed in the smoking room, alternating between sleep and imbibition in extravagance. But something told him he didn't want to overstay his welcome or explore Neville's tolerance for freeloading.

They walked the length of the hallway back toward the main store area. He must've slept longer than he first guessed because the end of the hallway was dark. Too dark.

"She was a fine specimen," Neville said. "I thoroughly enjoyed experimenting with her. A true beauty."

"Yeah, she's great." The noncommittal answer was simple and easy to give. Plus, he didn't feel like talking when the world undulated like this.

Neville didn't seem bothered. "It's rare to see someone like her," he smiled. "Especially nowadays. People abuse their bodies, wouldn't you say? Maybe I'm too long of this world, but I don't understand, nor do I appreciate, the idleness that seems to permeate our culture. We've become comfortable. Grown lazy. I imagine a man of your stature would agree?"

Rudolph wasn't listening. The unexpected darkness was distracting enough, but Neville's grip and the smooth softness of his skin demanded his attention.

"It's dark. I must have slept longer than I thought," Rudolph attempted to laugh at his growing unease. "Are you closed?"

Neville kept walking, staring ahead. The darkness approached. Was he avoiding the question? His grip on Rudolph's hand was unrelenting. *How awkward would this get if I yanked away?*

"Life can be unfair, wouldn't you say?" Neville broke the silence as they approached the open maw of the main room. "We are animals, nothing more. And our animal brains seek pleasure. That's not our fault, of course, it's part of the nature of our species. But it is unfair just the same."

They stepped out into the main floor, lit only by a few security lights scattered across the thousands of square feet, separated by the cabinets that looked like nothing more than dark boxes in this poor light. Rudolph didn't see Jennica anywhere, only expensive clothes and the parallel rows of mannequins that lined the main aisle, dressed in the rich garments. Yet they weren't. Not any longer. Something had changed. The effete light soiled their refined nature. The clothes sparkled less, looking suddenly ragged and aged, and the exposed skin of the mannequins took on a phantasmal sheen.

"Wh—where's Jennica?"

"So it's hardly fair to fault us for seeking that which we are designed to desire," Neville continued, either avoiding or not hearing Rudolph's question. "Take Jennica for example. She knows that you're married yet she willfully fornicates with you, even though she's disgusted by your actions. Why? Because it brings her things like this, the spoiling that you do to her. She's never been treated so well by anyone. It helps her escape the banality of daily life. It would be difficult to fault anyone for desiring that."

Rudolph couldn't believe what he was hearing. Was this old fucker judging him? Is that what the pair of them had been doing the entire time he was sleeping? The old man prying into their most personal details while trying to sell that stupid bitch outfits she didn't need? Rudolph yanked his hand away.

But couldn't.

Neville's grip remained firm. He didn't shift an inch. Not a single one of those pathetic strands of white hair moved.

Rudolph pulled again, but Neville didn't budge.

"And you," Neville sneered, all pretenses now erased from his expression, "the married man, with an adoring wife sitting alone in the condominium she owns with you. Probably wondering where you are at this very moment, having no clue that you spent today fucking a woman ten years her younger. The woman whose silence you buy with trips to Central America and these clothes that will surely rot as your morality has."

"Fuck you." Rudolph yanked, sure his relative youth and strength would overpower this obnoxious vendor.

But, for the third time, Neville's grip remained intact. How is this man so powerful? Years sitting behind a desk, handling deals worth tens of millions of dollars instead of the gym equipment, had softened Rudolph. He knew that. But he wasn't fragile, he worked out enough to attract whores like Jennica, after all. Yet ...

Off in the darkness, a door creaked open. Neville glanced in that direction but Rudolph didn't dare turn. Didn't dare look. Without understanding why he knew he didn't want to face what moved in the murky shadows.

"The world is a dark place, wouldn't you agree?" Neville stated. The elderly man wasn't seeking his insight; this was a game to Neville, a plodding, supercilious exploration of ego. And Rudolph wasn't going to play along. "It's full of egocentric, dare I say masochistic, creatures. Seeking pain and pleasure in equal measure, cognizant of neither, not fully."

"What do you want?" Rudolph imagined it sounded sterner to Neville than it did in his own ears.

Shuffling feet, light and uncoordinated, announced the arrival of a witness to the conversation.

"I have want for very little at this point my life," Neville admitted. He squared up to Rudolph now. The older man's chest rose and fell, his shoulders lifting with exertion. It was a sad sigh, and expression built by a lifetime of pain. "And what I want is so readily available, yet so difficult to obtain. I often wonder if it's worth pursuing at all anymore. Of course—" Neville loosed a rough bark of a laugh "— I cannot deny my own rudimentary needs and desires. I guess you'd say that makes me a bit of a hypocrite."

The dragging feet drew nearer. Rudolph heard a moan. It sounded like Jennica, but different, like those moments when you swore you recognized a voice on the other end of the phone but couldn't place it. Whatever approached him wasn't the woman he'd walked into the store with.

There were other sounds, too, farther behind him. Towards the front door.

Rescue?

"I'll deal with that in time," Neville contemplated, oblivious to all that moved in the darkness. "In my time. I've got plenty of it. It's both a blessing and a curse. The more time you have to think, to reflect, the more things about yourself you uncover. None of us are perfect, not even myself. But I'm working on it, improving where I can. You're going to help me with that."

Neville reached out and snagged Rudolph's other hand by the wrist. His grip was unyielding. Rudolph leaned back, trying to pull away, but Neville's grip refused to slip. He looked for anything that might help, but he was surrounded by racks of anachronistic clothes. Ancient. There was nothing near he could use to free himself from this maniacal store keep. Even the mannequins—

Oh my God, the mannequins.

In the dead light, Rudolph saw them for what they were. Instead of a mixture of synthetic plastics melted to replicate the human body, Rudolph now saw the true nature of the mannequins.

The true monstrosities they were.

Each mannequin, one like the other, had shed their clothes under the dead light, mourning their display in naked revelry. Their faces painted with the sorrowful gaze of unfulfilled destiny. Each one of them, in turn, stripped of that which made them human. Only hours ago, they were immaculate, perfect in their manufactured presentation. One looked at him, her eye socket empty, bleeding as if she'd just suffered the extraction. Another, a man, his entire chest stripped of the skin that made it full and attractive for the women he once pursued in his living life. Yet another fell from its pedestal, having no legs to stand on, and pulled itself along the smooth floor toward Rudolph by its burly arms.

"What the fuck?" Rudolph yanked. He pulled. He tried to shove Neville away. None of it worked. None of it brought him his release.

"It's futile my good man," Neville said. "Your struggle. Seeking that which you will never gain again. Your fight isn't worth fighting anymore. You have given the world all you will ever give it. Now is your time to give it all that you have left."

"Leave me alone," Rudolph screamed. "Let go!"

For a moment Neville looked remorseful, almost as if he was about to entertain Rudolph's command. In that split moment between hope and reality, Rudolph saw his future clearly. It was easy because the future was also his past, the lie of a life he'd been living for years. A future devoid of frivolities with Jennica. A future filled with faithful servitude to Rhonda. It was a future without enticement or excitement. The endless work weeks. The pretentious parties with equally empty people. Money only replaced so much misery. Booze too, booze solved a lot of his problems. How long had it been since he'd been sober? Life was a daily exercise in drowning in a bottle. Why else was he fucking around with that needy bitch? It was a future he didn't want to realize.

That wasn't the life he'd worked for, running around the city, secreting to side streets and alternate paths to avoid being discovered by his wife or one of her friends. He was a grown man acting like a teenage boy who didn't want to get caught exploring life's alternatives. Didn't that explain the alcohol use? The experiments with harder stuff? The lack of intimacy between him and Rhonda? If this was what fate scripted for him, then this was what it would be. The options were his no longer, if they were ever.

Even before he capitulated, Neville nodded. "It'll be better this way. You'll see." The promise sounded empty. But it didn't matter anymore. Nothing did.

The scraping shuffle was close now. Close enough to hear Jennica, or what remained of her, slobbering as if she couldn't control her own swallowing.

"I'll give you a prominent display, of course," Neville promised. "The customers will absolutely adore you. I haven't had a new male mannequin in quite a while. One can only view the female form, no matter how stunning, for so long before growing bored with it. Yes, yes. You'll be a favorite among the city's elite. Quite a favorite."

Those strong, soft hands held him. "What do you want from me?"

Neville lifted their arms together as if they were one, solid piece. "Well, I don't very well need your hands, as you can clearly see. These I gathered from Jennica. Such wonderful skin. Such fullness, wouldn't you say?" Neville paused to admire his new hands, the previously protruding bones hidden underneath a full layering of youthful skin. He seemed lost for second before responding, but when he did his eyes looked past Rudolph. "I can't very well do anything with your face. You have scarred that through the years with your alcohol abuse. Those red cheeks and nose won't do. But don't worry. Once I transform you with the dead light you will look as pristine as the others."

The shuffle came closer. Right behind him. Something slobbered on his neck. Neville finally released one of his hands. Just one. Even now, partially free, Rudolph didn't attempt to pull away. He couldn't. And where would he go? Why would he go? Neville's free hand ran up the side of

Rudolph's cheeks, tainted by telangiectasia, and into his full, thick hair. The hair Jennica used to yank and pull whenever he buried himself deep in her.

"No, I've been meaning to do something about this horrendous hairline for the longest time," Neville laughed. "It would shock and disappoint you to learn that women can be incredibly superficial, even in their older age. Always wanting a man with a full-bodied hair. I'll finally have that now."

Rudolph began to cry. "Will it hurt?"

Deep lines undercut Neville's eyes. He looked sad. "Only for a short while, my man. Only for a short while."

Two stumps landed on each side of Rudolph's head, pressing against his neck. It was like a slow vice, squeezing, cutting off his ability to breathe. The bloody stumps at his neck dripped gore and tiny chunks of pink meat down the front of his button-up shirt. Rudolph had the crazy thought that the stain might not come out in time for him to be put on display.

But the thought didn't last long. Jennica continued squeezing. The world darkened little by little as the mannequin zombies closed in around him. The zombie army he would soon join. The zombie army that would become his eternal family.

He wondered if he would black out before the pain came. He soon found out.

Jennica's death grip tightened. She choked on her slobber, exerting enough force to crush his spine. There was a distinct, sharp crack, sending sizzles of pain racing throughout his entire body in a single instant. His spine seized in paralyzing pain and he was unable to breathe until it was all over.

Then he never breathed again.

* * *

Renee Dykstra held her husband's hand as they walked down Fifth Avenue. He almost knocked her over when she stopped in front of a store window display. "You would look hot in that," she exclaimed.

Cary, her husband, shook his head. The suit in the window was decent enough, though he wasn't a fan of anything fitting tightly around his cylindrical chest. He hated feeling confined. But it fit the shaved head mannequin perfectly, showing off his broad shoulders and tapered legs. It even covered the mannequin's protruding gut. Since when did they make fat mannequins? "I guess," Cary admitted, examining the suit. "I don't know if it's my-"

He stopped when he looked into the plastic eyes of the mannequin. He swore they were wet as if it were— no, that was nonsense.

"Come on," Renee tugged at his arm, racing to the door. "Let's go in and see if we can find you something."

Before he could object, the doorman pulled the door open for Renee and she disappeared into the upscale store. Cary shook his head, taking one more sideways glance at that odd mannequin before following the love of his life into the store. By the time he stepped inside Cary still hadn't convinced himself that it wasn't crying.

END

Satan Claws

Did I leave the warmth and sun of Florida for this shit?
Adam thought.

But he smiled to meet his families' expectations, lifting a toast to his dickhead brother, Jon. The brandy warmed his throat. It was cheap shit, the kind you could buy anywhere in Hannibal, like convenience stores and gas stations. The typical swill of family gatherings, even for the Christmas holiday. If he'd quit on life, like his father, Adam would drink enough to dull his senses long enough to get through the next couple days.

The men sat in a small side room his father reserved for drinking and reminiscing about glories of seasons past. Over the years it had become a retreat for the men in the family and any company they had over. That was the way Ted, his father, liked it. That was the way most men in Central New York preferred it, from what Adam remembered. This small town community allowed them to place the blame of misfortune at the feet of fate. How else could they deal with their inability to get ahead?

"If only we got preferential treatment," Ted said when the frustrations of the world got to him. "You know?"

All too well. Ted raised his sons to be compliant, little robots. Jon fell in line like a lemming, Adam never had. He always questioned, always challenged. That's why he earned this 'second son' status. Where Jon's meager accomplishments were bragged about at neighborhood picnics, Adam's seemed to only get mentioned in passing. Where his parents somehow found the money to support a number of Jon's whims, like the time he had to have a dirt bike so that he could train to become a professional racer,

Adam struggled to feed himself through college. The theme had been repeated over and over, throughout the years.

Besides DNA, Ted contributed very little to the man Adam was. Growing up, Adam was always sensitive to how other fathers encouraged their children. Ted criticized. During sports, other fathers worried when their sons were injured. Ted yelled at Adam the few times he went down in a game, including the time he dislocated his elbow. The community never saw Ted as an abuser because Adam and Jon, and their mother, never bore observable scars of Ted's anger. But they were there, tucked away in the folds of gray matter. Permanent.

Counseling was never paid for. "They're all quacks," Ted swore.

Family self-help wasn't entertained. People didn't need to talk about their feelings because that's was what 'pussies and pansies' did, Ted reminded his sons.

In Ted's world 'men' simply 'manned-up' and moved on. Adam never saw Ted admit he might have gone a little overboard in his criticisms, nor did he ever acknowledge anything that might serve as evidence of a shortcoming.

So in the absence of therapy, Adam did the only thing he knew would help him; he moved. Florida's heat was oppressive, and the air stank of wet salt most of the time, but it sure as hell beat New York winters and her people. Especially when those people included family.

I don't want to be here, he thought as he watched his father and brother laugh about yet another story of local origin that was insanely uninteresting. To them, their stories were the epicenter of all that was culture and humor in this obscure world. Hannibal did that to people, made small people feel big. And it didn't only happen to the likes of Ted and Jon, it happened to almost everyone he knew here. Maybe it was the polluted waterways that were still recovering from decades of environmental crimes by the dead industrial base. Whatever the real cause, this snow land's people took a stubborn pride in their hometown and its stories. Adam imagined that was natural when there was nothing else going right for the populace.

"You should have seen it, Adam," Jon laughed, slapping Ted on the back. "I mean, it was sick. He takes the throttle and just *cranks* it." Jon embellished his story with the appropriately annoying hand gesture of a sideways fist revving an imaginary throttle. "And then he just hits the jump."

"Went flying over those handlebars too," Ted piped in, almost choking on his mouthful of Pabst Blue Ribbon.

"A'right?" Jon slapped Ted on the back again. "Take it easy, old man. You're going to keel over if you keep that up."

If we were only so lucky, Adam thought.

"Listen, man, you've got to come back up next time the festival happens," Jon turned to Adam once he was sure their father was not actually choking to death on canned beer. "You sure you can't hang out a few weeks until it starts again? It's going to be awesome."

"Got to work," Adam hid his groan. Was it that hard to understand that responsible people couldn't take weeks at a time away from work? It was hard enough getting away to come back for this funeral because almost everyone was out for the holidays. Most of the world understood that, but not Jon. He struggled with what it meant to be an adult. "Plus, I haven't been on a snowmobile since ..."

When? 17?

Ted tipped the gold-colored beer can lid at him. "You don't forget once you've done it. Stop being such a pussy. Stick around. You might have some fun. Then your mother will stop bitching about you never being here."

At the mention of her title, Adam's mother defended herself. "Don't bring me into this," Jennie said from the kitchen where she spent most of her time.

Some things never changed.

"Just saying the kid could stop worrying only about himself and come around more often," Ted yelled over his shoulder at her. "Don't need to wait for bad stuff like this to happen for him to get his ass up here. Plus, coming back would get him right again."

'The kid.' Adam was thirty, possessor of a career and home. He was anything but a kid. For that, Ted only needed to look to his eldest son. Five years older, with a history of unemployment that would make the Great Depression blush, Jon was a failure in every sense of the word. Except to Ted. Everyone knew Jon had a marijuana habit too, one he hid from the family priest they would be seeing later tonight. Father McElroy was a watcher, connected throughout the town, and seemed to know the 'sinful' comings and goings of everyone for well over twenty years. If there was any 'kid' in the family, it was Jon.

"Leave him alone," Jennie chided. "Flying isn't cheap. Maybe he doesn't have the money for it?"

"I'm fine," Adam started to say, but was cut off—ignored—by Ted.

"He's got the money for that fancy car he's posting all over Facebook. So he can fly up here more often so you're happy about something."

Jesus Fucking Christ, here we go again.

"I don't come up here that often because of my job, not because of money," Adam intervened before this turned even more awkward and regrettable. It was already hard enough dealing with the death of his adored Aunt Celia, the reason for the visit. He didn't need or want family drama piled on to make matters worse. This trip wasn't about Christmas. It wasn't about seeing the family he enjoyed rarely visiting. It was about a beautiful woman who left life too soon.

Fucking death. Aunt Celia was the sweet woman they were putting in the ground and he was here to honor her memory, silly as it was. Dead people were dead; they had no idea whether three people or three thousand attended their funeral.

For Aunt Celia.

The next three days couldn't pass quickly enough. Florida already beckoned.

"Forgot," Ted snarled under his breath with vinegar tone, "you're a big man at your company, aren't you?"

Adam shook his head. Round and round they went. "It's not my company, I don't own it," he reminded his father for the one-millionth time. "And I worked my ass off to get where I am."

"And we're proud of you," Jennie called from the kitchen. Adam had the sneaking suspicion she wasn't actually doing anything in there. More likely that she was using her 'work' in the kitchen as justification to avoid Ted and Jon while trying to enjoy as much of Adam's visit as she could. It was a healthy decision.

"You don't need to be using words like that either," Ted admonished him, returning the feel in the room to the appropriate level of distress. "We're a Christian family. That language isn't allowed. See? This is what I'm talking about. Can't wait until the Father gets his hands on you."

Adam hid the laugh begging to be released by bringing the beer can to his lips, taking a small sip. Numb from years of mental abuse, he wasn't bothered by this latest threat. When they were kids, Ted was driven to make them 'good' by scaring them into submission, sometimes even going as far as to tell them fantastic stories about the power of Satan being so strong that he could send demons into the real world. Messages that were reinforced at the church, as crazy as it was. In his teens, Adam simply rejected the nonsense out of pure rebellion. As an adult, he'd gotten angry over the twisted manipulation he and his brother had been subjected to. Though, only hours into this current visit, it didn't look like Jon wasn't anything but fully bought-into the family dynamic. Adam wondered how much of what he saw in his brother now was a result of decades of unfair manipulation by a father and a priest.

Demons. How had he ever fallen for that?

"Ted," came the cautious word from the kitchen. How many previous arguments had his mother stopped? Not even a full day into this return home and her tally began again. Like it always did when he came home.

Adam sighed. *Three more days. Just three more days. I'm here for Aunt Celia.*

He should have followed his gut and got a hotel room. He tried. But being the armpit of the world that Hannibal was, the closest hotel was a dump in Oswego, twenty minutes away. A straight shot past small farms and homes devoid of hope, the half hour it added each way wasn't a problem for him. But it was for his mother. Jennie asked—begged—him to stay with them. Adam didn't have a wife or kids to bed down, he didn't even have time for a girlfriend, so it wasn't like it would have required a lot of room, his mother argued. She'd even made up his old room. So he did.

And regretted every minute of it even before dinner.

"Yeah, I know," he responded, not remotely interested in having this conversation again.

"And I don't need any lip about it either," Ted set the cheap beer down on the end table with a dramatic *thunk*. "You can do all that devilin' stuff in your Sinland, but don't you bring it home with you. We don't want any business with that stuff you all do down there."

Adam laughed. He couldn't help it. Ted was counseling him while downing what was at least his fourth beer of the afternoon. Tonight they were all going to a dinner. Nothing formal but, under the circumstances, not something to attend drunk. Yet to Ted, drinking like this was only a problem when others did it. It was *always* about what other people were doing. He was a good Catholic in that way.

Sinland? Father McElroy's influence. Ted wasn't clever enough to come up with that term on his own.

"What's so funny?" Jon leaned toward him. It was a gesture Adam remembered quite easily and not-so-fondly. Jon's aggression was well-documented through bruises on Adam's body during their younger years.

"Nothing."

"Then why'd you laugh?"

"No reason."

Jon sat back, his can of beer bouncing on his own leg. "Yeah, well, it's not a laughing matter, Adam. Because you

24

turned your back on Christ doesn't mean you don't have to
show respect in Dad and Mom's house."

"Damn right," Ted echoed.

Adam held up his hands, a gesture that would feed their
egos without costing him anything. His pride was too healthy
for these little men to damage. "Sorry. I didn't realize you
were all suddenly religious." He wanted to say convenient, but
why fan the flames? Maybe they had changed over the years?
People did. The family had been the typical run-of-the-mill
Catholics, attending Mass on Christmas Eve and Easter and
virtually forgetting where the church was the rest of the year.
But those two times a year when they did go? They knew how
to put on a good show, taking Communion and talking up the
virtues of Confession like they were stalwarts of the faith.

It was all so Catholic.

Somewhere in Florida, there was a man walking a white
sand beach, enjoying the breeze coming off the Gulf of
Mexico. Sand between his toes. Lapping waves of an
afternoon tide. Adam envied that faceless stranger.

The pair across from him cast dark glances, holding back
words entangled in jumbled brains. This could take a while.

But he didn't need them to because, at that moment, his
mother walked into the room, drying her hands in a dishtowel.
His smile, already depressed, slipped. "Is everything okay,
Mom?"

Jennie looked at her husband and eldest son before
coming and sitting on the arm of the chair. "Honey," she said,
pulling a stray hair away from Adam's face, "we need to talk."

"Okay," he offered with a nervous laugh. This was beyond
typical family strangeness now.

Maybe they had fallen into the religion well, head first,
drowning in the empty promise of salvation without evidence?
At least then they committed to something besides the
retelling of local triumphs that didn't register anywhere
outside of Hannibal.

"Things," she paused, looking over at Ted, who shrugged
and tapped his beer can, "things have been different here

since you left. We've changed. Everyone has. It's been glorious."

"Okay," he drew the word out, hoping for understanding.

Jennie drew a deep breath, her gaze moving from his to where she played with that loose strand of his hair. She didn't say a word. No one did. Adam squirmed.

"It's probably best if Father McElroy talks to him," Ted said.

Adam tried to ignore his mother's lingering fingers in his hair. He looked up at her. She blinked, trance-like. "Yes. Yes, I guess we should," she answered.

Adam had no interest in talking to Father McElroy. As an awkward high school senior, Adam was forced into compliance with the ridiculous Catholic faith. That was the last time he saw the man. A laugh boiled in his chest at the memory. And he'd fucked with the priest, giving his confession that he masturbated no less than ten times a day. Every day. Adam smirked as he recalled McElroy's expression. All these years later, understanding the crimes of the church, Adam wondered what perverse thoughts that old bastard had rolling around in his lustful mind as he imagined that teenager pulling on his hard flesh-tube so often.

Their church was a fundamental Roman Catholic congregation. They didn't believe in using Confessional booths, that was how cowards and cheats confessed their sins to God. Hannibal's sons and daughters were proper Catholics, the type who confessed their sins face-to-face with their priest. The way God intended.

All pain, no actual gain.

He wasn't in a hurry to see the priest. But he'd have to at some point; McElroy was conducting Aunt Celia's ceremonies this weekend.

"What's going on?" Adam broke their silent strategy session.

No one answered. Even Jon looked morose.

"Come on," Adam urged, his heart thumped a little harder.

Ted examined him from across the room, his gaze unwavering. When he spoke the discussion ended. "We wait."

***

And wait they did.

Dinner was awkward, the conversation empty and forced. They talked about the same things they always talked about. Local news and happenings. Stories of old, when they were kids and the town was relevant.

And throughout it, Ted and Jon continued to drink. Adam didn't bother trying to count how many beers the pair shared. Their new drinking habits didn't interest him. Plus, it would have been nearly impossible to keep count. The more they drank, the faster they consumed. Newfound drinking buddies. Adam couldn't help but feel for his mother, cooking and cleaning up after the pair; who ate, drank and laughed like a knight and his squire. She was never independent. Her generation grew up on the tail end of gender and role conformity, the last of a people who refused to entertain ideas of fluidity. But now she seemed even more docile than Adam remembered. More subservient.

"We need to get ready to get down to the church," Jennie said softly when she finished.

Ted and Jon's laughing stopped abruptly. "Already?" his father asked, flicking his wrist in an attempt to get the watch to spin so he could read it. Ted squinted, struggling. "Damn watch," he grumbled, finally giving up.

"What are we going to the church for?"

"We have some things to take care of," Ted said, his statement followed by a harsh hiccup. It was harder than ever to take him seriously.

"What things? Isn't Aunt Celia's family handling everything?"

Jennie patted his hand. "Now, now, Adam," there was a charmed lightness to her tone, "they can't do everything. Celia's death ... it was hard on them."

Death was like that. Hard. Adam believed in appreciating every day while he was alive to enjoy them. He doubted Celia's family appreciated her until it was too late, but he wasn't about to bring that up. Aunt Celia was sweet, but her husband and kids could be downright assholes. To her and everyone they knew. The first time Adam took a punch it wasn't from his own older brother, but from Celia's kid, Tosha. In Celia's family, the kids were all equal bullies. That might have been a major reason why she was so good to him and all the other neighborhood kids; she was making up for the twats she brought into the world. They all took her for granted, a lot of people did, Adam's parents included. Later in his teenage years, when he understood the world a little better, Adam empathized with Celia. Her eyes were perpetually cast downward, her shoulders slumped. She walked with the confidence of someone who'd lose out on the lottery if someone told her the winning numbers beforehand. Her family had done that to her.

It was hard to feel for them.

Celia was the first one to congratulate him when he was accepted into Central Florida University. Ted was too drunk to care, Jon too jealous, and his own mother too mournful to celebrate. But Aunt Celia did.

So he would do this for her, even if it meant going to the church with this merry band of losers. "Okay," he nodded, "what do you need me to do?"

"Just be there," his mother answered in a dreamy voice.

Ted and Jon tapped their beers together and took long, silent swigs.

***

"Adam! It's so good to see you," Father McElroy's voice boomed across the empty church foyer. The man hadn't lost much vibrancy over the years. It was still the smooth voice of ages past, the same voice that told him demons were real and masturbation was bad.

The same gold font Adam told the priest he'd pissed in half a lifetime ago stood between them, a quirky reminder of a past when this place severed his sense of normalcy and taught him to hate himself. He hated this place, hated the fabrication, and great expense of creating an image to sustain a lie.

Adam played the part, wearing his best smile. *For Aunt Celia,* he reminded himself. "Good to see you too," Adam replied, intentionally leaving his greeting free of titles of reverence. The silence behind him and the slight quiver in the priest's face were all he needed to know that he'd struck first.

They weren't going to pull him into their little game this time. He was a grown man, someone who didn't owe any of them deference. The games of doctrinal hierarchy were of no interest. McElroy was a man, just like any other. There was nothing special about him and, in fact, Adam had a hard time understanding and trusting any man who chose the lifelong prison of celibacy. That shit wasn't normal.

To his credit, the priest's practiced smile returned quickly. "I hope your flight was a good one. It can always be tricky landing in Syracuse in the winter. It's just wonderful you were able to make it."

Adam grunted and Father McElroy moved on quickly.

"Come, let's start. I want to show you some of the changes we've made," Father McElroy slid his hand into Adam's before Adam could protest, pulling him into the chapel. McElroy pointed out an impressive number of improvements they'd made over the past decade. Adam swallowed the bitter taste as the priest gave thanks to God instead of all the actual people who made the improvements. Adam faked his enthusiasm all the way through.

They reached a door in the far corner of the chapel. Father McElroy stopped and finally let go of Adam's hand, pressing his own to his chest. A sign above the door read: Rebirth Baptismal.

"What's this?" Adam asked, pointing out the sign.

"Our pride and joy," the priest beamed like a new father, opening the door with a sweeping gesture, encouraging Adam to step inside. "We're in the hand of God in here. Come, let me show you."

Sure you are. When Adam paused, Ted whispered caustically, "Don't be a pussy. Go in."

Father McElroy didn't appear to hear the inappropriate comment.

Adam held his sigh and stepped into the room. The quicker he entertained their pietistic masturbation session, the quicker they could get to the reason they were here. Aunt Celia.

"Come," Father McElroy tugged his hand, "let me show you."

A black cloak of darkness hung over the room, making it feel larger than the entire church. Massive candles, as broad as an adult, lined a walled rectangle in the middle of the room. The candlelight didn't reach the edge of the room. A short wall, no more than three feet high and twenty feet wide, cut the space in half. They stepped toward it. A strong scent of iron made Adam pull back, pinching his nose. Behind him, in the descending shroud of darkness, the door banged closed. The stiffness in the room was palpable as if the rest of the world had detached itself, wanting no association with these proceedings.

"This cost us over one hundred thousand dollars, the entire project did," Father McElroy was saying when Adam could focus again. It was hard to do. "It took years of fundraising but, with the graces of God smiling down on us, we were finally able to start construction. Then it was a matter of the congregation jumping in and providing some sweat equity. And let me tell you, did they ever. God has been good to us."

They approached the structure. It looked like a long, rectangular wading pool. It stretched out beyond the candlelight and into the darkness beyond. A low and constant rumble came from the far end. Adam imagined the pool was being fed by an underground spring. But it was a weird sound, not rhythmic, like a pump or a spring. Erratic. Like the water was moving on its own, without mechanical assistance. Adam peered into the darkness, but the priest pulled his attention away.

"This is the baptismal," Father McElroy said, with an air of awe that Adam didn't feel. "It's our proudest accomplishment."

"Amen," Ted said behind them. The reverence in his voice was thick.

"Hallelujah," Jon echoed.

Adam swallowed a scoffing laugh forcing its way out at his family's newfound devotion. So much had changed in the past decade.

Father McElroy looked beyond Adam, to his family members, and nodded. "Your family is good people," he said. "Some of the best in our congregation. We're very lucky to have them."

Adam nodded, it was a slight gesture that wouldn't betray his disagreement.

Father McElroy smiled with eyes that devoured the humor. "And they're worried about you, Adam."

"I guess," he said. "It's tough for them with me living so far away."

Father McElroy shook his head. "It's not that at all. They're worried about your soul and, from what I hear, rightfully so."

"How so?" Instant bitterness. Adam hoped it cut the priest.

Father McElroy's eyes narrowed, taking a stony appearance. He spread his hands wide. "You have fallen away, Adam. The church ... she misses you. But you miss her more, whether or not you know it."

Adam couldn't help himself. He laughed, even though he knew it would piss off his father and hurt his mother. But this was garbage and he didn't have to tolerate it. "I promise, I'm fine."

But Father McElroy wasn't listening. The priest's eyes were taking in the baptismal as if it held the response he sought. "The wayward," Father McElroy started, "they don't realize that they're wayward. That's why it's so important to have a life centered on the church and its teachings. You have a family who cares, and a church community who wants you to come home."

The priest turned around, looking past him, and gave a slight nod of his head. Adam didn't have time to wonder what the gesture was about. Because in that instant Father McElroy did something Adam would have never anticipated; he reached up and pulled his white chasuble over his head, tossing it to the floor. Then Father McElroy pulled his alb down, leaving it piled at his feet. The priest was completely naked.

"What the fuck?" The moment couldn't recognize the delicacies of the church. If the Father McElroy didn't appreciate his language, then the priest could put his goddamn clothes back on.

Father McElroy wagged a finger, frowning. "See? The foul mouth is the foul soul. This language of the devil you've embraced in your time away? We weep for you. The church cries for your soul, Adam, and we want you to come home."

There was movement behind him, a light hand touched his shoulder. His mother's hand. "We want you to come home," she said, moving past Adam. Naked.

Adam stumbled backward.

"Mom?" He said, averting his gaze as she moved up alongside the priest.

She didn't answer.

"We want you to come home," now Jon, naked as the day he was born, took his place by the priest, opposite his mother.

"I don't know what the fuck is going on, but I don't want any part of this. You all can keep this shit. I'm leaving."

He bumped into something. Someone. "You'll stay here," Ted's voice was close. His firm hands grasped Adam's shoulders. Ted's steely erection pressed against Adam's back. "We want you to come home."

Adam froze as Father McElroy approached, laying his hand on top of Ted's, pressing down on Adam's shoulder. "It's time for you to be reborn, Adam. That's why you're here and it's what your family needs. You must do this for your family. It is what our Father commands."

But Adam had no intention of doing this for anyone, especially the people he'd run away from as soon as he was old enough to do so.

In one swift movement, Adam ducked and spun, breaking free of Ted's grip. Holding out an arm toward them, his voice shook even as he warned them away. "This — this is nuts. What the fuck is wrong with all of you?"

The four people moved, circling Adam, closing around him. "We want you to come home," they said in unison. "We want you to come home."

Tighter and tighter. Adam backed away, trying to avoid this becoming physical. He couldn't hit any of them. But this was beyond weird! It was perverse. If violence was the only way out, it was the route he would take. "Back up!"

But they didn't. They stepped closer, inching toward him as they chanted in unison, "We want you to come home."

With each collective step closer, Adam back away. They were shepherding him toward the pool, forcing him into this corner. He wasn't going to be part of their sick ritual. Never again. "Stay away," his voice shook.

"We want you to come home," four voices said as one.

Step.

Adam's heels bumped into the front wall of the pool, his hand braced against the top of it. "Back off. I mean it."

But they didn't. The four naked bodies closed in around him. Their vacant eyes no longer recognizing the son and brother he was.

"He has you in His grasp," the priest intoned, "and we mean to free you. Free you from Satan's claw."

The iron smell in the air was powerful this close to the pool. Adam's throat throbbed as the four pressed in on him. Panic rose. He was going to have to fight his way out of this. Fight his own goddamn family! This was their choice, though; they were making him do this.

Father McElroy stepped closer, ahead of Adam's family. The priest's erection was thick, pulsing. "Satan's claw has grasped your heart and we mean to free you."

Before Adam could ask another question, before he warned the priest away, Father McElroy grinned and shoved Adam, sending him reeling backward.

Adam fell over the top of the wall and into the pool. Bracing for impact against the concrete bottom, Adam only felt himself falling. He panicked, trying to upright himself and swim toward the surface. He opened his eyes as he struggled and couldn't see anything. The water was dark, thick. Adam couldn't make out the candlelight in the room above.

He kicked harder, now unsure where the surface was. As he did, Adam stretched out in all directions, hoping his hands or feet would brush against a surface so he could orient himself. But he felt nothing more than the viscous water.

Squirming and kicking, Adam tried to stand but his feet couldn't find purchase. In a moment of hysterical confusion, he wondered how deep the pool actually was. And the water was filmy as if it was polluted by an oil-based substance. It made his movements sluggish. He swam in what he thought was the opposite direction of his fall. Up.

The distance was impossible to judge without an indicator of which direction to head. Swimming in this baptismal felt like the inside of an oil barrel. Right before his lungs exploded, Adam's head broke the surface.

Gasping to draw breath, Adam pinched his eyes closed and tried to tread water with just his feet so he could wipe the goo from his eyes. Blinking away the slimy water was doing nothing.

When his opened his eyes his vision was blurred, burning. Adam gagged. The smell of rusted metal was stronger than ever now that his head bobbed above the water.

"We want you to come home." The chorus boomed with more voices. No longer four. Adam rotated around noticed that the congregation of the church, 50, 60, maybe more, lined the baptismal. All eyes fixed on him. Each member of the parish just as naked as the priest who led them into this madness.

"We want you to come home."

"Come home!" One young voice rebelled against the monotonous chorus, pleading with Adam to comply.

"We want you to come home." The chorus grew. Adam spun to discover why. Candles were being lit along the pool, running another 50 feet into this massive room. Hundreds of people stood near the pool walls as even more filed into the open spaces. They watched Adam tread water while he tried to —

— but it wasn't water.

With immediate recognition, Adam vomited.

What he was swimming in wasn't a pool of water at all. It was a pool of crimson blood. This structure, this baptismal, massive as it was, was filled with blood. Whose blood? How much blood would it take to fill something this size?

Crazy thoughts, he knew, but thoughts he couldn't avoid.

The blood rippled around him. There was no escape route with the pool surrounded by the congregation. Adam scanned the group, looking for the most elderly, the frailest. He would swim there, pull himself out of this madness, and fight his way out if he had to.

"Please come home."

"Please come home."

"Please come home."

Each time the iteration of the disturbing hymn was louder than the previous.

His skin itched.

Father McElroy stepped on top of the wall, his arms spread out in celebration of the gathering. "Brothers and sisters, we come together on this very important day to bring Brother Adam home. To rend the devil's mind! To rip out Satan's hold! Pray with me as we call on our heavenly father to free this young man from his sinful ways. His behavior spits in the face of God and his son and the Holy Spirit! Pray with me and call on the spirit to rid Adam of Satan's claw!" The priest's cock bobbed with each powerful proclamation.

Adam took in the congregation. There was no sorrow. There was no empathy or concern. Mindless compliance.

And something else in those eyes.

Joy! That's what it was! Everyone appeared to be nearing utter ecstasy.

He tread backward, toward an older couple. They would be the ones he would fight through, he decided.

Father McElroy dropped one hand, leaving his right arm extended by his side. Adam watched as his mother climbed up onto the edge of the wall. With a quick nod from the priest, she turned toward Adam. "We miss you, son, and want you to come home. We love you, no matter the wrongs you've done, no matter the sin you've committed. We love you just the same."

Adam didn't want to draw the attention to himself. To get away, he'd have to be subtle. Not even the older couple he was targeting could notice. So he remained quiet, allowing them to spread their gospel of weird.

Father McElroy dropped his arm and Adam watched as his mother stepped back down. The priest raised his other arm and Jon stepped up onto the edge of the pool. "You've heard the Father, you spat in God's eye and you need to be cleansed so that He can love you again."

Without another word, Jon stepped off the pool. Father McElroy shook his head at Adam's lack of reaction. "Let us pray for this sinner as his earthly father, the man who spawned him, joins me."

The group picked up their chant exactly where they left off. Lemmings. But one did not pray with the group. One did not stand in robotic compliance, mindlessly uttering the same phrase over and over. One was different. Ted.

Adam blinked the remaining blood out of his eyes, unsure that what he was witnessing was actually happening.

Balancing on top of the edge of the pool wall, Ted kneeled before the priest.

As the congregation prayed for Adam, he watched, mesmerized, by what happened between the two men. Ted, his father, the bigot who hated him and all he had become, turned toward the priest's crotch and opened his mouth, accepting Father McElroy's cock.

Louder, the congregation chanted.

The pool of blood. Ripples grew into waves.

"Pray brothers and sisters," Father McElroy shouted above the clamor. "Pray for the hand of God to purge Satan's claw from brother Adam!"

The priest shouted as Ted fellated him. The congregation, if it noticed what was happening between the two, didn't break their rhythm. Over and over, their voices rose, united, in their pious chant, "We want you to come home."

The pool of blood undulated.

Father McElroy threw his head back. Laughing.

Ted's head rocked up and down on the priest's cock.

Bubbles of blood exploded around Adam; huge bubbles, some larger than five feet in diameter.

Father McElroy thrust forward.

Waves of blood crashed against the sides of the pool.

The congregation prayed louder, drowned out by the noise around him.

Ted bobbed faster. Up, then down. Deep. Taking all the priest could offer. Like a good servant.

The priest gripped the back of Ted's head and, with one final thrust, released.

The chanting echoed off the walls, off the ceilings. It was as if the pool of blood could feel the energy in the room. Adam didn't care to hide his intent anymore. He swam as fast as he could, no longer caring if they were onto him or not.

Before he could make it to the wall, the pool erupted, sending a shower of blood piercing the air, painting the ceiling, and raining back down on the congregation. Their pristine skin bled.

The congregants screamed in joy, holding their hands up at the gift of the rain of blood.

And then Adam saw it, a shadow on the wall, cast by hundreds of candles. A shadow much too large for anything human.

For anything explainable.

A monstrosity rose out of the pool. The pool with no bottom.

Larger than life, a hand that spanned 40 feet rose up toward the ceiling, blocking out the candlelight. The congregation's chant grew louder, orgasmic, as massive fingers extended, scraping the ceiling.

"Our prayers have been answered and brother Adam is being cleansed!" Father McElroy screamed from the end of the pool, his cock still buried in Ted's mouth. "God has judged him and he will be cleansed!"

The vast hand descended on Adam, moving volumes of air as it fell. The assault of wind struck before the hand did.

There was nowhere to run, there was nowhere to hide. Adam couldn't avoid the reach of the hand of God.

His lucid mind acquiesced to madness as the hand slammed down, thrusting him under the sea of red.

The baptismal.

To be born again.

END

Walking in a Winter Harvestland

The winter of 1886 announced its arrival in September with snow. At first, it bothered no one. Snow in this part of central New York came in irregular and weird intervals. In the past, early snowfall was fleeting. After the novelty wore off, life resumed. The hearty people of Hannibal were accustomed to the odd snowfall at unlikely times of the year. This year was different.

In 1886, the snow that fell wasn't light. It was thick, heavy, and wet. It was, by all definitions, a true lake effect snow. Virginia Sterling watched it from behind the window of her family's small kitchen.

"Get'cha to work, now," her mother, Cecilia, called from across the small room. "Don't be wastin' time or your father'll be upset. You don't be wantin' that."

"No, Mother," Virginia answered and stepped away from the window, already missing the spectacle of thousands, *millions*, of big flakes drifting toward the earth. No one wanted Father upset. He was a loving man, but a hard one. Sometimes it was easy to forget his capacity to love once his temper took hold.

Virginia returned to her knitting. A few weeks ago, her father went into town and traded for wool, so she could make clothes and blankets. Virginia wasn't supposed to start knitting for weeks yet, but with three straight days of heavy snow, she couldn't do her outside chores. She filled her idle time with something productive. On the farm, idle time was a sin, so the choice to knit was made for her. Virginia didn't mind; it was soothing to knit by the fire.

"You'll need to hurry with those," her mother looked away from her own work to examine Virginia. "Snow don't appear to be letting up."

Cecilia was a worrier, proving that Virginia was barely her mother's daughter. Who had time to worry about so many things when there were so many things to explore? She knew she should take a few more of her mother's lessons to heart though. Pretty soon she would be courting and starting a family of her own.

Life in this part of New York was difficult for everyone. Isolated on the northern tier of a young country, it might as well have been the front edge of a Nordic frontier. The winters were long, gray, and harsh under the best of circumstances—hard on animals, people, and especially the soul. Even at sixteen, Virginia experienced enough New York winters to be mentally jaded and exhausted by the months-long wait for the first blades of grass to appear.

She sighed, her fingers dancing with her tools of needle and wool. It took a few minutes to get back into her rhythm but soon section after section of the blanket came together. Knitting helped her let go of the world's worries. She loved making something from nothing, creating order from chaos, and for providing for her family in a way that *she* could. Her father hunted and butchered meat, and built everything else they needed through trading and scavenging. Her brother worked the fields, ensuring they had crops to get through the long winters. He chopped wood to make sure there was fuel for a fire. Her mother did all the cooking to ensure the hard work everyone else did had an end result. She tended to the cows and fed the chickens when she wasn't busy being the foundation that held the family together. Meredith, her older sister by a year, helped by cleaning the small home and the animal stalls. Everyone did their part because everyone *had* to do their part.

Knitting was her role and knowing that work mitigated the winter discomfort was one of the few things she could be proud of. Her family woke each morning ready to get their work done *because* she did her part to ensure their comfort and safety against the conditions.

Indeed, what she did now *was* important, regardless of what her siblings said.

Virginia jumped when the door banged open.

Her father stomped the snow from his boots. "Good God," he barked, "snow's falling hard."

"It's not letting up?" Cecilia asked.

Roger shook his head. "If anything, it's getting worse."

Cecilia covered her flinch. Her father did too. "It'll be fine," he assured Cecilia. "Maybe another few hours and it'll blow over. It always does. Can't believe how quickly it's piling up."

"And if it doesn't?" Cecilia kept glancing toward the single window.

Roger shrugged. "It's September, it could snow for another three days and melt within the week. Don't worry, wife, it'll be over soon."

***

But it didn't end. Not that day. Not the day after. Not for the next week. With each passing day, the tension inside the home grew with the depth of the snow.

By the end of September, the decimation of the wheat and corn was complete, bringing a dark realization there would be no harvest this year.

As the snow deepened, the green world disappeared. First, the fields were buried, and then came the farm equipment and smaller structures. The snow devoured every sign of life.

And it kept coming.

Day in and day out the snow fell, wet and heavy. The blanket of white extended out and up, growing deeper each day.

Threatening.

Roger reassured them, and Cecilia lied to them. But the children were old enough to know the gravity of the situation. The snow wasn't stopping anytime soon, and they'd lost or already eaten most of their livestock. With each fading sun, their options dwindled. To make matters worse, the road to town was long gone.

They were alone and stranded as the world went dormant.

**

"What are we going to eat, Pa?" Jacob, her brother, paced the small room, looking like a caged animal.

Roger's face had aged over the past few weeks. Deep lines carved through what used to be smooth cheeks. His shrug, muted.

"We have a little from the last harvest," Cecilia said. Her statement sounded more like a question. "And ... and we still have the animals."

But they didn't.

Within an hour of Cecilia's hopeful observation, the family discovered the barn had collapsed under the weight of the snow, killing all of their livestock with the exception of a single horse and Blueberry, Virginia's favorite pig. With no other place to keep the animal alive, Virginia brought it into the house. The family fell into a dark silence, idly staying busy with the fire or occupying the pig. When the door banged open an hour later, the three women turned to see Jacob enter the house, alone.

"Where's your father?" Cecilia snapped.

"Gone," Jacob shook the snow off, hanging his jacket on a hook.

"Gone where?"

"Town. Took Thunder into town for help. Said we—"

"Don't matter what he said," Cecilia interrupted. And it didn't. They all knew. The barn collapsed, the animals killed. Most of the firewood buried under feet of snow.

They knew.

**

There were breaks between storms, but the cold ensured none of the snow melted. The road and fields remained buried beneath the thick white blanket.

By the end of December, things were much worse. The hay used to feed Blueberry and their firewood was disappearing as the snow continued to pile. They had to be even more prudent with it. It felt like the fire was rarely fed. Virginia never knew what it meant to not be able to ever get warm. She did now. Even huddled together around the hearth, holding their hands as close to the flames as they dared, the heat never seemed to reach them.

***

Blueberry never saw January.

The preserves and rations were gone sometime around the turn of the year. Blueberry was a necessary sacrifice, but it was still painful to say goodbye. When that litter was born no one thought Blueberry would live past the week. Virginia was allowed to take a little time away from working around the farm to tend to the piglet. They bonded and, even though Virginia was no child, she unabashedly held a childlike hope that Blueberry would be able to make it. And she had; she'd outlived all the other pigs. Blueberry had been born into the world a weakling and left it as a paragon of strength and selflessness.

As February approached, the snow came in batches and Roger still hadn't returned. If he made it to town he likely didn't make it out. Virginia saw how everyone forced themselves into believing he would return as soon as the weather lifted and the roads reappeared. They refused to believe anything else because to think anything else was to recognize the very real possibility that he was gone. Virginia sensed none of them were strong enough for that.

Cecilia was no help. With her husband gone and the unbroken months of dark winter, Virginia and her siblings could only watch as their mother descended into her own dormant season. She rarely spoke, she hadn't for weeks, and when she did have something to say it was often nothing more than a few grunts and short bursts of aggression.

They kept as much distance from her as they could. To Virginia, Jacob seemed to be the only one capable of supporting the family now. She appreciated his ceaseless work to keep them alive until help arrived.

As March approached, the gift that Blueberry provided was gone and they only survived the past few weeks on salted meat Jacob cured. He never mentioned where he got it and she didn't want to ask. She was too hungry to care if it was horse meat or something worse, like a rat. She was grateful for his forward thinking but that didn't mean she wasn't absolutely sick and tired of eating it. Her disgust at what they might be eating soon gave way to disgust at the taste of the same sustenance, meal after meal.

Halfway through March, she would have done anything for some of Jacob's salted meat.

**

By early March when everything edible was gone. Virginia tried to pass the short days busying herself straightening, cleaning, and fiddling. Avoiding idle minds also allowed her to avoid her mother.

Cecilia was no longer a contributing member of the family. Instead, she'd become a living ghost, spending most days in front of the window. Virginia knew what her mother was doing; she was hoping to see Roger racing Thunder back down the road, laden with every supply imaginable. Her mother would be daydreaming about them being together again, feasting over their reunion and the promise of the coming spring. But her mother wouldn't get that wish. Not for weeks yet, at best.

Virginia doubted her father was coming home. Something in her gut, some awareness, told her he was out there, buried under the snow that obscured the world. He likely got lost in the white-out storms on his way into town. She promised herself she would mourn come springtime; for now, she needed all her energy to survive another day.

***

Near the middle of March, Virginia didn't have to worry about her mother anymore.

Jacob was making repairs to the damaged barn roof and Meredith and Virginia were attempting to clear snow from the roof of the house. After struggling for a grueling hour, they headed inside for much-needed rest. It was so easy to get tired when you hadn't eaten for a week. When they got inside they noticed Cecilia was gone.

"Where's Ma?" Meredith asked.

Virginia didn't know. They waited, trying to warm themselves by the doleful flames that clung to life in the fireplace.

Though the imminent arrival of spring meant longer days, the sun was already setting. Their search would have to wait until the morning when they could follow her tracks and uncover her fate.

As luck would have it, or as fate demanded, it snowed that night. Virginia's heart sank when she woke to another cold morning and a fresh coat of snow.

They tried to find their mother's tracks. Even Jacob helped. But they soon gave up, realizing it was futile.

Their mother was gone.

Meredith got sick a few days later and started sleeping most days away. Virginia lacked the strength to be much help. Weakened by starvation, she could only watch her sister fade into her own premature winter. Jacob spent most days snarling at the fire, cursing God under his breath and doing what he could to keep snow off the roof when he wasn't out repairing the barn. He spent a lot of time out there, which angered Virginia. If she was going to die, she wanted to die with her remaining family near her. She understood Jacob's anger at the cruel fate God had fashioned for them but that didn't override her need to have him near.

Jacob's anger seemed to fuel him. Whereas she hardly had the strength to get up and urinate outside, he worked hours on end on the barn and house. A few days before he even dug out a wide trail to the woodpile and started bringing pieces into the house and splitting it into smaller slivers in hopes that they would catch and keep the fire alive. Enough of the splinters did, bringing a withered smile to Virginia's face at the newfound heat, puny as it was. Jacob sacrificed so much for them.

With the warmer fire, she knew she could let go and rest. And rest she did. Virginia woke a few days later to find Jacob kneeling next to Meredith.

Praying.

Virginia bolted upright.

Jacob turned at the noise. Tears stained his red cheeks. "Gone," Jacob cried, and Virginia felt her heart clutch.

She screamed in denial.

She screamed at God for being so cruel, taking one so young.

She screamed with all she could, knowing it would do nothing for Meredith and only irritate Jacob. She couldn't fault him when he lifted their sister's body, telling her he would take care of burying their Meredith. She didn't want to be around her broken mind either.

Exhausted, Virginia fell into a deep sleep. She slept ... and slept ... and slept ... and ...

Slept.

***

Her eyes flitted open sometime later. Virginia felt melded to the straw-matted pallet they slept on. It felt as much a part of her as she was of it.

Her father. Dead.

Her mother. Dead.

Meredith, so young. Dead.

Virginia and Jacob were all that was left of the family, the only two to make it this long. And her time was drawing near. She didn't want to die. She wanted to live. Not for the enjoyment of a new day or for seeing the promise of the first blade of grass or for the far-off prospect of marrying a nice boy.

No, she wanted to live so Jacob wouldn't have to carry on alone.

A scraping rang from across the room. Virginia turned, wincing against the bright light invading the house.

The sun!

Her weak heart leaped to life. She had no idea how much time had passed but she knew that was sunlight and that was all she cared about at the moment. The sun. She needed to feel the sun. Virginia struggled to throw off the blanket covering her. The room was warm, warmer than it should be from the weak fire that—

The hearth was dark.

She struggled to her elbows and to understand what was happening.

Jacob sat in front of the window. He was shirtless and his muscular back was sweaty.

"Jacob, how long have I been sleeping?" She swung her feet off the pallet to the floor. A spell of dizziness passed over her. She placed a hand on the pallet to steady herself. It was wonderful to not feel an icy coldness race up through the soles of her feet. It was so warm in the house; that realization alone brought some of her strength back.

"A few days," he answered, without turning around. The scraping continued.

Virginia watched him work, amazed at his fortitude. His strength was remarkable. Commendable. The way his muscles flexed, the way he appeared to have grown healthier over the winter when everyone else succumbed to it, herself included; it was almost inhuman.

Virginia struggled to her feet, wobbling as she tried to get her balance. It was an achievement to stand and there was Jacob, furiously working. She wore her shame like a shawl.

How did he do it? she thought.

Did it matter? He was healthy; he would survive even if she didn't.

And he might have the strength to find help.

47

Virginia stumbled, almost fell, catching herself on the hearthstone.

It was ice cold.

Her heart raced. This could only be a good sign, a sign of the nearing spring. She took a prudent step in Jacob's direction, trying to find a wall, the table, a chair, *anything* to hold lest she kill herself from a fall. They were too close to surviving to die now. She could taste it. She could smell—

That's when Virginia noticed the open window ... and the fresh air blowing into the house.

Her body groaned as she hurried over to smell the breeze. The fresh, warm breeze!

What she saw at the window stopped her immediately.

Icicles that had hung from the porch roof for an eternity were gone. The fat snow that clung to tree branches for endless months had regressed, exposing bare branches. Virginia could see through the graveyard of hundreds of naked trees that were no more than skeletons now, casualties of the winter war. But there, beyond the trees and across the road was a—

The road!

She could see the road!

The snow was no longer deep. It retreated so far that the porch was free of its grip and the wild bush tops jutted above the white blanket. A bird called from somewhere off in that graveyard of trees. Life was returning to Hannibal!

Excited, Virginia spun to hug her brother and ... gasped for air as the meat hook he held ripped open her stomach.

Everything came to her in a rush.

This was what he'd been working on when she woke.

The meat hook he'd been readying ... for her.

Virginia's hands went to his broad, muscular shoulders as she looked into his dark eyes. She leaned against him as her blood drained from her already weak body, pooling at her feet. She slumped against his solid chest as the world wavered, her vision blurring.

She now understood everything.

She understood where her father and mother had really gone.

She understood what happened to Meredith after she died.

And she understood how Jacob had remained so healthy throughout the brutal winter.

"Why?" she choked on the blood filling her throat.

Jacob bared his teeth. His dark eyes never faltered.

As her last breath faded, Virginia slumped, caught in Jacob's thick arms.

"At first I did it because we needed to survive," Jacob held her up, kissing her on the forehead and taking a long, deep smell of her hair. "But then I started to like the taste."

END

The Snowman

"I'm the mother fucking snowman."

Chelsea could barely make out the words; the world was a painful haze of booze and cocaine. Her head felt thick like someone filled it with concrete. Hard to hold up. In the haze, Eddie the Snowman was talking; she was sure of that much. She just didn't care.

The world was pain; her body was the canvas upon which it was conceived, outlined, filled in; where dimension was added until it was finally realized.

She had the Snowman to thank for that.

"Fuck man, I can't get comfortable," the Snowman—*did he even remember his name anymore*—squirmed on the rotted sofa, spreading his naked legs and grabbing his hairy balls in a grip that looked tight. That had to hurt, didn't it? Shit, even if it did, Eddie—the Snowman—would simply enjoy it that much more.

The Snowman was masochistic.

"That's because you're still flying," she moaned, her skull vibrating with each word.

He flicked a hand at her. "Shut up, bitch."

One of these days she was going to escape. One of these days she was going to find a real man who knew how to treat her the way she deserved to be treated. It was just a matter of time, but it was a time that would come. She would make sure of that. If she believed in a god she would pray that the day would come tomorrow. Today. But there was no god.

No god would let her fall like this.

Plus, waiting was difficult. She yearned to be respected by a man again, by anyone. But to Chelsea, that was a dream too far. Impossible.

From the floors to the ceilings, the apartment they shared with three other people was decaying. The peeling paint, neglected holes that dotted the walls, their home was a silent exposé on the effectiveness of violence and subjugation. She was pretty sure the cockroaches had become immune to the mold problem.

Numb to it the same way she was numb to life.

It hadn't always been like this. Once upon a time, she was the model of a woman with a plan. She had her shit together. Driven and young, Chelsea once possessed a dangerous mix of intelligence and beauty that smart women leveraged to make millions on the backs of the misogynistic culture.

But every chance she ever had, every gift she was given, she'd wasted on narcotics-filled needles and nose candy that provided an escape from the strife of living. People didn't understand. They didn't appreciate how miserable it was to see the world through her eyes, to feel its decay on her skin. They looked at her and pitied her, not caring to understand the pressures which ultimately compressed her into a ruined mess of constantly disheveled hair and cracked makeup. Her perpetual mask of emotional desolation.

But her recovery, the promise of feeling alive again, was close.

She only had to melt the Snowman.

"I'm hungry," he rolled over onto his stomach, his hairy, pimpled ass exposed to the daylight for the first, but not last, time today. "Go make me something."

"I don't feel like it."

"And I don't feel like being hungry," he snapped his finger. "Now, go make me something, Chelsea."

She moaned, hating him, but got up and crossed the twenty feet of linoleum to the kitchen.

The Snowman always got what the Snowman wanted, thanks to being the lifeline for every junkie in Olympia.

A few cheap beer bottles lay, toppled over, at the back of the bottom shelf of the refrigerator. The empty milk container mocked her. She had three eggs in the carton. That wouldn't feed both of them.

Looks like I'm eating out, she groaned as her stomach protested its delayed fulfillment. Or her stomach was smart enough to realize there might not be enough money in the account to pay for a fast-food breakfast. *Fuck, what if he says we're broke?*

"When aren't we?" she mumbled to the uninhabited refrigerator.

The Snowman grumbled, still face down on the couch. "What?"

She shook her head. "Nothing."

She grabbed a pan from the cupboard and threw it on the stove top. It clanked on the iron grates and the Snowman grumbled his displeasure. He hated noise. Chelsea did her best to ignore him. There was a time when she would cry anytime he got upset. Now, she was too dead inside to care.

When will his heart explode? she wondered. Could putting thought to it make the dream come true?

But snowmen didn't have hearts. Years of liquor, coke, cigarettes, barbiturates, and cheap beer eroded anything that might have passed as a heart, replacing it with an impermeable core, untouched by corrosion.

Chelsea realized she was daydreaming. Too late, registering the sizzling pan. *Shit, the eggs!* Chelsea turned them over. Burned.

He's going to fucking kill me.

How was she going to tell him? Infernos were calmer than a hungry Snowman. But if she was honest maybe he'd finally give her money to buy groceries. It wasn't something he usually did, even when times were good. Chelsea didn't even know where he stashed all the cash he made from pushing coke on business owners and politicians downtown. But if he knew they had nothing to eat, odds were good he'd be looser with his cash. Maybe he'd even part with a little extra and would forget about it long before he was sober again. Enough cash so she could buy herself a second pair of jeans, maybe?

The thought excited her. She scraped the eggs into the garbage and didn't even bother to wash the pan. She'd scrape out the burned parts later. The iron was hot; she needed to act while he was still coked out of his mind or the moment would pass and he might do something worse than not give her enough money to feed herself. The last time she pissed him off it took her over a week to walk without a limp. A week of staying inside so people didn't guess at what he'd done. She couldn't be cooped up with him again for that long.

Chelsea glanced at the Snowman, sprawled open on the couch and, in that split second, felt something she rarely ever felt.

Hope.

Rushing across the bedroom, she changed into her only pair of jeans and a sweater, grabbing her jacket on the way back to the living room. The world outside faded into white as snow fell. The shopping trip was going to be cold as the Snowman's love. She didn't care. A shopping trip meant a few minutes of feeling alive again.

He was still asleep. Chelsea shoved his shoulder. Once. Two times would get her a fist to the gut. "Hey! Wake up." Her tone was moderate, appropriate. Or that punch would surely come.

"What?" the Snowman spit into the pillow.

"I need cash."

"Fuck off."

"Come on, Eddie!" she slapped her thigh. She wanted him to see that she was upset. She wanted him to see that she was alive. "Just give me—"

Chelsea didn't finish the sentence. The Snowman vaulted to his feet. Before she realized he was standing, his fist was flying toward her head. A thick thud made the world swoon and then she was falling over the torn arm of the recliner. Her back hit the chair arm, the part where the cloth cover was worn away years before and most of the stuffing ripped out by the Husky they used to have. The Husky that Eddie took off the leash when he was supposed to be walking it. The Husky Eddie allowed to run into a neighborhood where the rich people in Olympia lived, the sort of people who saw dogs like that and kept them, and put chips in their necks, and took them for monthly grooming. Probably even some doggie daycare shit too. She never saw the dog again. Chelsea loved that dog, a lot more than she loved Eddie.

"You stupid cunt," spit foamed in the corner of the Snowman's mouth, "don't you ever call me that again!"

Chelsea leaned up on an elbow, holding the side of her face that felt as if it was on fire. "What? 'Eddie'? That's your name, isn't it?" It felt good to poke him from the safety of the other side of the chair.

"Don't do it, bitch," he snarled. "I'm the mother fucking—"

"Snowman, I know," she finished for him. In a million years Chelsea hadn't imagined she would provoke him like this. But, goddamn, this felt good. Really good. The Snowman waggled back and forth like a toddler who was about to piss his big boy undies. His usually narrowed gaze was wide with irritation and disbelief. Who was the last person to stand up to him? Chelsea wasn't sure anyone besides Eddie's junkies ever dared to speak to him like she was now.

"Are you fucking joking?" Eddie lunged over the chair to grab her. Chelsea scurried backward, out of reach, into the kitchen. It was a bad decision; the kitchen was an open area except for the four-chair table placed dead center in the small room. Still not on her feet, it was simple for Eddie to get to her. Enraged, he quickly closed the space between them. "You fucking cunt. I'm going to fucking kill you."

Then Chelsea did something that pushed him over the edge, threw him into a dizzy rage unlike any she'd seen and wasn't even sure he was capable of.

She laughed.

It was easy. They were fighting and Eddie was pissed. Again. And this time over the all-important issue of ruined eggs and her calling him by his actual name. It was as ridiculous as it was jaded. No other couples acted like this, not even the coke addicts that came around from time to time, trying to score a free flight from Eddie.

But not her and Eddie. This was them; this was how they were. Chaotic fragility.

"Are you fucking laughing at me?" Eddie knocked over one of the chairs.

Chelsea's lips trembled all on their own.

He closed the distance.

Chelsea backed up.

Eddie raised a fist.

Chelsea flinched and cowered against the counter cupboards.

"I oughta kill you," he threatened. He was close; his stale breath fell on her in a thin film. "You know that, bitch? I oughta kill you."

Then Eddie grabbed her by the throat and Chelsea knew he would do it.

He squeezed.

She gasped.

Chelsea didn't want to show him that she was afraid. He'd threatened to kill her a thousand times. Before her fall, she never imagined a world where she'd be okay with being threatened by anyone. Times changed when life stripped you of options and dignity, she guessed.

Here she was now, serving as a warning to those who made poor life choices. She never thought she'd die because of them.

Eddie's grip wasn't relaxing. Her throat felt thick, like those times when she'd partied too hard and urgently needed to evacuate a stomach full of booze and pills. Chelsea opened her mouth to draw a breath she desperately wanted, but nothing came.

Eddie pulled and she scrambled to her feet before he ripped her head from her shoulders. They were face-to-face now. Chelsea grasped for anything that would ground her to the world. The countertop was cool. Wet. Her hand slipped, stabbing the basin of the sink, sending jolts of pain up her elbow. She couldn't even cry out.

Eddie's face closed in on hers. "I'll fucking kill you."

In that moment his eyes burned with the desire for blood, there was no question about that. He was going to choke her until she was gone and he was free. He'd crush her windpipe like he enjoyed crushing beer cans he spent nights emptying when they were too broke to snort some of their extra inventory.

Chelsea knew she was seconds away from blinking out of the world in the middle of a shitty apartment in snowy Olympia, Washington. Memories of her life in Los Angeles, back when she was flying, flickered across the big screen of her mind. She'd almost been someone. Now she was about to become a faceless statistic, another number in a domestic violence report sitting on some enervated cop's desk.

Chelsea's hand, still in the sink, bumped the handle of the pan she'd burned the eggs in. The black iron wrapped itself inside her fingers. The handle was sturdy, so unlike anything else in her life. She brought it up in a quick, shallow arc. The side of the pan connected with Eddie's face. A satisfying *clonk* filled the small kitchen and Eddie collapsed in a heap against the table. It shuttled a few inches across the floor, sending one of the chairs toppling over.

He's going to kill me, Chelsea reminded herself, looking down at the man who always followed through on the promises that benefited him while ignoring any that didn't. Hundreds of nights of sobbing herself to sleep served as her evidence that he gladly failed her over and over.

And in that second of reflection, she knew everything she needed to know to make this life-altering decision. If she didn't kill him, he would finish his work when he regained consciousness.

Chelsea jumped on Eddie's chest, raised the pan, and brought it down on his head. The first strike was the most difficult, but she'd swung it out of instinct to survive. The second swing was much easier. It was a strike filled with rage and revenge, the toll she'd paid for his self-loathing and addiction. Nothing more than any animal would want for itself. She needed to respect herself enough to realize that.

And it was easier with each subsequent *thunk* against his head.

Under the assault, Eddie didn't move, didn't cry out.

Each swing delivered freedom.

She felt lighter, knowing that the only thing separating her from finding the person she used to be was dying here on the kitchen floor. When he was gone she would find his hidden case of drug money. It wasn't a fortune, but it was enough to get her away from this decrepit life and buy her time to figure out what she was going to do next.

Snow piled up on the small balcony. A full-blown storm now. By the time Eddie's face had turned to mush, Chelsea knew she needed to act fast. She had to find the money and escape. The city would start shutting down if it wasn't already, and their roommates would be home as soon as the city bus could bring them back.

Eddie was dead. No amount of egg pans to the face was going to help her escape. So Chelsea spent the next few hours tearing apart the apartment. Under a set of loose floorboards by the television cabinet, she found what she was looking for. Two olive green military bags stuffed to the top with cash were jammed into the narrow space. Ones, fives, and tens. Thousands of dollars!

A new life.

Chelsea snagged the bags and loaded the new BMW Eddie never let her drive. He bought it six months ago and she'd never even sat in the driver's seat. It was his baby, he told her whenever she had 'the guts', as he said, to ask permission to drive it. Now she was taking it. He couldn't protest and this would convince the cops of a robbery if the money and the car were gone.

It was exciting to spit in the face of the man who'd ruined her. Even if he was already dead.

Chelsea loaded the money and her single bag of clothes, leaving everything else she owned behind.

There was one last thing to do.

Dispose of Eddie the Snowman.

The snow was falling fast, which worked to her advantage. People hid from it, remaining inside, making it easier to get his body to the car. The most difficult part was dragging him to the elevator—thankfully it worked again, enough tenants complained to finally get the landlord moving again—and out to the car. By the time she'd loaded him into the trunk and slunk in the driver's seat, her hair was matted to her face. Her chest heaved, filling and emptying in gradually-decreasing breaths. Chelsea's heart rate slowed enough to convince her it was excitement and not death she was feeling. Finally composed, she pulled away from her personal hell.

She didn't stop until she was east of Tacoma.

Out here the cities curved away toward Canada.

Out here, people spread as far and wide as the Cascade Range took them.

Out here, up in the hills, she could get rid of Eddie.

In her previous life, she skied. A lot. During college, Chelsea spent weekends chasing thrills with the money her parents sent her every few weeks. That was when she was an athlete, young and healthy, with an ass that drew more gawking than the last ten years combined had.

She was at home in the mountains, like she'd never left. But she wasn't here to ski; she drove these winding back roads to find a place remote enough to dump Eddie.

The snowstorm chased her all the way out of Olympia and continued its eastward path. She needed to be back to sea level before it hit the mountains or she'd be stuck. The BMW was shit in the snow, a lesson she learned as soon as she raced away from the apartment and almost side-swiped a pedestrian.

A trailhead stretched toward the road, emptying into a small area where hikers and hunters parked their vehicles before heading into the mountains. No cars dotted the parking area. Chelsea didn't want to test her luck. It was dusk and getting darker with each passing second. She needed to be out of the woods before darkness descended. A parked car would raise suspicions. A parked car here when night fell would draw someone from law enforcement.

The sight of Eddie's broken body assaulted her as soon as she opened the trunk. The drive was relatively short, less than two hours, but it provided her with an opportunity to mentally cleanse herself of what she'd done. Seeing him like this was an uneasy reminder of the cost of her freedom.

Pulling Eddie's body from the trunk required two free hands. She took a deep gulp and got to work. Eddie's cologne drifted into her nasal passages, reminding her of the times he would lay on top of her and grunt himself to satisfaction while she was tripping.

She wasn't going to miss him.

His head bobbed against a raised arm as she yanked him, step-by-excruciating-step, up the path. His particular shade of death became more prominent by the minute. Chelsea's stomach heaved. Eddie's demolished cheek and collapsed eye socket made her gagging worse. He deserved nothing less. Maybe he shouldn't have fed her volatile drugs, getting her hooked, and secluding her from everything in her life that made her happy. If he'd let her live, maybe she would have let him.

Eddie deserved every bit of this and she deserved the spiritual and financial windfall that was coming her way.

No remorse. No regret.

Chelsea's feet slipped out and she landed hard on her ass, making her shout in pain. Glancing over her shoulder, she exhaled; the trail gained elevation quickly. There was no way she could get him up another fifty feet. Eddie's corpse was heavy and uncooperative and she tired quickly after the adrenaline of killing him flushed from her system. Years of abusing her body weren't helping either.

This was going to have to be the spot.

A steep drop off beckoned. Chelsea couldn't see how far down it went in the fading light, but it was steep enough to meet her needs. She didn't have to pull him up the mountain; all she had to do was drop him over the side of it.

Inching him toward the edge, Chelsea's lungs burned. Her thighs quivered. The plan was to get to Seattle tonight and buy an expensive hotel room, the most expensive she could find that would take cash. But her life of exciting flings would have to wait another night. Tonight she'd have to find something close and start her elevated experience tomorrow.

Falling to her knees next to Eddie's body with all the energy she had left, she shoved.

Eddie's body rocked forward and then back toward her. Chelsea gave a cry of frustration that sounded odd against the silent mountains. He wasn't going to deny her this. He wasn't going to get his way this time.

In that brief second, she screamed with all the pent-up rage and pain of wasted years, slamming into him with every bit of force one hundred and forty pounds could muster. When Eddie the Snowman rolled over the edge, Chelsea cried.

His body tumbled, slowly at first, and then picked up speed as it descended. She watched his corpse tumbled down the slope. Even bouncing off trees didn't stop the momentum created by the pitch of the mountain.

Chelsea remained on her knees, at the edge of the trail, gasping for breath. She didn't need the dying daylight to ensure Eddie was gone for good; she could hear him falling. Branches cracked. Twigs snapped. *Thumping* as his corpse bounced off hard snow-covered mounds. Down and down Eddie tumbled until she no longer heard him over the cleansing wind.

Only then did she stand and begin living again.

Eddie was gone from her life.

***

Four years old. *How is he four already?* Where had the time gone? It seemed like just yesterday that she and Jerrod found out they were pregnant, and now she was watching Jacob, the light of her world, race around the kitchen.

"Mommy, can I have one?" Jacob tried to stretch on his toes to peek over the counter.

Chelsea laughed. "No sweetie. You've already had three." Jacob was a ravenous boy. The fact that her mother kept feeding him brownies wasn't one of her better ideas. Chelsea didn't blame her. They'd missed so many years of life over the fallout that was so distant now as to be a dream. This was them enjoying being a family again, so unlike that time before.

It was another lifetime. I was a different person.

More than a decade removed from that drug-induced hell she'd survived with Eddie, her life was hers again. The money helped. A lot. It paid for a small home in Shelton, where real estate was cheaper. It paid for a drug treatment program she completed on her first attempt. It paid for some of her education, but not all. Tuition was ridiculous!

Erasing her previous life was so much easier but also so less rewarding than carving her professional path. The only people who missed Eddie were probably the roommates she'd left behind, though their perpetual high probably prevented them from thinking too much about him. Cops came around once, within a few weeks of her leaving. They had a difficult conversation; not because it was difficult to lie to them—it wasn't—but because she was suffering through miserable withdrawals. They seemed more interested in getting her the help she needed than they did tracking down drug-pushing scum like Eddie. The treatment center was, at times, worse than living with Eddie. But she'd gotten through it and came out a whole person, ready to make up those lost years to those she'd hurt.

Like Mom.

Cynthia made reconciliation a breeze compared to what Chelsea had just been through. The Snowman and a treatment program lacked the one attribute her mother possessed in abundance: love. They'd erased years of pain with long conversations, filled with a few hundred tears and even more hugs. Cynthia didn't ask much after Chelsea explained that she'd left Eddie for good. And now Chelsea understood why. Some things were too painful for a parent to bear.

It all paid off. She had been clean for years now, held a four-year degree, and married to Jerrod. And she was a mother now. *A mother!* Success after success came for them. It was a fairytale, the past decade. They opened a cabin resort outside of Mt. Rainier's national park, to which she was about to return.

She was the different woman she always wanted to be.

"You be good for Grandma," Chelsea smiled, kneeling to get to Jacob's level.

"I will, Mommy."

Her mother patted Chelsea's hand, loosening its grip on Jacob. "Go, before it gets dark."

Chelsea stood and hugged her. "Are you sure you're okay with this? Keeping Jacob for this long?"

Cynthia laughed. "Oh, please. A week is nothing. Plus," she wagged a finger at Chelsea, "you and Jerrod deserve the cruise. You've been working too much. It's time for you to relax for a bit. Enjoy it."

They shared a final hug before Chelsea kissed Jacob one more time.

Waving goodbye to the two outlines of people, one large, one tiny, standing in her mother's door squeezed her heart.

The disappearing house encouraged her onward even as the evening began to shroud it.

The drive was short, but the night was quickly blackening. And it was snowing again, as it had been for weeks. Starting in late October and, two months later, the snow still hadn't abated. Every year since moving to the mountains they'd had a white Christmas. This one would be no different.

And she loved every minute of it. So different than the dreary Christmases in Olympia.

Chelsea was excited. It took more than money to operate the business. In fact, money was the thing that launched the business, it didn't maintain it. Almost overnight she had to become a receptionist, booking clerk, groundskeeper, and plumber. Those were the real skills that kept the cabins booked and patrons returning season after season. And working for two years straight without a day off had worn her down. The business was fulfilling but exhausting, and this cruise was long overdue.

The thought of an all-inclusive drink menu, days spent lounging poolside with a good book, and ocean-side port stops at exotic locations helped get her out her mother's front door. It was the only way she could be okay with leaving Jacob behind. Chelsea hadn't been separated from him for more than a single night when he had a sleepover at a friend's house. A week? She wasn't sure she could survive that.

At that moment the world went white.

Chelsea slammed on the brakes. She'd been daydreaming, half paying attention to the road she could navigate in her sleep. The sharp bend was a few hundred yards in the distance one second and, the next, her windshield was a blanket of white.

A mountain slide, she thought, her throat gripped closed with fear.

The car kicked sideways.

Chelsea corrected, in the opposite direction of the side of the road that dropped away. The back wheels caught and whipped the car in a one-hundred-eighty-degree turn. Her head slammed against the window, stars exploding to life in her vision. She hit something, and the car spun rotated in a dizzying circle, too quickly to remain oriented.

Then the world gave way and she fell.

The car went over the edge. Without a barricade, there was nothing to stop her from tumbling down the mountainside. The car struck a tree and flipped. Side windows smashed. Chelsea screamed at the assault of shards, wind, and snow that filled the car. A tree branch snapped into the cabin, catching her square in the face. She lost all but the slimmest of senses that she was still falling. For an eternity of seconds, the car bounced through young trees, bouncing and spinning off the larger ones, gaining momentum as it fell.

She was going to die out here.

The snow-covered landscape became the sky. The blackness became the ground above which she floated. Turning over and over, tumbling further from the road.

And then it all ended. The car came to a rest on its roof. Chelsea was alive but in too much pain to think through what she needed to do. Her face felt hot; there was a pool of blood forming on the roof of the car underneath her. Everything and nothing hurt.

And the night was silent.

At some point during the accident, the engine stopped running. The bitter smell of gas filled the cooling night air. It was quiet. The headlights that revealed millions of glittering specks of snow dust, the only sign she was still alive.

Chelsea knew she was in trouble, serious trouble. This part of the road wasn't a main thoroughfare for the skiers and snowboarders. There was no reason for anyone to come this way at this time of year except to get to the various cabin resorts. And at this time of night in the middle of the week, those types of visitors would be few and far between. Only a great stroke of luck was going to bring a motorist in this direction.

To make matters worse, she had no safety gear in the car. The trip to her mother's was supposed to be quick so she hadn't bothered to grab blankets. At best, and only if she could get to the trunk, the flares might still be there. She could use those to light her way back up the mountain and alert someone.

Assuming I can walk.

The pull of gravity placed her weight on the seat belt. The tension eliminated any slack she might have used to unhook it. Panic rose at the realization that she might be trapped in her own car, upside down, in a tight valley at the foot of a mountainside road. Passing motorists might now even be able to see this far down.

Tears began to stream down—up?—her forehead. *Jacob? Jerrod? God, no!* She fought the seatbelt buckle, but it refused to come loose.

"Help!" her cry disappeared beyond the illuminated part of the forest. No one answered. No one should. The nearest house was a few miles away, at best.

But she cried out again anyway. Throughout her life, she'd been a fighter and that wasn't about to change now. She was in a desperate situation, but she wasn't going to sit and wait for the reaper. She would do what she always did, even when things seemed hopeless.

"HELP!" Her message carried through the night.

Silence.

Despair grew to an overwhelming force. A blackout was coming. That might be the best way to go, to fall asleep and never wake up. Painless. She wouldn't suffer the anguish of freezing to death, watching the world become grayer until her will to live was sucked from her. Sleep, even eternal, would be better than that.

Her eyes closed. Heavy.

Chelsea hoped her final sleep would be filled with visions of Jacob and Jerrod. They rescued her belief in humankind after years of hell and torture. They saved her. Would they miss her as much as she already missed them? *They would, right?* They were a loving family, small but close, working past the scars of the past together.

Surely they would re—

—a branch snapped. Chelsea's eyes rocketed open and she stared into the white waste of the falling night.

Again, another crack and ... and something else.

Scratching.

A bear? *Shit! Shit! Shit! My gun, where did I put the gun? The glove box? Can I reach—*

More scratching, this time closer, just out of range of the lights.

But that wasn't scratching. It was too persistent, too rhythmic.

Not scratching ...

... shuffling.

In the beams of the headlights, something moved. The deep darkness was thick, but not impenetrable. A hint of something out there.

The gun might or might not be in the glove box, but she wasn't going to wait. She reached, stretched, strained against the hold the seat belt had on her. Her shaking hand stretched as she willed her joints to give just a little more.

But the glove box was too far away, forever out of reach as long as she was restrained.

The thing in the blackness shuffled closer.

In a desperate last move, Chelsea yanked her car keys out of the ignition. Finding the thickest one, she began sawing at the belt. She wasn't sure it would work but what other options did she have?

The shuffling now came from the edge of the world, where her headlights met the eternal blackness. Chelsea risked a glance into beams of light, not sure she wanted to see what was coming.

Her hand went numb at the sight, the keys falling onto the roof of the car.

Out of the woods walked a ... man.

A man who wasn't a man.

A man whose naked legs were as white as the snow that blanketed the ground in her car beams. No, they were whiter, as if the cold that destroyed his legs was deeper, older, than the snow on the ground. Ageless.

A man whose bare feet tortuously crunched the ground in a festering creep.

A man who strode through the world as naked as the day he was born, his frozen white cock swaying back and forth as flaccid and loose as if blood still surged through it.

A man whose flabby stomach betrayed the fact that even in death neglect still had consequences.

A man whose half-face had frozen in the perpetual state of the moment of his death. The moment he was assaulted by a frying pan containing burned eggs. The face that was beaten and battered after he fell into a sleep from which he never woke again.

As the frozen half-face smiled, the eyeball hanging from the crushed socket wiggled, laughing all on its own.

Eddie.

Chelsea screamed, yanking at the seatbelt, commanding it to separate. She slithered, pushing against the roof. Rip. Tear. Yet it didn't give; it refused her that which she lusted for. Escape.

Inch by inch, the frozen corpse of her former lover moved toward the vehicle. Crunching snow. Step by lethargic step. Mere feet away, he lowered himself to clear the hood of the car and crawled toward her with a depraved lopsided grin on his face. She'd seen that smile a million times. It was the smile Eddie only showed when he'd screwed someone out of a deal or scored a big hit.

It was the smile he wore on those nights when he beat her.

The corpse drew closer, its white arms extended outward. His sky-blue nails promising to dig into her. Deep.

"Hello, bitch." Frozen death had robbed Eddie of his voice, leaving only a wispy emanation to it.

His claws made the first contact with her skin. The ice-blue nails closed around her throat.

"E—Eddie?" she choked.

The corpse shook its head, the loose eyeball swaying side to side. "No, cunt," it answered, "I'm the mother fucking snowman."

And then the nails dug into her skin, beneath her skin, into her esophagus, into her.

And the world went white.

END

I'm Dreaming of a Whiteout

"When are we going home, Kai?" Dad asked.

Again.

It was the fifteenth time in the past hour. I know because I counted.

Both me and Mom knew when we were going home. It was the same as every trip to the cabin.

"Soon, Jim," Mom answered. It was her fifteenth time as well. I know that because she says it every time he asks, even if I've already answered him.

We smiled at each other across the cabin. Knowing, patient smiles, filled with a mix of pain and love for the ghost of the man who sat in the front room with me.

"Why isn't Max here yet?" she asked me. I was hoping to get through my first coffee before she brought him up.

"I don't know, Mom," I tried to make my reply sound absent, disinterested with the topic. But Mom was always good at picking up on subtleties except when it came to me and my love life. She got better at it over the years, mostly because she let go of her biases. While I was in college she was all over me. If it wasn't my major, it was my grades. If it wasn't my major or my grades, it was my love life.

That was a lot of fun.

I'd hidden the fact that I was gay from my parents throughout high school, even dating a few girls to throw them off. But leaving to attend the University of Washington delivered freedom on a level I didn't think was possible. Not only was living in Seattle a hell of a lot better than living in the small town of Centralia, two hours down the road, but the people of the city and the campus itself were much more open and accepting of its gay, lesbian, and trans members. It was the first place in the world where it was okay to be anything but straight. I could have stayed there forever.

Some of my excitement about this new identity liberty slipped through in a text to my mother during my freshman year. I don't even think I was into my second semester when I mentioned finding someone attractive. It was at a party. In my drunken stupor (*or was it courage?*) I told my mother the secret I'd hid from her my entire life. She didn't reply. When a few weeks passed and I still hadn't heard from her, I knew we'd crossed a threshold that redefined our relationship.

That's how conservative families operate. The expected blowups and accusations, yelling matches filled with painful comments from parents not yet ready to deal with having a gay kid, followed by months, if not years, of silence. We didn't start healing until I came home after that freshman year. I guess it was a lot harder for them to ignore or reject me when I was standing on their doorstep.

To her credit, Mom came around. Who said you couldn't teach old dogs new tricks?

Dad ... well, he never changed, not until that decision was taken from him.

By the time I returned to Seattle the following September, she was at least convinced I wasn't torturing small animals in my spare time. Before long she was even ready to meet my boyfriend. Dad had a serious aversion to thinking about his son planting a hand on a man's ass the same way he'd done to Mom my entire life. He seemed fixated on the image he'd created. Back then, the hypocrisy of straight people infuriated me. After too many years, even after college, and too many screaming matches, I gave it up. If he didn't care about the true me, I wasn't going to care about what principles grounded his opinion.

I was okay with that; time was on my side. He was the older one, the parent who was missing out on his child's life. The weight of it bothered him, even if he tried to never show it. At least he tried to deal with something.

We almost ended up being a decent family.

Sitting here, with him, I grimaced at the memory of us. The family we never quite became.

"What's that about?"

"What?" I put the mask back on.

"That look?"

"Oh," I laughed. It was fake and I knew she'd notice. "Nothing."

"Hmmm, okay. Well, I hope Max gets up here before the storm," she commented as she washed the last of the dishes. I breathed again. "I don't want him getting caught out in it. He's a city boy, after all. You might want to get into town and grab him."

This time my laugh was real. I loved when she talked like this about people from cities as if we were mountain people. We were as 'trashy white' as everyone else in Centralia, a decent-sized town in its own right. But in Centralia, we were as satiated with the comforts of modern living as someone from Seattle. The only difference? Seattle had mass transit.

"We're city people too," I reminded her, glancing away from the book I was reading long enough to smirk at her.

She flicked her soapy fingertips at me. "You're a brat."

"And you're a snob," I said, being playful. I set my e-reader down in my lap. "But, I promise, I'll head into town in a bit."

She glanced out the window that exposed the Pacific Northwest's majesty. A shadow passed over her face as if she saw something out there. "You should call him. If he's not close, tell him to turn around."

I didn't like her change of tone or her suggestion. Lifting myself off the chair, a challenge since I'd draped my legs over the arm, I reached into my back pocket and pulled out my cell phone, wagging it at her. "Kinda hard to do without reception, Mommy."

Now she flicked a spatula covered with soapy water at me. "Don't say that," she chided. "It's gross. Plus, I can't help that you're addicted to that darn thing. Use the house phone."

I laughed. "It's not about being addicted," I groaned. "It's about being connected. You know? To the world? The big, round globe we live on?"

I stopped immediately. That was a stupid thing to say. What happened with Dad wasn't her fault. Mom's face blanked. "I'm sorry."

But she only shook her head, concentrating on that small, soapy pile of dishes and utensils from the night's dinner. "It's okay."

It wasn't. It hurt. I should have been more sensitive. I crossed the small living area to the kitchen. Mom continued washing the dishes. Putting my arm around her, I leaned my head until it touched hers. She softened immediately. "Does he still do it?"

All Dad seemed worried about was that stupid desktop globe. It had to be everywhere he was. Mom kept one at the cabin, convincing him it was the same one from the house. He didn't know. But he needed the globe, Mom said. It helped him feel grounded because his way home was illuminated in the lights in the globe.

It didn't have lights.

But Dad saw them. Ever since the accident.

Going home. He always worried about going home. Even when he was home.

The accident really fucked him up.

The soapy water served as a wonderful distraction for her. After a moment of silence, we shared a look at Dad. He sat in the rocking chair facing the tall windows. Back to my middle school years, I could remember him enjoying the view, almost at an unhealthy level, like he had some deep connection with this part of the world that went beyond normal. But now, decades later, it was the only thing that brought him out of his vegetative stupor. And that only happened on rare occasions. Maybe that was why Mom brought him up here so often. Maybe that was why we were spending Christmas here at the cabin, instead of back at the house in Centralia.

Below us, the dark green canopy of western Washington forest darkened with the oncoming winter evening. It was four in the afternoon. Night came early in this part of the world. The night promised our first snowfall of the season.

"Yeah," her soft reply was barely audible above the sound of running water hitting the dishes under her hands. She stole a glance at my immobile father.

"It'll get better," I served up the platitude with practiced ease. It wasn't going to get better, we both knew it. It hadn't since the accident that took my father from us and replaced him with that shell sitting in the living room. He'd been in the Olympic Mountains when it happened. No one was with him; Dad had so few friends out here. A steep grade on a mountain, a misplaced foot, we guessed, and the man we knew tumbled from the world, replaced by this reserved and incomprehensible person. Rumors from town about an ancient evil being responsible for Dad's disappearance filtered out to the cabin, out to Mom. People said inconsiderate things, ridiculous things. Blaming some ancient creature. Spreading stories of how it terrorized the region and that Dad was its latest victim. Irresponsible things. How many times had she called me in tears because of the stupid things uneducated people said? I hated that she came up here with Dad. I hated that she stayed here when he disappeared. I hated the people in town for tormenting her like that.

And I hated myself for not being there for her. For them.

But Dad proved them wrong, wandering to safety after days of being lost.

How it didn't kill Mom, I'll never know. When he came back though, he wasn't the same. He never was again.

Docility easily switched to rage with this new man. After the medications mutated his brain's pathways, he started disappearing for hours at a time, getting lost in the neighborhood where he'd spent his entire life. It caused Mom endless heartache. But she stood by him. Even when he'd wander off during a dark period when Ember Lake was terrorized by a serial killer a couple years ago. Every year since the accident, he'd disappear on her. Most of those times were up here, too far away for me to help. She was alone in more ways than one. When most people would have broken, she stayed strong.

"I know," Mom said, just as false as I'd been with her. I imagined she was distracted by visions of what her life was like before the accident and subsequent drugs filled her husband's head with hallucinations. "It's starting to snow," Mom broke my thoughts, gesturing with a butter knife toward the windows. "The first snow. The white night is coming. You need to get going, Kai. No two ways about it. Go. Get Max. It'll be time to feed your father soon. I want you home."

She was right; flakes danced in swirls outside the windows.

"Okay, okay. I'll head into town," I leaned in and kissed her on the cheek.

The side of her mouth curled up. Did my coming out here make her happy? I hoped so; she had so little happiness in her life these past few years. "Good. Get going," she counseled, her tone lighter now as she gave me a tender shove. "I don't want you and Max caught out in it. You're bad enough of a driver and he's never been up here. Don't make him do it on his own. You know how it can be."

I did. The road going into town was a tight two-lane with no shoulder. All the roads around Ember Lake were slivers cutting through the forest. Even on summer days, it was perilous. Winter made it worse. Driving them in the snow, for someone who'd never driven up here? I didn't want to do that to Max.

Even if we'd been fighting.

Even if he was being a complete asshole.

"Don't dawdle," Mom smiled, draining the sink. "We've got nowhere to go until the Montmore's party tomorrow. But I want you back soon. Then we can all have a nice, relaxing weekend. You two have been under a lot of pressure lately."

We had.

I kissed her cheek one last time and headed down the short hall toward the room I was going to share with Max. If he ever got here. Snagging my North Face jacket, I made a quick exit and got the car warming. Refusing to sit and wait for it, I headed back inside to let Mom know I was leaving.

She sat next to Dad in front of the windows. Their gray-haired heads peaked over the chairs. Mom's knitting sat in her lap and Dad was asleep. He slept a lot these days. Mom put a finger to her lips, shushing me. I noticed her other hand was on his. Knitting had given way to a connection between the lifelong partners.

My chest swelled. After all these years they still had intimacy. She'd lost so much with him, time and memories, but she hadn't lost that at least.

I winked at her and headed out. Even if the car was cold, I'd start toward town and give them some quiet. Half of me ached that they didn't have many other people in their lives. But I was relieved to be away. I loved my father, even though he never came to peace with who I was. Maybe that's why seeing him like this bothered me so much. It was a reminder that I would never get his acceptance.

I drew a breath. The past couldn't be changed, and I had to take care of me now. That meant keeping my remorse over what happened to him balanced with healthy things.

Things like having Max near me.

The night sucked the warm glow from the cabin windows into the growing darkness as I drove toward town.

Toward Max.

A half hour passed before I turned onto Main Street, the main thoroughfare cluttered with every business required to satisfy the immediate needs of a mountain community. On the left, beyond the shops, was the Inlet. The right, a few houses scattered across the uneven hillside, reaching away from the road.

In Ember Lake, all life happened on Main Street.

Max and I had agreed to meet at Smithy's, the local coffee and ice cream bar. A single car parked in front of the building betrayed Max. He was late again.

I pulled in and headed inside for coffee and an overdue conversation. In all honesty, I was sort of glad Max wasn't here yet; it would give me time to catch up with a lifelong friend.

Smithy made the best damn coffee in Ember Lake; it didn't matter that Smithy's was the only place in Ember Lake that served coffee except for the gas station. Plus, the gas station was technically outside the village limits.

"Hey, Kai," Smithy greeted me with a perpetual warm smile. "Chocolate Mocha?" Smithy knew my drink even after almost two years since the last time I saw him. Some people had bartenders who knew everything about them. I had Smithy and his knowledge of my inclination toward sweeter blends. This wasn't about fitting gay stereotypes; this was about enjoying the beautiful experience of a perfectly roasted mocha.

"Yes, sir," I beamed back, giving him a quick hug over top the counter. He had to stretch; his stomach had grown since I'd last seen him.

Smithy was in his 50s and had owned the shop as long as I could remember. He was also the sole employee of the shop. Smithy never got away. That's why everyone considered him an icon in town. The man was a rock. As I hugged him, his bulbous shoulders were solid, his grip, crushing. Smithy still shaved his head. I don't think he ever had hair. Most amazing of all about Smithy, for a man who ran a coffee and ice cream shop, was the fact that he had the most gorgeous set of teeth I'd ever seen on anyone. They were straight, square, and bone white. He was handsome for an older man. If I was into men his age, he'd be a target.

I stood at the counter while he made the drink. I was the only customer in the place except for a woman who sat in the corner, typing away on a laptop. She didn't look like the type of hardened person who lived in a place like this. It takes a certain level of fortitude to be a mountain person and she wasn't carved to fit that mold. A professional blogger? Her midnight hair was straight and fell well past her shoulders. She was slim and fit. Her skin was dark. Whoever she was, she definitely wasn't someone I expected to see in Ember Lake.

Smithy steamed my coffee, stirring it before moving to the back bar and adding his custom cream design, which was nothing more than the shop's iconic logo. He did it all within seconds, perfect and clean. Every single time. "Thanks," I said as I took my mug. "How's business been?"

Smithy smiled. He always smiled. "Decent enough," he answered. Waving at the empty room, he continued, "Little slow right now, but it's offseason and getting close to the evening. You know folks aren't going to be out past dark. Especially with the first snow supposedly rolling in."

"Yeah, it's rolling in behind me," I commented. "That's why I came into town today. My boyfriend is coming up and I'm going to meet up with him. Wasn't planning on it, but Mom wanted me back at the cabin before the storm hit."

Smithy nodded, his smile tightening. Something was wrong. "Was it snowing already up at their place?"

"Yeah."

Now the smile slipped completely.

"You need to head on back to your cabin, son." He nodded at the woman, "I'm about to tell her to start packing up too. You and I? We can catch up after the white night."

This wasn't like Smithy at all. Throughout my teens when I bought coffee and ice cream—I was a boy who could eat anything—I'd routinely stay past closing time. He never minded. But people changed and Smithy wasn't getting younger. Maybe he was just tired?

"I swear your sign said you closed at 6?" I asked.

Smithy stepped back from the bar, running a hand over that slick dome of a skull. "Yeah, I need to get that changed. Just don't have time to get down to Olympia to get it done. Figure it's easier to tell people."

I was confused but tried to not let it show. I didn't want to interrupt the woman from whatever she was working on. This was Smithy's store; he could do whatever he wanted, even if it meant closing early and losing out on business. It's not like my four-dollar cup of coffee was going to make a difference in his ability to feed himself tomorrow. The only issue was Max.

"How much longer are you going to stay open?" I asked. "I'm waiting for my boyfriend. We agreed to meet here." The woman on the laptop stopped typing; I felt her eyes on me even without having to look at her.

Smithy almost looked sad, his smile turning into a slight frown. "Soon, son. I'm sorry, but it's the first snow."

"First snow?" I watched him. "Why does everyone keep saying that?"

Smithy paused and then nodded toward the front windows of the store, out where my car was parked next to this woman's. Beyond that, the street was quiet. No one was walking. No vehicles passed by. I hadn't noticed it on my way in because I was focused on Max and my family. But the way Smithy was acting made me feel uneasy. His need to close early had me imagining all sorts of apocalyptic scenarios.

But this wasn't the apocalypse; this was a mountain town with mountain people who worked hard and spent most of their time at home with their families. I figured since this was Christmas week that's exactly what everyone in Ember Lake was doing.

"I'm not sure what you're —" I started as I turned back toward Smithy, only to notice he was no longer behind the bar but making his way around it, toward the front window. The black haired woman now watched him unashamedly. He stood in front of the window, arms crossed, checking as much of the sky as his shop's awning allowed.

"First snow. The white night is coming," Smithy said. It was a dark comment, full of foreboding.

Or maybe misery over the coming months of cold, I thought. Ember Lake's warmer weather meant a fatter bank account. The cold months had to be tight for his wallet.

"Can I stay here until Max shows up?" I asked.

Smithy didn't turn around. Erect, he kept standing there, arms crossed. Whatever had his attention, it had it completely. I began to think he was going to ignore the question. This wasn't the Smithy I used to know. If I left, I could drive around town finding a cell signal. It was an option, but one that would deprive me of catching up with a friend I hadn't seen in too long.

Smithy shook his head back and forth, not saying a word. I couldn't tell if he was shaking his head in answer to me or at this strange revulsion over some snow.

Smithy then shocked me. Without looking at either of us, he told the woman, "I'm going to need you to pack up your things. Going to close up shop."

The woman scowled but began gathering her loose notes spread across the small table.

I moved closer, leaning in to whisper, "What's going on, Smithy? Is everything okay?"

He squared up to me. When I looked into his eyes I saw an abyss. "First snow is comin' and you best be getting home. Get inside. Stay inside. It's going to be a dangerous one. No one needs to be out when the white night comes. Even you."

"Smithy, I need to wait for Max. I get it if I can't stay here, I'll head over to the gas station. I'm not going home. But I'm more worried about you. Are you okay?"

One sharp shake of his head. "Don't head to the gas station, don't head anywhere. Get yourself home, son. And ma'am," he turned and acknowledged the woman, "same goes for you. Wherever you're going, get there. And get there soon. I failed both of you." He returned his gaze to me. "Failed both of you, I did. Now."

"Smithy," I laughed, "what are you talking about? You didn't fail us. And, in case you forgot, I've been up here in the winter before, you know that. Remember how Dad used to make me drive in the snow to get used to it? I went off the road into your front yard. Tore up your bushes. Remember? A little snow isn't going to be a problem for me."

Smithy stared at me. The woman was done packing her things up and turned sideways to get by me, out the door. I watched her go. She fumbled with her car fob, dropped it, and disappeared behind her car as she bent to retrieve it.

I turned to Smithy. "See what you did? You made a nervous wreck out of her. She's probably going to drive like hell out of town, back to wherever she came from. She gets in an accident, that's on you."

Smithy nodded. "Better an accident away from Ember Lake than sticking around here. You need to get going, son." He turned away and mumbled. "Before the evil wakes."

I shook my head, unsure if I'd heard him correctly. "I'll go, but I would rather you tell me you had some hot date lined up. No need to be acting all weird."

Smithy moved behind the counter powering down the signs, lights, and equipment. "You wouldn't say that if you knew what was coming."

"What? What's coming?"

Still distracted by closing down the store and collecting his cash drawer and receipts, Smithy shook his head, not making eye contact. "The white night son. Things—things happen in Ember Lake. Have been for the last couple years. No one knows how or why, but that doesn't change this or that." He fumbled the cash bag, dropping it. Disappearing below the counter to retrieve it, he slapped the bag on the counter in frustration when he reappeared. His stare made me fidget. "There's an ancient evil coming, Kai. Always does on the first snow. You need to get somewhere safe, son. And this coffee shop isn't it. Go."

I zipped up my jacket. "Okay," I said, not trying to push him. Smithy looked frayed. "I'm going. I don't imagine you're going to be open tomorrow, with it being Christmas. So have yourself a good one, Smithy. I'll see you again before I head out of town."

Smithy stopped. "I mean it, Kai," his stern voice removed all ambiguity. "Call that boyfriend of yours and tell him to turn around and head back to Olympia or wherever he's from. And if he insists on making it out here, you get in that car of yours and go right back down the mountain, stopping him on your way if you have to."

I would have laughed but this wasn't a joke. Not to Smithy. I didn't think it was funny either. It was time to leave.

A brutal chill in the air struck me as soon as I pulled open the door. The temperature had dropped since I left my parent's cabin. The sharp smell of snow, stinging and chilling, hung in the dying day. It seared into my nostrils. The storm would be here soon.

"The first flakes," Smithy gasped, suddenly at my shoulder. I could smell the fear on him.

Then he shoved me into the storm. I turned to see Smithy shivering, his eyes wide. "Call your boyfriend and get back to that cabin! Get back before it comes," he shouted through the door.

I stood outside watching him run behind the counter, tuck the cash bag under his arm, and dash into the back of the store. "Crazy," I shook my head before stealing a second to smell the air. There's nothing as satisfying as the brisk smell of winter air that hinted at the arrival of snow.

I was in the middle of setting my phone in the carriage suctioned to the front window when Smithy's pickup truck surged up the incline of the driveway. Without yielding, he pulled into the road. These weren't the actions of a reasonable man. It was snow. Nothing more. He was a damn native.

But he wasn't reasonable, was he?

Smithy's behaviors made me think of Max. He wasn't a native. His world was one of cultivated roadways and mass transit, not narrow mountain roads and black ice. Throw in the oppressive darkness of the night sky without city light illumination, compound it with the driving snow, and it would be nearly impossible for Max to make his way into town. Max wasn't made that way. He'd never make it to the cabin, not without us having a huge fight when he did arrive. I should have told him I would see him after Christmas, but I missed him as soon as I pulled away from our apartment and wanted to be together for the holiday.

I pulled out of the parking lot and headed toward the grocery store. There were a few cars parked there. People doing last-minute grocery runs for their Christmas meals. I could wait him out in here.

But the doors didn't open when I stepped on the mat. I moved off it and tried again. They remained closed.

"Shit." I peered inside. Sparse security lights illuminated strategic parts of the store. Closed, even though the sign said it would be open for another five hours. Like Smithy's. Now I was going to have to figure out where to meet Max. With my options narrowing, I might have to drive down the mountain to catch him on his way up. But doing that would keep me out in the weather. At least I could squeeze in another episode of my favorite thriller podcast, *Subject: Found*.

Two voices sounded from around the corner of the building. Under normal circumstances, I wouldn't have thought twice about it, but nothing about the evening was normal.

Faced with a slew of unattractive options, I decided I was going to see what I could find out from whoever owned those voices.

Two employees, a woman and a man in their early 20s, strode out a side door. They stood close together. The female was busy locking up while her male counterpart hung close, watching her while taking quick glances around the parking lot. My appearance startled him.

"Jesus!" he exclaimed. His tone frightened the woman. She screamed, spinning, her eyes wide. The man held a hand across his chest. "Fuck man, you scared the shit out of me."

I held my hands up in apology. "I'm sorry about that. Are ... are you closed?"

The two glanced at each other before she answered, "Yeah. What ... what are you doing out?"

Their expressions made it clear this wasn't something to laugh off, even if her question sounded ridiculous. What the hell was going on with everyone? "I'm meeting someone and was hoping I could wait for them here."

The man looked at me like I was standing in the cold, naked as the day I was born. "We're closed, dude. Remember? The first snow?" He made the last comment sound like it should explain everything.

"Yeah, I get that," I answered. This was probably the last chance I was going to get tonight to get any help with waiting for Max. It wouldn't hurt to at least ask. "Any chance you'd let me do some shopping?"

"Are you crazy?" the woman asked. "You need to get the hell out of here."

"Why?"

The man's lips moved wordlessly as if I'd stunned him. Turning to the woman, he said, "Janie, we need to go."

"I know." Janie finished locking up.

The window of opportunity was closed.

The man turned to me, his tone bordered between male aggression and hidden vulnerability. "Look, dude, I don't know what your deal is, but you need to leave. Go back down to Olympia, or Tacoma, or wherever the hell you came from. I don't really care. But leave us alone. We're not to gonna get caught out here. Not for you. Not for no one."

Janie, for her part, was more sympathetic. "You're not from here, are you?"

The man moved to his car. He paused at his open door. "Janie, come on. Seriously." His voice shook.

When the woman named Janie looked at me again there was a marked sadness in her eyes. I knew I only had seconds of her attention left. "Please, I don't know what's going on, but ... my boyfriend is coming up. We were going to meet him at Smithy's, but that got weird ... he kicked me out and closed early. If you're closed too, I—"

She looked on the verge of crying. "You shouldn't meet him here or anywhere. The —" she lowered her voice, "the first snow is coming."

What the fuck was everyone talking about?

"The white night." Tears filled her eyes. Stunned, I wanted to tell her I was sorry even though I didn't know what I was apologizing for. But she was already racing to her own car. Her coworker saw her running and hopped into his, slamming the door and peeling out of the parking lot. Within seconds, her car joined the race, kicking up loose clouds of snow and leaving me alone on the side of an empty grocery store with no clue what was happening.

"The white night?" I headed to my car, checking my cell phone signal, hoping for a sliver of a chance to call Max.

There! Two bars. Enough for a call. I launched my phone app and punched in Max's name. I don't think I breathed until I heard the phone ring.

"Hello?" Max's quivering voice was distorted by noise. Wind, maybe?

"Hey babe, is everything okay? I wanted to call—"

"I can't get through. They're making us turn around," Max whined. The urge to save him from everything was overwhelming.

"What? Who?"

"Fuck if I know. State troopers? Sheriffs?" His anger was a facade for his fear. "I was going to try to get back into the Hoodsport and see if I could get enough of a signal to pull up my GPS. See if there's a way around."

I sighed. There wasn't, and I told him so. Turning around would only take him farther away from me.

"What you want me to do?" Max bit. I let it pass.

"Can you ask them to let you through?"

A battering of strong wind cut off his reply. Something else, a piercing sound, lay in the deep background, well underneath the interrupting sound of wind.

"Max? Are you there?"

When I heard his voice again, it sounded scratchy, distant. Only broken phrases came through. "Not likely ... Closed ... An accident ... Cops ..."

"Max?" I shouted as if that would make it easier for him to hear me. "Max, are you there?"

"Messy ... Something ... Flying ... Telling us ... Abandon ..."

Abandon? Abandon what? "Max? Are you there?"

"Running ... Oh, my God!"

And then he was gone. The phone, dead. I still had two bars.

"Max? Max!"

I looked around the parking lot as if it was going to provide me with the guidance I needed. Max sounded panicked. Frightened. And what was he talking about? What

83

was he supposed to abandon and what was that comment about running? Without an idea of where he was or what he needed, I was helpless.

And I was alone. The entire town felt vacant. No stores opened. The dark interiors of the houses on Main Street sent clear signals that my troubles weren't welcomed. Under normal conditions, it was thirty minutes to my parent's cabin. Tonight, with the snow rolling over the area, it'd be an hour, at least. They couldn't help.

Max was out there alone, and I was helpless. The possibilities of what might be happening to him chilled my skin more than the freezing night air.

Fuck the storm. I could drive in the snow, even with my sports coupe. I would have to be careful, but Max needed me. That was the only thing that mattered.

***

Ten miles outside of town, the snow blanketed the frozen landscape around me. The conditions forced me to take it slow, though my heart pushed me forward faster. The lack of tire tracks on either side of the road was disorienting, making the winding road over the mountain difficult to navigate. As difficult as navigating my way through a struggling relationship. The indented layer of snow to my right informed me of the ditch hidden there, a cautionary guide. Without a shoulder, I had little room for error. Night had fallen. The cloud-covered sky spewed millions of snow pellets curving toward my windshield. I stayed near the middle of the unmarked road to remain safe. But mile after mile, with no traffic coming the other way, my fear grew. What I was seeing was an aftermath of the events of that phone call.

Another fifteen minutes I wrapped around the mountainside and saw red and blue dancing off the snowscape. Pulling my foot off the gas, I drifted to a stop. Those lights belonged to police cruisers. An accident?

My throat seized when I came around the bend.

Two police cruisers barricaded the road, crisscrossing the narrow lanes to prevent traffic from getting through. There were no cars in front of me so I was able to pull up to them as close as I dared. For some reason, I felt safer being in their presence.

Until I got out of the car.

The night held an uncomfortable weight, urging me to turn around and head back to my parents' cabin. A sense of growing dread sank into the pit of my stomach. Those lights flashed blue and red in an alternating silent dance. Shadows flashed across the hillside to my right and against the trees to my left, where the hillside dropped away toward the lake.

The cruisers stood alone. No accompanying cops.

"Hello?" I called out. Only the wind answered me and it wasn't willing to help. "Can you hear me?"

Dread washed over me as the snow hit my face. It wasn't icy and harsh like it had been when it started falling, but wet and cold. The flakes were getting bigger; that meant a true storm was rolling in off the ocean. And when storms hit, Ember Lake shut down. I needed to find Max and get the hell back to the cabin.

But it was hard to keep my cool when it felt like I'd stepped into a dead world.

Shielding my eyes against the snow, I approached the police cruisers. The flashing lights prevented me from seeing much of anything. The world beyond them was pitched into complete darkness. I shielded my eyes to make out as much as I could. It was too quiet here. Too devoid of life. When I got within a few feet of the cruisers I wish I'd never had seen anything at all. I should have stayed in my car or even listened to the two employees at the grocery store. Or Smithy. I should have never left the cabin.

The passenger side door of the nearest cruiser was open. The dome light was out, pitching details into obscurity. What I could see made me thankful to be as blinded as I was.

A police officer's limp body slumped halfway through the open door window. Dead.

"Oh my God," I groaned. A dark pool of blood shadowed the bottom of the door.

Putting a hand to my mouth, I glanced at the other cruiser. Two police cruisers meant at least two officers. One wouldn't allow the other to suffer like that.

Unless something happened to him as well.

Moving backward, one methodical step behind the other, I kept an eye on the dead officer. The irrational part of my brain watched for signs of reanimation. Nothing about this entire experience was rational.

Fortunately for me, not the cop, he didn't move.

I glanced over my shoulder as I backed up. Snowflakes reflecting red and blue lights weren't helping. I was exposed. Vulnerable. I couldn't see anything beyond what was immediately in front of me. But if whatever had killed the cop was out there it could most likely see me. The only thing that stopped me from scurrying to safety was the fact that Max was out there, beyond those cruisers.

It was the thought of Max that held me together.

Until I saw the second cop.

Vomit curled in my throat at what remained of him. Strewn across the hood of his car, a half torso, identifiable as a human only by the torn uniform. A display, a testament to the evil lurking in the blackness. I gulped for oxygen as I began crying. I'd never seen a dead body ever before. In the last minute, I'd seen two.

But this ... this was beyond imaginable.

A human body torn in two?

Unsure if I was trying to satiate my morbidity or not, I looked at the ground in front of the cruiser for the officer's lower half.

"Max ..." I groaned a reminder. I needed to get to Max.

My instincts screamed against my sudden decision to go back to the officer slumped through the cruiser's window. I thought I saw a holster on him. If he had a holster, he might still have his weapon.

Fortune smiled through the black. His right side was exposed, the holstered weapon still there. I reached out with a shaking hand I couldn't control. When my fingers wrapped around the pistol grip I gave it a yank, ready for his cold hand to slap down on mine.

Somewhere in the blackness, a horrendous screech ripped through the storm, a pitch outside the human range. A screech from the depths of hell.

I pissed down my pant leg.

The holster refused to release. I yanked harder. My chest heaved with exertion and a primal plea to flee.

Then I saw it. A leather strap between the grip and the hammer held the gun in the holster. Stupid. With a simple snap, I pulled the gun free, blindly aiming it into the darkness. I had no idea where that screech came from, no idea even what I was aiming at.

The gun felt heavier than I imagined it would. This was the first time I'd held one and didn't know how to aim the damn thing. I saw people on television closing an eye when they shot but I never knew what they were actually looking at when they did that. This wasn't the time to learn either. I'd aim the best I could because I had to.

I moved through the narrow gap between the cruisers. I wanted as many obstacles between me and the thing that had done this as possible.

A long line of cars stretched down the hill. The traffic that Max was tied up in. Was he in it, waiting to get to me? But Max wouldn't do that. He was stubborn but he wasn't stupid. Something had happened to those cops and Max wouldn't have waited around to figure out what it was. The bravest thing he'd ever done was agree to move in with me, and that took a year of effort. The driver's door of the first car in line was open, the dome light illuminating the empty interior. A popular rap song thumped from the speakers.

The next car was also empty. It's engine, like the one in front of it, still running.

Car after car, I made my way down the line. Each vehicle was running as if their drivers were expected to return soon. My hope for Max grew. His car wasn't in the line. I passed at least forty vehicles without seeing his. Each vehicle, empty.

But that feeling crumbled toward the end of my search. Max's Infiniti sat near the end of the line.

Empty.

I scrambled to it, searching the back seats, hoping he was sleeping. I knew better, knew I wouldn't find him. But I searched just the same. It was futile.

How had everyone disappeared into the night? Did the deaths of those two cops have something to do with the disappearances of so many people, including Max?

Wait. Not finding him meant he was alive, didn't it? Besides the shredded cop and his limp partner, there were no signs of struggles around any of these other vehicles. So everyone must have fled after word spread down the line of what happened to the cops. And the narrow road didn't give them space to turn their vehicles around to flee. They would have been forced to run. So, if Max's car was in this line, I could take solace in the fact that he was out there in the night, somewhere.

Then I heard the screech again. My heart stopped beating.

I didn't think it through. I didn't mean to abandon hope of Max. But I was out in the open and there was something unnatural above me in the black night sky. I was alone.

I turned and sprinted back toward my car.

I was halfway up the hill when it rang out again. My skin prickled and my spine went rigid with a sharp tingle. Distant, that sound still pierced my psyche. Nothing from nature sounded like that. My thighs burned, the accumulating snow on the road making the uphill sprint difficult. As it deepened, my footing slipped more often than not. I almost fell on my face, catching myself, stinging my hand in the process.

The dancing red and blue lights beckoned me forward, encouraging me when I didn't need it. Somehow I knew, whatever made that sound was responsible for the disappearances of all these people and the deaths of those two cops.

The screech cut through the night, this time much closer. I spun, raising the gun into the blackness hidden behind the driving snow. Above the trees, a rhythmic beat that sounded like a single bass drum being struck in time. At first, it was low, barely audible behind the wind, but second-after-second, it grew in volume and density. It wasn't a drum.

It was ... wings.

Massive wings. Flying toward me.

The screech sliced through the night, this time above me. I fell to the ground, covering my head. The tree branches shook. From my new vantage point, the world had grown larger. The cars now provided more shelter from the storm as I lay in the snow, wishing I could disappear.

The wings beat on, passing by as if the thing was surveying the area beyond just this part of the mountain pass.

I needed to make a break for the car. I could use these vehicles as shelter. The close mountainside protected me, ignoring the reality that something had frightened all these motorists into the night and they had been in the same situation as I now was. My car was another hundred yards away. I needed to get to it. It would get me to town and a stronger cell signal. Worse case, I'd have to call Max when I got back to the cabin.

I refused to acknowledge my cowardice.

Without another thought, I stood and sprinted uphill. Fifty yards. The thumping was growing again. That demon in the sky was coming back. It called out, the high-pitched screech mixing with an animalistic growl.

Thirty yards.

The beast swooped down close enough to beat air against my face. I glanced up but couldn't see it.

There was something besides the beating of the wings.

Rushing of air.

Something fell out of the sky toward me. I dodged the blackened shape, barely moving before it hit the road with a wet thump.

A carcass.

I retched right there in the middle of the road, staring down at the remains of a human being. I couldn't tell if it was male or female. There was no head, both feet were missing, and the chest cavity was ripped open. Bones encased in chunks of meat jutted out in a grotesque proclamation of a feast enjoyed. The open chest looked emptied of its organs.

Tearing my eyes away from that obliterated corpse, I ran, slipped, and got to my feet again. My thighs felt like knives were being thrust into the most vulnerable weaves of sinew. Between the physical exhaustion and mental terror, I couldn't catch my breath. Slipping again, I tried to focus on my only hope for escape. My car.

The wind howled as it split around the mountain, a burst weaving its way down the tight confines of the road. Tree branches cracked in protest as the night howled its rage. I didn't notice the cold anymore.

The screech sounded, moving away. In that sliver of hope, I found renewed energy. Ignoring my burning muscles, ignoring the thick queasiness below my rib cage, I surged ahead, dashing between the police cruisers. There was a brief respite when I yanked open my car door and jumped in the driver seat. The car roared to life, blaring *Rudolph the Red-Nosed Reindeer* into the tight interior. Panicked, I ignored it as I backed up to a driveway marked with reflective light sticks. I aimed for the smooth white lane between those two markers, trying to suffocate the anticipation of hearing that screech again.

Seconds sludged by, urging me to move quicker, but I denied the temptation. I tried focusing my thoughts on my family and the love of my life. They anchored my fading sanity.

How many more times would Dad ask Mom when we were going home? Did she even feel alive with him anymore? Would Dad's innocent repetition distract her from worrying about why I wasn't home with Max yet? Where was Max? Was he someplace warm? Safe? My poor mother. She would be an angel if angels were real. Poor Max. Putting up with me. Loving me like he did. *Does.*

Thinking about them helped me keep an even, safe speed heading back into town. Haste would put me in a ditch, forcing me back out into the night, exposed to that terror in the sky.

I tried to stave off the tears for Max. There was no way I could help him if I was stranded or worse, but that didn't do much for the pain of knowing he was out there, lost and freezing.

Hopefully, he stayed with the other motorists.

Hopefully, he had someone to help him where I couldn't.

The streets in town were completely empty. The houses that hugged the road were dark. My familiarity with the town was the only thing that made navigating the streets possible. The deepening snow blanketed everything, covering the road, making it indistinguishable from the sidewalks. The soft orange glow from the streetlights made this all the stranger.

Keeping a firm grip on the wheel, I pulled up my phone, hoping against hope that I'd get a break and a signal. The indicator displayed two bars again. I swallowed. Careful to avoid putting myself into a skid, I slowed to a stop, dialing Max's number. It rang six times before going to voicemail. I called again. Voicemail.

Throwing my head against the headrest, I began crying. Even a simple phone call might have made the difference.

I tried one more time. This time I left a voicemail.

"Max, honey, it's me," I cried. "Please pick up. It's me, baby. Please. I—I haven't heard from you. Please, please call me as soon as you get this. I ... I just need to know you're okay." I ignored how desperate I must have sounded. Desperation served the moment.

But then my thoughts were ripped from my mind. Ahead, the snow-covered road exploded, a cloud of white erupting into the air. I put the car in reverse in case I needed to make an escape from whatever was happening in front of me.

An escape to where? half of my broken mind laughed. A dark form emerged in that cloud as the snow settled.

The creature was hard to make out between the street lights and heavy snow, but I could see enough to tell that it was over eight feet tall. Its long arms reached well past its knees, past thighs three times thicker than its calves, twice as thick as a human's torso. The creature's legs would have reminded me of a mountain goat's legs if they weren't so massive.

As the cloud surrounding it was blown away, the monstrosity became clearer. It shook itself, clumps of snow falling off in small frozen pieces. Then, straightening its back, the beast stretched out its massive wings.

Something inside the car whimpered.

I was still alone.

The wingspan of this monster was at least 30 feet.

I didn't think to move. I didn't think to back up and try to race away. There was no way to get away from something like that, not in these conditions. If I tried it would chase me down. I slowly reached over to make sure the car doors were locked, doubting it would do anything to stop this beast.

The gun.

Without taking my eyes off that thing, I searched the passenger seat. When my hand wrapped around the grip, I pulled the gun into my lap, feeling a sense of confidence I didn't deserve.

The creature stepped toward me, tufts of soft snow exploded with each powerful foot it planted. All I could see was a dark outline of a demon from hell. Somehow, I knew that thing could see me.

The wind whipped around my car, howling through the tiny seams as if this beast controlled the weather too and was trying to shatter my mind.

It stopped, standing taller and beating its wings as it tilted its head towards the sky and loosed a horrendous screech. Even at this distance, through my sealed vehicle, I winced. The sound was so loud, so clear, it was as if I was standing outside next to it.

Covering my ears, I refused to let go of the pistol. The pain was excruciating. My teeth rattled. It felt like someone was prying into my ear canal with a stake.

The screech went on and on.

And then it was gone, cut off as quickly as it started.

For a brief moment, I heard nothing but the promise of a truce. It had left. I shivered, just me and the power of nature as the first snow blew through Ember Lake.

I'd survived. The thing had let me live.

My car shook in rhythm with the thumping of the demon's wings. Pulling my hands away from my ears, I risked a look up. The creature had lifted itself off the ground. There, in the middle of Ember Lake's Main Street, this beast of hell hovered ten feet off the ground, facing me. Behind its darkened face, I imagined it examining me. I felt violated. As if it wanted me to watch, the beast turned and flew into the night.

I waited as the thumping of its wings faded. Sitting in my car for what felt like an eternity, I was unable to think or move. What was that thing and why did it spare me?

When it had killed others.

Had it spared Max too?

Whatever the answer, I was alive and it was gone. But it might be back. I had to get to safety. But where was safety?

Then I remembered what Smithy told me. He told me to get inside, to get out of the white night. He knew! He knew what was going to happen and instead of explaining the horrors that waited in the storm, he served cryptic warnings to save himself. Was the white night the same reason my mother urged me to get to Max?

My mother.

I had to get home to them. That thing might come back and, when it did, it wasn't going to find me sitting here, a sacrifice.

Putting the car in drive, I gunned the engine; the tires spun. For a second, I thought I was stranded. Maybe the demon anticipated that. That was why it left, to go kill more difficult prey, saving me for later because it knew I was stuck?

Throwing the car into first gear, I tried again, breathing once more when the familiar sound of snow crunching under tires told me that I'd succeeded. The car jerked when I reached the place where that thing launched itself into the night. Its powerful flapping had cleared a broad swathe of snow from the road. In fact, as far ahead as I could see, the gray surface of blacktop carved through the white world around it.

Within a few minutes, I was driving up the mountain, the town—and Max—falling behind me.

I felt guilty about leaving Max, but there was nothing I could do for him. Not with my car, not with this small pistol. Once I got back to the cabin I would try to call him. Even if Max didn't answer, I could take Dad's truck and his guns. I'd be ready and capable of saving him then.

I had a plan. There was something I could do.

So why was I bothered?

Then: clarity.

A disturbing thought no more.

The road was clear of snow except for the fresh dusting falling from the sky. Completely clear. From the spot where that monstrosity faced me down in the middle of town to all the way out here.

Just for me.

It made no sense. The town bunkered down against the storm. Only me and that thing were out in the elements.

It had cleared the road.

Why?

I couldn't deny what I was seeing. Blacktop cleared of all but the newest dusting of snow. I picked up speed, dismissing the obvious problem in my urgency to make sure my parents were safe and to prepare for my search for my boyfriend. Urgency required speed.

Gripped by fear, I pushed the gas down and pushed myself through the apprehension of being too risky. I was less than a mile away from the cabin when I noticed the end of the cleared road. It stopped just behind my turn-off. The demon was done doing me any favors.

It didn't matter; I was almost home.

Using the trees that lined the road as a guide, I navigated up the path to the cabin.

Halfway up, the car got stuck. The only way I was getting to my parents was on foot. Mentally exhausted, I got out.

As I opened the door that horrific screech filled the night air again.

This time I didn't cower. My parents needed me.

The creature was here. Close.

"No!" I pulled the pistol up and aimed at everything and nothing at the same time. This far out into the mountains there was no artificial light. Here, the world was untouched, untainted by mankind. The night was at its blackest. I couldn't see anything except the few feet in front of me. The single light glowing in the living room was my only guide. The blackness cloaked the demon.

I found the energy to slip and slide my way up the driveway. I couldn't hear anything over top of my breathing, but once I bounded up the stairs I noticed how silent the night was.

Too silent.

Branches cracked back down the hill. I spun, aiming the gun where I thought I'd heard the noise.

Nothing moved on the ground, but the night sky was alive with malevolence.

Close, but distorted by wind cutting through the forest, the thumping of the creature's wings filled the night. Slow and methodical, they beat against the cold air.

It was here and it was on the other side of the cabin.

I reached out for the door handle. It seized up and my mind imagined all the horrible ways I was going to die at the hands of this beast. My chest relaxed when I cranked on the handle and it spun. The door popped open, rubbing against the uneven floor. I jumped inside, slamming and locking it.

My mother sat in the same chair I left her in, staring at me as if I was a madman.

How had she not heard anything going on? Why wasn't she half as frightened as I was? "Mom," I huffed, "are you okay?"

She smiled, setting her knitting aside. "Of course I am, honey. But you look like you've seen the devil."

Had I?

"Mom, something, something happened. Is the back door ... the windows ... are they locked?"

A quizzical, half-humored, look passed over her face. "Heavens no, honey. Why?"

How could I tell her about the horrors I'd seen? Dad's accident had robbed her of more than her share of a normal life. I dashed across the cabin to the back door, throwing the deadbolt. A sense of security came with the pleasant sound of the metal cylinder sliding into the lock. My heart stopped thudding so forcefully that it no longer moved my rib cage. Taking deep breaths, I tried to control my heavy breathing. Mom didn't need to be upset. She didn't need to know. I would stay up all night if I needed to, making sure my parents were safe. In the morning, if we survived, we'd leave. No matter how much snow the white night dumped on the world.

The door had six small windows framed in it. I backed away, feeling too exposed. Standing inside the cabin meant that whatever might be out there could see me and I couldn't see it.

Something thudded on the deck. The window in the kitchen next to me rattled. The lump in my throat caught.

Another booming thud.

The creature was outside.

Reaching as far as I could without moving in front of the door, I flicked on the deck lights ...

... and stared into the face of a demon.

Its black, leathery skin was wrinkled and hairless, matching the utter absence of color of the night. The creature stood taller, as it had when it faced me down in the street, filling my view through the door. Its wide mouth opened. I swore that it was smiling. Looking at its gaping maw, its pointed teeth were covered in blood. I whimpered. Chunks of pink meat were caught between some of the teeth. Even without horns, this thing looked like something out of the depths of hell.

It stepped closer, ponderous footfalls splintering the deck, reaching out with its ridiculously long arm. Its fingers were knuckled and jointed in at least three places. Graceless, black nails—claws—extended three inches beyond the ends of its fingers. The nails scratched the iron door handle.

I backed away, raising the gun at the creature, looking into its eyes.

It's intelligent eyes. Familiar eyes.

Almost human.

The gun shook loose from my grip, thumping to the floor.

Mom called out from the front room. She sounded annoyed, like when I was little and interrupted her shows with my playing. Or all those times since Dad's accident when he asked her the same question over and over about going home. "What are you doing, Kai? Don't lock the back door. Your father will be home soon."

Dad would be coming home? From where? He didn't go anywhere alone; she didn't let him. He couldn't. He hadn't driven since the accident in the woods. Since his first disappearance. How would he get around? He couldn't be walking around in the storm; he'd get lost, like all those times before when …

Mom answered my unasked questions as the realization struck. My father never came back out of the mountains after his accident all those years ago.

Something else had.

She said, "He went out to get a bite to eat."

END

Hung by the Fire

Blood surged through its loins as it watched the human. The Sender bit down, its fang piercing its bottom lip.

It didn't even wince.

Pain was life.

Satisfied that the game had begun, it turned back toward the forest. The trees parted as it approached as if they feared the Sender's touch.

***

Jeremy Baker let the front door drift closed after grabbing the paper someone left on his door stoop. He'd heard something from his sofa, where he was comfortably masturbating to girl-on-girl porn on his sixty-inch television. The noise interrupted what was otherwise a wonderful jerk session. But this was the Christmas season, and he'd ordered a few things off the Internet, and that sounded like someone dropping a package. Leaving packages sitting on the stoop, especially around Christmas, was a sure way of helping an order disappear. Living around a bunch of white trash neighbors almost guaranteed that. They'd steal the package before it even collected a few water droplets from the spitting sleet, stealing with the same hands they clasped in prayer every single Sunday.

Bastards, each and every one of them.

What he saw when he opened the door wasn't what he expected. A tightly rolled piece of yellowed paper lay on his doormat, almost like someone placed it there with great care. The scrolled paper sat parallel with his doormat and front door. A red wax seal, centered on the scroll, peered up at him. Someone had intentionally laid this here for him to find.

As he squatted to pick it up, a stiff breeze blew up his open robe. It felt good, encouraging his cock back to life after the ruined masturbation session. He wondered if any of the neighbors in the apartments across the way were looking out their windows at this moment. Exhibiting his man-meat for some horny unemployed housewife or girlfriend was exhilarating. The apartments held more than a few sluts; he knew that from watching them at the community pool during the summer. If they liked this sight maybe he could entice them to come over for a visit? Or invite him to their place? That would be fun too, especially if their husbands or boyfriends were working.

Jeremy smiled at the thoughts of debauchery as he ran his thumb over the seal. Something was written on it. Letters bordered an outer circle, spelling out something he couldn't decipher.

Probably Russian. He couldn't be sure.

What he couldn't make out in the lettering, Jeremy could easily see in the picture within the seal. A small figure in a forest scene. The figure had thick hind legs and looked like a goat with a human torso. Its face was indistinguishable. The details were so fine he could see matted hair on the figure's thighs and its split hooves. Whatever the picture was supposed to depict, this was impressive artwork.

Why did someone leave the scroll?

An accident?

The leathery feel of the aged paper and the fine detail of that seal implied opulent grace and, even Jeremy would admit, that was something he lacked.

Surely it was someone else's delivery.

This was not meant for him or someone really fucked up their Christmas shopping. But then the thought hit him. As a teen, he went to the mall often, and not just for the girls. There was a comic book store that sold the hentai books he would soon become addicted to. Later, when he was older and after the advent of the Internet, he started buying them online. They were edgy and exciting, delivering on the promises of discrete, nondescript packages. Months later he found a visionary of an artist and started a monthly donation to support him in return for exclusive content. Jeremy wondered if this scroll was the surprise bonus the artist promised his patrons months ago. The artist promised to feature girls he didn't typically release publicly.

That could only mean one thing.

Sweat formed on Jeremy's top lip at the thought. Saliva bubbled in the corner of his mouth.

Jeremy grabbed his hairdryer. He wanted to keep this seal intact as much as possible, it would probably be a collector's item one day.

This could be a gift from Haley. That little slut had promised him something special for Christmas, supplementing it with that cute giggle she used to hide her particularly perverse nature. The younger guys didn't get it; that level of aggression from a woman was incomprehensible to teen boys. But Jeremy did. He loved it. She was mentally well beyond her chronological age, and that body...

Oh, what a body!

Now heated, the wax seal popped loose, still intact. His heart skittered as he set it off to the side to make sure that it remained that way.

Taking one last, long breathe—god, how he loved the way Haley teased—he slowly unfurled the letter. The rich paper gasped at its release.

Jeremy held the letter away from his face, arm extended. He'd left his glasses on the coffee table—porn was better when you could see it in clear detail—now forgotten at the promise of this new adventure with a real life slut.

Moving the letter back and forth, further and closer, Jeremy squinted to read the few simple words written on it.

I've called you by your name; you are mine.

Oh, Haley truly was being naughty this Christmas, Jeremy smirked. What wicked plans was she concocting?

The mall would be crowded this afternoon, filled with last-minute shoppers absentmindedly trying to fulfill the insatiable appetite of their equally insatiable, materialistic loved ones.

The perfect type of night to hang out there.

Hundreds of young, tight bodies in even tighter pants, idly milling between stores, hanging out at the slushy stand, picking up waffle cones filled with high-calorie ice cream. They could afford that; youth was on their side. For now.

He was planning on heading to the mall after he was done jerking off anyway. This new opportunity solidified his plans. He hadn't anticipated seeing her so soon after their last exhausting fuck. Jeremy wiped away the spot of blood from the bottom lip he hadn't realized he was biting.

I'm going to tear into her, he thought as he undressed in front of the mirror and started the shower. Waiting for the water to heat, Jeremy examined his naked body. He wasn't in the shape he used to be in during his 20s and now, as he approached 40, time was winning the battle. A healthy diet and regular exercise were never high on his list of things to do, but he'd at least maintained a decent shape for the girls during his younger years.

Now he was becoming circular, bulges appeared in places where he couldn't tuck them away in a waistband to hide them from an unreasonable and hypercritical world.

He slapped his flabby stomach in disgust. Thankfully there were still young women out there who didn't care about men with enhanced bodies. They just wanted to be treated right. And he could do that. He had an income that boys their age couldn't dream to match. Had a nice car, he'd made sure of that. Cars were whore magnets. And his respectable home outdid what most of the cunt's parents could offer them.

As long as they stayed away from his office there wouldn't be any problems.

His mouth filled with spit; his cock stiffened even as he looked at his flabby form. After a few hours at the mall, watching tight bodies saunter between stores, he'd devour Haley. She'd learned so much since she started college in the fall.

Tonight, he planned on teaching her a few more things. This was going to be a good Christmas.

***

The Sender stretched, waking from its slumber. Each muscle fiber burned to life as he extended his thick legs. Muscles this size always hurt more when they were cold.

The Sender emerged from his cocoon, back into the world of the mortal.

The air was crisp and the night was dark.

It was time to hunt.

He smiled before letting loose with a ravenous howl that shook the night.

***

"You wouldn't believe what I got today. A package, well not really a *package*," Haley said from the bathroom, where she was doing whatever women did in preparation for being sexually ravaged. "It was the weirdest thing. Someone left this thing on my—wait, did you hear that?"

Jeremy sat up on the bed, the sheet falling over his extended stomach to his groin. "What?"

She peeked out at him, her hands busy in her hair. She wasn't smiling. But he would make her smile in a few minutes. "I said," she said with a sigh, "did you hear that?"

Jeremy shook his head. He didn't hear anything, too distracted by his throbbing cock and everything he was about to do to her. Nothing else mattered. Plus, it was Christmas Eve. All of his neighbors were fake Christians, the type who went to Christmas Eve mass and pretended to be part of the pretentiously pure. He knew better, of course. Every day he saw them doing things that proved their true character, things that couldn't be erased no matter how many torture sessions they attended. None of them would be home tonight. Haley was just hearing things, delaying the pounding she was about to take.

"No," he answered. "Just hurry up and get your ass in here." Jeremy rubbed himself, careful not to rub too much. He wanted to see her wince tonight and that wouldn't happen if he spent himself before she even climbed into bed.

The bathroom light flicked out, darkening the bedroom, now lit only by the soft glow of the fire he started as soon as they got home. Younger women were so fascinated by his romanticism, another advantage he had over those teenage punks and their tight bodies and bulging muscles. Seconds later, Haley stepped out of the bathroom. Her thin frame wasn't hidden by the black nightie she wore, the one he bought her a few weeks ago. He intentionally bought the most transparent one the store had in stock. She looked better then he'd anticipated. Haley stood at the foot of the bed smirking, a finger lightly pinched between her teeth. That was the flirtatiousness that the whore hooked him with. Haley was so different than all the other women.

She was special.

Jeremy didn't believe in love, but Haley was making that position untenable.

"Do you like it?" she asked, swinging her hips back and forth making the bottom of the nightie sway, exposing a few inches of naked thigh each time.

"I love it," he grinned. "Now, get your ass in bed."

Haley winced. Jeremy didn't care. Girls—women—like her needed to be told what to do. That's how dirty women liked It.

Haley crawled onto the bed just to the side of his feet and slowly made her way toward him. The nightie hung open, exposing her breasts. Even in that position, when gravity pulled on every ounce of skin, her body refused to give. Her firm breasts were round, just as they were supposed to be. Her stomach, flat. She was perfect. "I don't like it when you talk to me like that," she said as she laid on her side, tracing a finger down his chest and over the hump of his stomach, toward his cock.

Jeremy laughed.

"What's so funny?"

Her question made him laugh harder. "Nothing." *Stupid girl.*

She began to stroke him. Her grip hurt. Just like he wanted it. So young, but so advanced.

Worth all the trouble she causes.

Few, almost no, young women were. But not Haley. She never disappointed.

Slowly, she stroked him. Somehow, she made him harder than he already was. The way she jerked him could make a faggot cum, the perfect grip and cadence. *So good.*

He didn't have time for her games tonight though. It was Christmas Eve and he'd waited all day to get his hands on someone. She happened to be the fortunate winner. Plus, the trip to the mall made him inpatient about feeling the smooth skin and tightness of a woman. Having to wait made him crazy with frustration and she was going to pay for that.

Jeremy shoved her off. Haley squealed. But he didn't give her time to complain, rolling on top of her and kissing her hard, biting her lower lip. She liked that. He bit a little harder.

"Ow!" she whined, trying to pull as far back as she could. "That hurt!"

"Shut up," he ordered, placing a finger on her lip and then sliding his hand down to her throat, squeezing, just enough. His thumb found the indent just above where her collarbones met. Haley's mouth opened. No words came out. He liked her better that way. And she wasn't hating this either. Her wetness betrayed that. He pressed up against her, into her, and her shock turned to ecstasy. It was in her face.

When he rammed his full length into her, she gasped.

That made him smile.

It was going to be a fun night.

***

The Sender stayed in the hallway, listening. It was always weird, times like these. He never knew when the appropriate time was to interrupt. This wasn't the first time he'd done this. Thousands of times over the past millennia he'd stood in similar domiciles, waiting. Humans were a strange species, their desires and motivations obscured by social conventions. But understanding them wasn't the Sender's job.

There were other things he could spend his immortal energy on.

Like figuring out how to make this all end.

The mental exercise did make for an interesting game while he waited. There were only so many occasions he could do this without being dulled by the entire experience.

What the male and female in the other room were doing was natural; he understood that as well as he understood the nature of any species in this realm. They all did it; this species just seemed to be more masochistic about it. They enjoyed self-enforced limitations and torturing each other physically, while torturing themselves mentally.

The Sender didn't care, he was here not because of what the two were doing, but because of what the male was doing. While the act itself may be completely natural, his decision to manipulate the young female wasn't. That was why the Sender had been sent.

To correct.

To teach.

To deliver consequences.

A mission he'd grown tired of long before this realm saw things like the automobile, steam engines, or even their lord and savior.

How many times had he contemplated asking for a reassignment only to never follow through on his own urges? The Sender was aware that he was here, doing the duty he despised, because of his own cowardice. This work was supposed to be temporary, part of the onboarding process that each new one of his kind went through. But more than 2,000 human years had come and gone and here he was, standing in yet another domicile, readying to deliver justice.

It was unfair to expect him to have to continue on this long. There were others who could do it. He knew they weren't as good as him, but who was? Was he to pay for his superior work ethic for all eternity?

It was time for something new. The excitement of this job was gone, it had been for the past few centuries. Even though his work was restricted to just this time of the human calendar, it was a busy period. Hundreds of assignments each time. It was grating. The Sender was jaded.

Where was the fun? This species didn't learn, they didn't change or strive to be better. What was the point in all of it? Worse yet? The work had changed him. A thousand human years ago he wasn't so aggressive. There were occasions when he'd let the species explain themselves, even let them walk away. So much of that had changed though. The Sender was no longer what he used to be, and that was because of this unending mission.

Maybe after this season, I'll ask to be released, the Sender thought, knowing he wouldn't.

The couple's animalistic machinations continued, ramping up toward the inevitable climax. How many times had he heard this? It played out the same every single time. While the utterance made the job easier, it jaded the Sender even more. The teenage female was faking it for the man's pleasure. Why couldn't this species' males perceive that?

The Sender wondered what this female got out of fornicating with a male who was old enough to have spawned her. This scene had played out thousands of times over the ages. He guessed understanding their motivations was beyond his immortal mind.

You're not here to contemplate this, he reminded himself.

He was here to do a job.

A job that exhausted him.

A job he despised.

But a job that needed to be done. And it was his to do.

Each of his kind was responsible for particular areas of the human species. Others had more glamorous responsibilities. Some were incredibly tame, just as unrewarding as his own work had become. But some. Oh, how some of his kind got to perform glorious work.

Right now, listening to the two humans, he would gladly accept any other assignment.

Soft moans drifted into the hall, overlapped by masculine grunts. The Sender's breeches began to tighten as his cock thickened. He grimaced. *Already?* Usually, he required a little more. This couple had a strong effect on him.

He snarled. Confused.

The hallway closed in around him. He couldn't pace outside the room because the pervert had wood flooring, and the Sender's hooves would announce his presence. He couldn't afford to give the couple any advantages. He hated this task, but he was going to do the job right. That was the only way to ensure promotion out of it. If he was particularly cruel, it would curry enough favor that he might be allowed to finally move on to something worthwhile.

The sounds from the bedroom grew louder. This made the Sender happy; his work here was almost done. The last season he would do anything like this, he hoped. He was tired of listening to this species fulfill their endless need for empty procreation.

He was ready to make an example out of them if it meant he could move on.

Edging down the hallway, careful to softly land each hoof on the off chance these disgusting humans were listening.

They weren't, of course. The male was too busy enjoying someone he had no business being with, and the female was too busy pretending everything about the male excited her. Neither one of them were aware of him.

The bedroom door was cracked open. The Sender crept closer and peered in. Firelight cast flickering shadows against the walls. The light would make his appearance even more paralyzing.

Disgusted at the vision of the pair copulating, the Sender turned away. Humans were a foul species. The male was on top of the female and the bed sheet had been pushed down to below the male's feet, exposing his fat ass. Up and down, the pervert thrust into the young female with all the skill and finesse of an apprentice woodworker etching out his first scroll saw design with a hatchet.

And she, the female, who should be worrying about the comings and goings of her people instead of spending time with males like this, winced. Her face poked up over the pervert's round, pimple-covered shoulder.

The vision angered him.

He was angered that the pervert would take advantage of someone who was too young to understand everything she was getting herself into.

He was angry that she allowed herself to get into these situations because she was infatuated with the self-loathing that pervaded this species, the type of hatred that ran so deep and raw as to drive them to the brink of non-existence.

He was angry that after serving for centuries as the arbiter of these things, at spending eleven human months every year tracking the improprieties of this species. Angry at the betrayal and pain, the ugliness of infidelity that rotted away their core that refused to be diminished.

He was angry that after generations of humans destroying each other's lives, suffering despair and loneliness on the good days, and being driven to hate and kill on the bad days, humans never stopped doing the simple things that would help them avoid their own self-destruction.

The act didn't bother him, there was a certain beauty to it. Even though he had no reproductive needs, he appreciated the fluid splendor of human fornication. What this pervert was doing wasn't beautiful. He was a jackhammer, not a paint brush. A cold Pacific Northwest day, not a day spent under a sunny Caribbean sun.

"I have called you by your name; you are mine," he snarled.

The Sender could have pushed the door open quietly, could have slunk into the room using the shadows as cover. He could have used a million diversionary tactics he'd perfected over the millennia since his creation. But he didn't want to. He wanted the thrill of cruel trauma.

I want out.

He wanted to etch fear on their faces for all eternity.

The female screamed when he flung the door open. She tried to push the fat pervert off, but he was lost in his thrusting. This was going to be too easy. Dissatisfying.

The female's legs shoved outward. The male pushed himself up on extended arms and looked down at her, smirking as if he was conducting a magical show for his teenage lover. He never saw the Sender coming.

The Sender strode across the room, the woman kicked again as she attempted to get out from underneath the male who, for his part, twisted, his eyes widening as he became aware of the immortal presence.

The Sender had seen this type of reaction each and every time for thousands of years. His presence was threatening. Minds broke when eyes took in the vision that was him. Maybe it was his goat legs or his thick human-like chest that always unsettled. More likely than not, it was the Sender's human face with the elongated snout filled with large, flat teeth. The two large horns protruding from the top of his head also seemed to push this species beyond their limited understanding of creation.

The male fell off the female, his blubbering gut failing to hide his dying erection. The female pushed herself against the headboard, pulling her knees to her chest and wrapping her arms around them. Trembling.

"Get—get the fuck out!" the male ordered, backing away against the headboard in an attempt to put as much space between him and the Sender as possible.

Space wouldn't help though. Nothing could.

"Stay away!"

But the Sender came. Slow. Methodical. This was what he enjoyed; this was where he got his thrills. He loved seeing the panic in the human's eyes, their disorientation as they tried to comprehend how a living nightmare could be corporeal.

Then the male rolled to his side, yanking open his nightstand drawer. The Sender didn't need to see the small handgun to know it was there. In a swift motion, he hopped onto the bed, right at the feet of the lovers. The woman yelped. The pervert swung the handgun.

But the human was too slow, as was typical of their species. The Sender delivered a powerful kick to the male's arm, snapping it in two. The male screamed in pain and the female screamed in horror at her lover's newly angled arm. The handgun fell to the bed between the pervert and her. All three looked at the gun. It was the center of their universe for the humans, their hope for salvation.

The female snatched it and aimed at the Sender. Her arms shook. "Please ... please leave me alone," she stammered.

The Sender lifted one thick leg and slammed his hoof down on the middle of the male's leg, snapping his femur. For the second time, the human male screamed, falling to his side. The male's breathing was ragged as he attempted to clutch a shattered leg and decimated arm.

The female jumped to the floor in naked glory, backing away from the bed while locking her aim on the Sender. "I ... I didn't do anything."

"I've called you by your name. You are mine," the Sender barked, hopping from the bed. His hoof stomp split the strips of flooring. The fireplace crackled. A log popped.

Tears rimmed the female's eyes. "I just ... I just want to go home." She backed up toward the door. The Sender followed her. He didn't mind toying with her, giving her the impression that escape was possible. It's what made this all the more thrilling. The female risked a glance at his stiffened cock. The thrill of this chase evident to her.

The excitement of purification. Even after all these years, he could still find joy. But the Sender knew this lust was temporary. The promotion out would be his.

A broad smile spread along his snout as he lunged at the female.

His sensitive ears exploded with the eruption of two distinct *pops* as the woman fired the pistol. The slugs buried deep in his wide chest, jerking him to a halt. A bitter smell in the air assaulted his sensitive nostrils.

The Sender looked down at the two new holes in his chest. And then at her. The female shook violently, noting the lack of blood from the wounds she inflicted. "No," she whimpered as she backed away. He lunged at her a second time, and this time she didn't bother to fire the weapon.

He grabbed the female, her naked form shivering in cold fear, and tucked her under one arm, spinning back to the bed. The pervert couldn't even be bothered to watch, he cared so little for the female he pursued so voraciously over the past year.

The Sender would need to work a little harder.

He bounded over to the fireplace. If shattering the pervert's body didn't get his attention, if possessing the female wasn't dramatic enough, the Sender would gladly break their determined minds.

Whoever found the pair after this was done would never see the world the same again.

The woman kicked but couldn't loosen his grip.

"No!" she screamed as he lifted her body with ease and flung her toward the fireplace. The grate collapsed inward and her back struck the corner of the fireplace, piercing the air with the cracking of her spine. She fell on the marble.

The female's low moan filled the silence. The pervert's wide eyes were fixed on his trophy that now lay, wrecked, at the foot of the fire.

The Sender was done with conventions and rules. He'd had enough of this. Humans would never learn.

He spun to face the broken female, placing a hoof against her heaving stomach. With a powerful shove, he pushed her into the fire. The small pile of logs collapsed as her body sailed into the firebox. Sparks spit out. The dazed female grabbed the tiled corner with a trembling hand to pull herself free. The Sender kicked her hands, crushing them, her bones popping like fireworks, and bent over to grab her legs.

Fear and recognition registered on the female's face.

"You are mine," he reminded her and then jammed her legs back into her chest. Her skeletal system obliterated, the female was dead long before the flames began to singe her skin.

With a single bound, the Sender leaped back onto the bed, grabbing the man by his throat.

"Please, I'll give you anything," the pervert gasped.

The Sender didn't respond. Instead, he jumped off the bed, still holding the male by his throat. One hand swatted at the Sender's grip.

A funny thing about humans, they put more energy into resisting consequences than they invested in making better decisions to avoid them in the first place.

The never-ending cycle.

He was here to teach.

To purify.

To make them learn.

But they never did.

The Sender dropped the male on top of the bent grate. The pervert's eyes widened at the compacted form of his lover crammed into the small crevice atop the burning logs. His disgusting mouth quivered.

The Sender reached into the small pouch tied around his waist, withdrawing a spike. "I've called you by your name. You are mine." Then the Sender grabbed the pervert by his throat again, lifting him to his feet. The male leaned to one side, unsupported by his crushed leg.

"I — I have money," the male bartered.

The Sender laughed. Immortals had no need for money. How could he expect this pathetic creature to understand that though? The human didn't even understand that targeting teenage females was morally abhorrent.

The Sender spun the male to face the warm tiled mantle. The pervert's naked ass quivered, the loose skin rippling like water in a puddle.

If this was what it took to free himself from this duty, it was a pleasure he would gladly rejoice in. He'd never been this cruel to this species before. Maybe that was why he was still a prisoner to this cruel fate. Maybe cruelty had been the secret all along?

The secret to his salvation.

The Sender leaned in against the pervert.

"No! No!" the human male cried.

There was no time for subtleties. No time for understanding or compassion. He was an immortal creature tasked with bringing balance to an imbalanced world. His duty was to teach empathy to the apathetic. His calling was to inject morality in the immoral. There was no quarter to be given to the likes of this pervert. The male's screams turned to whimpering cries as the Sender slid his erect cock against the pervert's ass. The head of his cock acted on its own, seeking out the pervert's greatest vulnerability. Once found, the Sender thrust with all of the apathy the pervert showed earlier in the evening to one who was young enough to be his daughter.

Invaded, the pervert shouted once and collapsed against the warm tile. But the Sender didn't stop. He violated the male until he climaxed. Only when he was done did he back away to reflect on what he'd accomplished. Looking down at the destroyed remnants of the male who once preyed on the vulnerable, the observer grabbed the stake and lifted the pervert off the floor.

He hefted the still form, laying him atop the mantle. A wood brace cracked inside the wall. He held the pervert there while leveling the stake and knocking against the wall in search of a stud. Finding one, the Sender adjusted the pervert. This time, the pervert's cock lay between the two. With one last thrust, the Sender slammed the stake through the male's flaccid penis and into the wall stud. It wouldn't hold forever but it would hold long enough so that the pervert could serve as a warning to whoever found him.

Word would quickly spread in this small community about what happened to males like the pervert.

And humans might finally begin to learn.

He didn't care any longer. He just wanted out.

The Sender backed away and examined his work. It was some of his most artistic, hopefully enough to satisfy Him. For if He were satisfied, maybe then the Sender could find his own release.

Content, the Sender left the male hanging by the fire.

The night air held a chill that made the Sender's heart swell. Christmas was in the air. The celebration of the birth of the Savior. He would be pleased.

The trees spread apart as the Sender stepped toward them, welcoming him home to rest.

There was still so much work to do.

END

I Saw Mommy Killing Santa Claus

"Are you serious, Bill? Are you fucking serious?" Brenda shouted.

Bill mumbled something in response, but Kyle didn't care to decipher his father's drunken slurs. He was almost to his bedroom, away from the cacophony his parents were creating in the kitchen.

This had been coming.

Kyle closed his bedroom door, grimacing when the latch clicked. Only when he realized that neither of his parents was following him down the hall did he relax enough to exhale. His mother was on the warpath, a path he wasn't willing to cross. Difficult to deal with in the best of times, she was impossible to tolerate when she was pissed.

Pressing his ear against the door, Kyle listened. Their kitchen argument could go on all night; they wouldn't bother him for a while.

Great Christmas Eve.

They were so stupid. Sometimes it felt like the only thing the two of them did was fight and scream at each other. At least the neighbors would get more free entertainment. But if the neighbors could see his parents in the middle of their screaming match, that would be hilarious. Mom, drunk. Dad still dressed in his Santa Claus get-up.

What a joke.

Kyle slumped against the door but then shot up, patting his hoodie pocket. It was empty. His cell phone, his connection to the world, was still out in the living room.

"Shit!"

Both of his parents were drunk. That's how the fights always started. That was usually what preceded him hiding in his room. It happened a lot. He should have enough practice avoiding them to not accidentally leave his phone on the chair in the living room. But tonight's shit storm came without a warning, exploding with a loaded question from his mother about his father's whereabouts. In an attempt to avoid collateral damage, Kyle fled to his room without a thought. And now, without his phone, that was going to cost him. It was going to be a long night without his connection to the world.

"Fucking great," Kyle collapsed into his chair, careful to not kick the desk. He had to place it in the corner of the room to accommodate its lean or it would collapse.

Not only did he forget his phone, but he didn't grab anything to eat before escaping. When his parents went at it like this it was almost a guarantee they'd argue for hours. Horrible insults would be spat, tears would flow. Either Dad would yell, or Mom would shriek right at the climax of their mutual verbal assault. The resulting banging on the rehouse wall from their neighbors, accompanied by scathing encouragement to 'shut the fuck up' would signal the full escalation of their fight. And he'd spend an entire night holed up in here until they finished breaking plates and each other's hearts.

Just like always. Nothing stopped it. Not even Christmas.

"Well, at least they won't bother me," he mumbled, scooting closer to his computer and double-clicking the mouse. The cheap desktop would have been considered slow five years ago. By today's standards, it was embarrassing. One more thing he hid from his friends.

The computer clicked and buzzed rapidly, finally whirring to life. For today, at least. It wasn't going to last much longer. Tyler, his computer geek friend, told him it was because of all the porn he watched was filling his hard drive with viruses. Kyle argued that he only looked at porn on reputable sites; Tyler said that wasn't how it worked.

The hard drive's lights blinked as it buzzed in protest. The hourglass icon on the monitor mocked him as the circuitry struggled to breathe life into itself. He could go take a good shit and be back before it booted up. But that wasn't going to happen. A bathroom trip meant passing his parents, who were still throwing insults around like kids at school threw handfuls of cafeteria slop during weekly food fights. The last thing he wanted was to be dragged into one of their stupid fights again.

Mom always did that.

And Dad takes it.

From the rising voices surging down the hallway, it wouldn't be much longer before she pushed him to snap.

The thump of something hitting a wall melted through the door. A wood chopping block this time? A shoe?

"You fucking bastard!" his mother shouted.

Metallic clanging. A drawer maybe?

Kyle came up with this guessing game when he was still in grade school.

Great, I'll have to clean that shit up.

Kyle wasn't even sure what his father had done this time. Bill didn't hit Brenda. He didn't have a home-away-from-home in the pub across the way like a lot of men in the neighborhood. He didn't even belong to a bowling league. The only thing that pissed her off this time of year was the side-hustle he had playing Santa Claus at the mall. The money was shit but it paid a few bills. His father took as many hours as he could each holiday season and this year was no different.

He worked. A lot.

She got lonely. A lot.

Someone had to do it. Brenda's life was one of comfortable ignorance where money wasn't something to worry about if there was an open balance on the credit card. The crumbling neighborhood they now lived in on the west side of Syracuse should serve as a reminder of their financial instability. It didn't. And it didn't stop her other bullshit either, like drinking a concoction of pills and alcohol when she thought Kyle wasn't watching or cutting herself when she got overwhelmed. She thought he didn't know about that. But he'd known for years. A few of his classmates cut themselves. One of his closest female friends, Jess, showed him her scares once. Since then, he knew what to look for and his mother wasn't so good at hiding her self-inflicted damage.

There had to be a part of her that knew it was wrong. None of her girlfriends were aware of how bad things were but she was good at keeping her destructive side cloaked behind the curtain of complaining she did about Bill. No, her shit was kept in-house.

Family secrets and all that.

So what the fuck was she mad about? That his father was drunk? So what? He'd worked every day for the past two weeks. He even pulled a Santa Claus shift tonight after working all day. Who cared if he had a few beers before coming home?

The answer came in the form of something, a drawer, clattering to the floor in the kitchen. Clanking utensils providing the dramatic impact, like cymbal crashes in a drum solo.

They were destroying the kitchen this time.

Bill raised his voice to match Brenda's. "Fuck yooou!" he slurred. "I don't hav-ta listen to ... to your sssssssssshit!"

"Remind me to not be a fucking idiot when I get away from this shit hole," Kyle instructed his computer screen. It replied with the tenacious hourglass icon that informed him he wasn't going to start using the Internet anytime soon.

For the time being, only his thoughts could distract him from the idiots in the other room.

Once upon a time his father had been someone, someone Kyle wasn't embarrassed to claim as his own. But that ended before Kyle reached high school. The window factory where Bill worked closed its doors, preferring Mexico as an operations base. That decision sent the community into a downward spiral. Since then Bill flopped from job to job, never holding down anything longer than a year.

Fuck, remember the time he got fired after a month? That was some epic shit!

Some of the guys in school still didn't even know about his father's struggles. Kyle intended on keeping it that way. Anytime someone asked, he lied, telling them that his father was a cross-country truck driver. They didn't need to know the truth about his father being a failure and his mother, a lunatic.

What changed? Was it the job loss that created a fragile ego? Months of feeling sorry for himself that propelled him into severe depression? Or was it mom's neediness? The way she'd go shopping for shit they didn't need every time she couldn't deal with life? Or the fact that her girlfriends didn't check in with her as often as they did with each other? Or that Dad thought she was fat?

Did any of it matter anymore? They were both beyond fucked.

Graduation needed to get here. Then he was out, leaving this city and its people behind. Plus, it didn't snow in LA. He only had to make it another half year. In LA, the weather and women would be hotter. There were jobs and a better chance to find guys to start a band with. No one in Syracuse knew what music was and most of them didn't have the courage to move away and chase their dreams. Central New York was where dreams died.

Just a few more months, that's all he needed to tolerate. Then he'd be free.

His excitement was accompanied by a throbbing squeeze in the middle of his chest. Kyle pushed the thoughts away. As embarrassing as the man was, his dad was still a provider, a mentor, and a coach. Kyle still remembered the time he thought of his father as a friend. It wasn't that long ago. Maybe that's why this fall from the perch hurt to watch. Leaving in a few months would create a hole Kyle wouldn't be able to fill.

But hadn't that hole already been there for years?

A few months ago, they had a conversation Kyle wasn't likely to forget. His father was drinking and in one of his rarer vulnerable states, a mix that usually led to a bonding session. He urged Kyle to take chances while he was young.

"Grab it and hold on with all your strength," Bill had said, draping a drunk arm around his son. "Don't be like your old man. Don't waste it on some bullshit like marriage and babies. Not until you're ready. It's shit, Kyle. What the world tells you. Absolute bullshit. You don't need a woman. You definitely don't need to be bringing more kids into this fucked up world. Just live your life, son. Don't be in a hurry to join the workforce or tie yourself down to one person. Live while you're living."

Kyle rocked back and forth in his chair, that tender memory rolling around in his head. *Live while you're living.*

Finally, his computer's login screen popped up and Kyle punched in his password incorrectly at first. He pounded the keys harder the second time as if force determined his accuracy. The memory of his father's lessons faded. Porn would take his mind off of what was going on. He needed that tonight. They'd ruined Christmas.

"Who was it?" Brenda shrieked, making Kyle jump. The shrill sound waves cut through the barrier he placed between him and the two demons who spawned him. "Who the fuck was it?"

Earbuds.

Kyle plugged them in. If the computer participated, he'd be watching porn soon. The hidden sounds of women having sex would drown out the bickering adults in the other room.

"Does it matter?" Bill yelled, some of his drunken slur disappeared in the heat of rage.

"Jesus Christ," Kyle grumbled.

Jesus Christ indeed. All over the city families were gathered, celebrating the season and the opportunity to be together. A foreign world. What would it be like in a noisy house filled with family and love? His friends complained about their holiday obligations, having to hang with relatives who were virtual strangers and older ones who smelled weird.

His friends were stupid; they didn't know how lucky they were.

"I fucking hate Christmas," he told his computer screen. It answered by popping up a number of browser windows he rushed to close before they dumped viruses onto his hard drive. All he wanted was to see some tits and ass to make this miserable night at least tolerable. Was that too much to ask?

Through the wall, through the closed door, even through the rubber filter of his earbuds, something collapsed in the kitchen. It sounded like everything in one of the cupboards fell to the floor at once. Almost.

Kyle pulled the earbuds out to listen closely. It didn't sound like plates and bowls. It was too solid. Too big. Definitely not glass. Enough glasses, beer mugs, and plates had exploded against walls in their apartment over the years to make it easy for Kyle to distinguish those sounds.

Whatever it was, it was heavy.

Kyle started to stand. This was going too far. If things were getting physical again ... his feet tangled around the feet of the chair when the power went out and his room was immediately shrouded in darkness. He reached out for something to keep him upright, finding the top of his desk.

"Fuck!" Kyle slammed his hands on the keyboard. One of the keys popped off, hitting the floor and bouncing away. Kyle dropped to his hands and knees, searching for the wayward square of plastic. In the dark, he didn't see the bed leg posing an imminent danger until it was too late. His hand bent the wrong way when he jammed the leg.

This was his parent's fault. If Dad hadn't lost job after job they would've moved out of this part of town by now. If Mom hadn't pissed away so much of their money on shoes, purses, and whatever the hell else she bought, they could have rented a house instead of cramming into eight hundred square feet of filth. And now his father was busy dipping his cock into someone? Was that why his mother swallowed her toxic mix of booze and pills for dinner each night? Was it worth caring about?

Ho, fucking ho, asshole, Kyle sneered, giving up his search for the key like he'd given up any hope his family would ever be normal.

It was time to make a decision. Sleep or slip out of the apartment and walk around the dark neighborhood? It was way too early to go to bed. He could go see Tyler but Kyle wanted to stay in his room, away from the world, and look at some naked women.

His lustful adrenaline wouldn't allow him to sleep now anyway so, the decision confirmed, Tyler was going to get an unannounced visitor.

Shoes tied, Kyle approached his bedroom door with apprehension. Pressing his ear to it, he listened. The apartment was silent. They're probably having a fuck fest. Those awkward moments almost always followed the big fights. They were so gross.

It was time to take a chance, to risk the awkward to escape the suffocating. He cranked down the door handle, listening as each spring creaked. It was ridiculous to think they could hear him, but he winced with each metallic crackle just the same.

Devoid of any streetlight, the hallway was a blanket of black.

The air smelled different. It popped with unease.

Something was wrong.

Step-by-step, Kyle worked his way down the hall without reaching out to feel the walls, hundreds of late-night parties taught him how to navigate a dark apartment. The night was soundless as if the world forgot how to breathe. Even the street noise was sucked into the black void.

The school's empty library was louder than the apartment.

Kyle stopped at the archway where the hallway opened to the small area that contained both the living room and the kitchen. The combined space was smaller than his bedroom in the old house in the suburbs.

He hated this place.

Something moved in the blanket of black.

In that instant, he didn't want to be there anymore, not because of his parents but because of the wicked scent in the air. It announced itself without making an appearance. He didn't need to see it, but he needed to get away. Far away.

Kyle took a cautious step forward.

And the sound approached.

At first, he thought it was one of the resident rats finally clawing its way through the thin walls and into their dump of a home. Their slight movement was part of life here. The nasty rodents were all over the apartment complex, scratching at everything and scurrying inside the walls every single night. But he'd never heard them scratching so clearly. They could be anywhere.

Kyle choked back the image of stepping onto a linoleum floor filled with hundreds of diseased rodents.

This was the way to the front door. It didn't matter if his parents were done fighting, it would start up again after they finished this round of sex. This was his one chance to leave, and he wasn't going to waste it.

Closing his eyes, Kyle readied himself to hear the squeal of a rat. A squeal was better than feeling one — or more — scurry over his foot. He stepped —

— on the cool, cracked linoleum floor. No rats.

A quick sigh of relief washed over him.

Scratch.

Scratch.

Scratch.

Something softer. The wisping of clothes?

Closer now. The chipped countertop corner signaled his arrival in the kitchen. The sound was almost at his feet.

Kyle stepped.

In the blackness, something moved.

Something big.

Here, it sounded ... wet.

Kyle felt along the counters, looking for the drawer where they kept the rolling pin. The neighbor's dog might have broken in again. It happened a lot. The front door didn't always catch, especially when one, or both, drunk parents came home too wasted to remember to close it properly. Dad always blamed the landlord for never bothering to come around and fix things. Mom always blamed Dad.

Both of them failed at life. A lot. Failure came naturally to this family.

A rolling pin would scare the stupid dog, hurt it a little maybe. Kyle didn't want to stab it, just give it a good whack and send it on its way out to the dump of an apartment next door, where its owners wasted life by shooting up while waiting for their next check from the government.

Kyle's hand paused on the drawer. If the contents moved when he opened it his parents would hear him. Even if they weren't boning, his mother was sloppy drunk. She'd want to hang all over him and cry about how bad everything was, and how she's not appreciated and loved. He didn't have time for her drama.

If the thing moving in the dark was the damn dog, he'd kick it. Give it a good scare. It was chicken shit anyway; a swift kick in the ribs and it would howl all the way back home.

Slurping. In front of him, near his feet.

The dog. It must have knocked the garbage over again.

He didn't have time to clean even more shit up.

The kitchen stunk like—

Kyle took another tentative step. His foot jammed into something solid and unmovable. He toppled forward, crashing into the plastic trashcan. It kicked out away from him and bounced against the wall. The lid popped off and tumbled away. The still-warm and wet remains of their Hamburger Helper dinner landed on the back of his head.

Forget kicking it, now he wanted to kill that damned dog.

All he wanted to do was get out of the house.

He was going to have to explain this mess to two drunk parents when they found him with half a pan of cheaply-seasoned hamburger meat running down the back of his neck.

Kyle growled and rolled over.

And froze.

Thwack.

Thump.

Thwack.

The sound was inches away from his feet.

Kyle pushed his back against the wall, away from the sound. Underneath the thumping, a child-like laugh chilled his skin. It held a deepness that only came after passing puberty and spending the intervening decades abusing your throat.

There was no neighbor's dog in the apartment. That was the tight giggle of an adult. It was low, almost inaudible under the sound of his heavy breaths.

Kyle's hands shook all on their own.

His palms flat, he felt the floor around him. The garbage can's contents everywhere. Plastic wrappers. Small cardboard containers. Something soft and squishy. Then, something firmer. Metal. It was thin and slightly bent. Kyle wrapped his hand around it, careful to not slice his fingers open. It was circular. The lid of a can. He cupped it against his palm. Whoever was in the kitchen was going to get a nasty surprise if they came at him. He might slice his hand open in the process, but they weren't going to do anything to him without getting a dose of pain first. The lid would do some serious damage.

Thwack.

Scratch.

Thump. Scratch.

Giggle.

Thwack.

Scratch.

Thump. Scratch. Scratch. Giggle.

Kyle's heart raced. His throat throbbed.

He pressed back against the wall. It didn't offer an escape, but he felt a lot better knowing nothing could sneak up behind him.

Kyle peered into the darkness. The thing moved. Scurried like a rat. The animalistic fluidity of its movements provided a rich soundscape. Normal people didn't move like that.

He had to get out. Fuck his parents and their stupid shit. They could fend for themselves.

Kyle inched himself up, careful to keep the wall to his back. He held the lid up like he was about to throw a baseball. It felt ridiculous, but it was all he had. And having something was better than having nothing at all to defend against whatever moved in the darkness.

The scratching ceased. Underneath the absence of noise, Kyle heard something else.

Deep, heavy breathing. The type of breathing people did after sprinting further than they were physically able. The type of breathing he heard animals in documentaries make when watching them tear a carcass apart. It was not the type of breathing you ever heard in a shit-hole apartment in the middle of a shithole city, occupied by shitty people.

He swallowed the dry lump in his throat.

At that instant, the lights flickered back to life. Kyle ignored the beeping of reanimated appliances, clocks, and the neighbor's television that suddenly blared to life through the thin walls. He was too mortified by what he was looking at to care about the rebirth of the electronic world.

There, in the middle of the kitchen floor, splayed out in absent glory, was his father. Bill laid on his back, his arms over his head and one leg cocked at an awkward angle. Bill's dead eyes stared up at the cracked paint on the ceiling.

Kyle forgot to breathe.

A carving knife jutted from the middle of his sternum, piercing the shredded sea of red polyester of his Santa Claus outfit. Kneeling next to his father's corpse, Brenda dug between the shredded cloth and into Bill's chest cavity, pulling out bloody organs like a kid looking through her Halloween basket.

She giggled as she reached under Bill's rib cage, fingering something that might have been a lung.

She's fucking giggling.

"Mom?" Kyle croaked.

Brenda didn't respond. She continued searching until she pulled out a pale flesh tube covered in blood and slime. A piece of it broke away and plopped on the thick, black costume belt.

"Mom?" Kyle's voice quivered as the reality of what was unfolding screamed through his numbed brain.

Brenda rocked back and forth on her knees, shaking her head. Her normally wispy brown hair lanced the air in red clumps. Blood and small chunks of tissue smeared her forehead. Brenda reached out and wrapped her fingers around the carving knife handle, yanking it from Bill's chest. Kyle jumped when his father's body jerked.

"He's ...," Brenda rocked back and forth as she searched for what she wanted to say, "he's not going to hurt me anymore, Kyle. No more."

What was she doing? What had she *done*?

This couldn't be real, it couldn't be.

"He's not going to hurt me anymore," Brenda repeated in slow, measured grunts. With each word, she slammed the carving knife back into Bill's chest. Blood splattered upward at every thrust, disappearing into the red of the Santa jacket. Kyle was almost thankful.

Thwack.

Thwack.

Thwack.

Over and over, she thrust the blade deep. Kyle vomited on the floor before he realized that his stomach was churning.

"You won't be like him will you, honey?" Brenda rocked back and forth stabbing over and over, without looking up at her son. "You'll be a good boy. Promise me you'll always be a good boy."

Thwack.

Thwack.

Thwack. Thwack. Thwack.

He gasped for breath that wouldn't come.

Over and over, each time harder than the time before, Brenda impaled the knife. "Always promise me that you'll treat women right."

She looked happy. The happiest she'd ever looked. The smile she wore walked the invisible line between madness and release.

"Mom ... stop ... please," Kyle begged. His father's body rocked with each piercing blow.

But she didn't.

She wouldn't, or couldn't.

Her giggle turned into a cackle, growing in volume and fervor. He had to go, go now before his mother's madness reminded her of the times Kyle hurt her.

127

He scrambled out of the kitchen and into the small living room. Fire exploded in his thigh when he crashed into the end table. He lunged for the front door. The loose handle spun in his grip and Kyle panicked. If the latch was broken inside the door he'd be stuck in this apartment with a madwoman.

But it was just loose, a piece of crap, like everything else in his world.

Finally, the latch released and he yanked the door open, sprinting out into the constricted hallway. Kyle didn't wait to scream for help from any of his uncaring neighbors. They wouldn't respond and it would only draw the madwoman's attention. As he descended the rickety steps, Brenda's cackling faded into the background of his life.

She was finally happy.

And Santa Claus was dead.

END

Roasting On An Open Fire

"Burn, motherfucker, burn," DeMarco Morales laughed.

Chikae shook his head at the idiot who also happened to also be his best friend. How DeMarco survived life was still a mystery to Chikae. DeMarco was a good guy, but he was still an idiot. "Back the fuck off before you burn yourself alive," Chikae laughed.

Dozens of times over their teenage years, Chikae watched DeMarco set things on fire. DeMarco was a bit of a pyromaniac. Everyone knew that. Most people grew out of the stupid things they did as teenagers, but not DeMarco. DeMarco would be a mental teenager for the rest of his life.

But in his own way, Chikae loved his friend. DeMarco embraced life every day he breathed. He was irresponsible and juvenile, but his personality provided a good balance to Chikae's own structured and careful approach to existing. That balance had outlasted the years since graduation and the exodus of friends from DeMarco's circle. Where the world dulled, DeMarco still held onto its promises of prosperity. Where Chikae settled down in a cubicle kingdom, DeMarco hopped from job to job, claiming he was still trying to find his future. The future where he would make $1 million a year and live in all the splendor it could provide. It was naive, of course, but refreshing. Part of Chikae believed that was why he enjoyed spending so much time around DeMarco, even all these years later, when most people distanced themselves. If it bothered DeMarco that so many of their childhood friends had turned away, he never showed it. But there was something there, something hidden, repressed. Something unhealthy that DeMarco hadn't dealt with. And that was one of the reasons why Chikae overlooked a lot of the dumb things that DeMarco did.

Like setting a trashcan filled with garbage on fire.

DeMarco backed away as the flames jumped into the sky, his gaze locked on their weaving dance. Chikae understood it, there was a beauty to the way fire destroyed. But there was a difference between appreciation and reverence.

"It's beautiful, bro, isn't it?" DeMarco uttered.

It was, but Chikae didn't want to encourage him.

"I mean, look at it," he pointed at the blazing trashcan. "The way it consumes. That's pretty fucking cool."

"Yeah, man, it's cool," Chikae replied. "Just back up a little more, will you? You're making me nervous."

DeMarco laughed. "Everything makes you nervous, bro."

Chikae avoided responding by taking a small hit of the pipe. It was amazing, DeMarco always knew where to get the best pot. One of the benefits of running in bad circles, Chikae imagined.

Chikae blew the cloud out into the warm night. The middle of Maryland was a moderate existence all year long. None of the insufferable heat of the South, none of that horrendous cold of the North. The ocean kept things normal, consistent, the way Chikae liked it, even as he dreamed of a life in California. Tonight, there were no thoughts of California. He was back home, under an open sky. The warmth teased, better suited for May than December. But Chikae enjoyed it just the same. Nights like tonight, where they could sit outside, smoke some great marijuana, and watch DeMarco act like a teenage idiot, were as enjoyable as they were simple.

He needed more of them.

Chikae thought about his job and the life that did nothing to stimulate him, as he watched DeMarco, still entranced by the fire. Wasn't life about the thrills and excitement of your twenties? Chikae couldn't remember the last time he was excited. And here was DeMarco, a grown man, adoring the flames as they leaped into the warm night. What must it be like? DeMarco didn't have a lot of close friends anymore, couldn't hold down a job, still lived with his aunt; but still seemed happy. Fulfilled.

Chikae had done everything he was supposed to do. He went to college after school, earning a degree and landing a respectable job; he had family and a few close friends and dozens of associates in his professional network; he had everything successful people had at this stage of his life. But yet, if a stranger watched the two of them, they would guess DeMarco was the more successful of the pair.

"I got an idea," DeMarco broke Chikae's silent reflection.

"Yeah?"

"Let's head down to the club."

DeMarco's smirk held the promise of trouble. Chikae knew the signs well; he'd seen them a million times. Throughout their teen years, DeMarco tried to get away with things that ended with them getting their asses beat. But even beatings didn't stop them from at least attempting to find trouble to fill their teenage weekends. More times than not, DeMarco was the epicenter of those plans, planning and scheming what he called 'harmless fun'.

Chikae proceeded with caution. "What do you have in mind?"

The club was a dive bar on the outskirts of town, an obscure blight on a dead industrial area. The owners had liked it out there because they could get away with things to make a little extra profit. And that approved deviance made it a popular spot for teenagers back in the day. It was a place where they could buy alcohol and pretend they were something they weren't. Everyone knew the club owners conducted shady business, but what teenager cared about that if they had a spot to dance, flirt, and get their drink on like their fathers did eight days a week?

But that legacy was the club's death knell. One night, Jack, the majority owner, served a little too much booze to the wrong teenager. That kid, Jamaal, took it upon himself to try to drive him and his girlfriend home, killing both when he failed to stop for a red light and ran straight into the oncoming path of a semi-truck. The tragic end of two young lives was also the end of the club and any hope for the kids in town to have a drinking spot again. Outraged parents made sure of that. Without a spot to waste his weekends walking the razor's edge of trouble, Chikae was forced to focus on other aspects of his life. Like his education. He was the first one in his family to finish college. He had a career. Everything turned out for the better.

That was almost 10 years now. What in the world would DeMarco want to do out there now? They were two grown men; they could go to any bar in town or head up into Annapolis. Either was a better prospect than the club.

"Yeah, let's head down there," DeMarco said, spinning back toward the car.

"Wait. Are we going to put that out?" Chikae indicated the fire raging inside the trashcan.

DeMarco smirked. "No man. Why? It'll burn down."

Chikae paused, unsure this was a wise decision.

DeMarco laughed at him. "Man, you're always so serious. Chill. It'll be fine."

Against his better judgment, Chikae got into the car and soon found himself partying in an empty parking lot outside the abandoned club. "Man, that's depressing," he commented, taking in the deteriorating building that once was the coolest place in his small world.

"It fell apart real quick after you left," DeMarco said, firing up another hit. "No one comes out here anymore."

Chikae remembered his parents talking about the collapse of the industrial center. A domino effect killed the economy when one of the bigger employers closed their doors and moved to Mexico. One after another, businesses followed that lead or went under, spreading unemployment like a disease. It was one of the reasons he didn't like coming home anymore. DC held a much more positive life. Out here it felt like someone hit the PAUSE button on the world at the worst part of the movie. Hopeless. Here? What could anyone hope for?

"You ready to do this?" DeMarco asked, breaking Chikae's tail-spinning thoughts.

"Do what?"

DeMarco hopped out of the car, releasing the last of the marijuana hit he held. A large, soft cloud filled the air. A sweet smell. DeMarco leaned down, one arm resting on the top of the door, "To burn it down, man."

He laughed, hacking up another small cloud of marijuana smoke, and slammed the door.

This was one of the worst ideas DeMarco ever had, but that didn't stop Chikae from getting out of the car to join him. If nothing else, he needed to protect DeMarco from himself.

"What are you doing?"

DeMarco rummaged around in the trunk. The parking lot was dark; the property manager probably wasn't interested in paying to light this abyss. Two of the light poles lay across the blacktop.

"Give me your light," DeMarco said from somewhere behind that trunk lid. "Wait, never mind. I found it."

"Found what?" Chikae asked, flicking on his flashlight app, shining it as he came around the back of the car.

"This," DeMarco held up a gas can.

It was one thing to burn shit in trash cans in the middle of some field, but it was something entirely different to burn a building, abandoned or not. This was real shit. This was a felony.

"Come on man," Chikae chided. "You're not serious."

DeMarco answered by slamming the trunk closed. "Last one in is a pussy."

With that, DeMarco sprinted for the building.

Chikae stood by the back of the car watching his friend disappear into the black hole where the front door used to be years ago. Now that he was alone in the parking lot, staring at a building that was rotting into extinction, he realized how creepy it was out here. The exterior bore the scars of time. Here and there, without rhyme or reason, slivers of the siding were torn off, making the building looked marked. It served as a signal to the world how quickly something could lose its beauty once it was no longer cared for. The few windows that faced the parking lot had the glass busted out. Jagged slivers grimaced at their fate. One end of the roof sagged.

Chikae couldn't believe he used to look forward to coming here. But this was worse; he was an adult, too old to be here, doing this. This was asinine. This was criminal. He could either leave DeMarco or he could talk him out of this. But everyone in their circles had left DeMarco. That was half the reason he was as fucked up as he was. Approaching thirty and still acting like a 13-year-old. Chikae wasn't going to join that queue.

"Shit," he slammed the car door, only checking for the keys afterward. Thankfully, he still had them.

The sound of his footsteps skipped across the parking lot as he approached the club, reminding him how isolated they were from anyone who could help if things went bad.

That black opening of the club swallowed DeMarco. Chikae paused, looking around at the parking lot one last time before carefully stepping through the rotted door frame and into the place where dreams had become reality for a teenage boy.

The club was nothing like a place of dreams now.

The dance floor was warped after years of exposure to the weather, thanks to a partially collapsed roof. The half-wall the bouncers used to sit behind was still there, but everything else had been stripped away, sold off or stolen. There were no barstools and even the glass mirror they used to use to covertly check out women was gone. The shelves that once held the promises delivered through bottles of alcohol now lay bare and broken, leaning at angles against one another. Chikae laughed when he saw the disco ball still hanging from the ceiling over the dance floor. How much had he learned about himself and what women liked underneath that damn thing?

Death had come to the club. It was a sad sight. "DeMarco, come on. Let's get out of here." He couldn't see his friend but could hear him moving around in the darkness. "What the hell are you doing?"

The sound stopped.

Chikae swallowed, thinking for the first time that they might not be the only ones in here. He couldn't see anything beyond the five feet his phone light illuminated. "Come on, man. This shit's not funny. Let's get out of here."

Things moved, shuffled in the darkness.

He thought he heard a sound to his right. It was light, skittering. Before he could spin, another sound teased him from the left.

And then the world was ablaze.

In one corner of the club, booths where the older kids used to flirt and talk about college, the spot high schoolers weren't allowed to be, moaned as they were consumed by fire. Flames leaped up the walls, accelerated by DeMarco's can of gas.

Then DeMarco was running by him. "Come on, man!"

DeMarco raced across the dance floor and straight out of the club. It took a second before Chikae understood everything that was happening. All around the back of the club, the flames spread.

"Come on, Chikae!" DeMarco yelled from the safety of the gaping doorway.

Chikae didn't need to be told again. A trail of fire surged up out of nothingness across the floor. The gas can had leaked. And it led straight to his only escape route.

Breaking into a sprint, Chikae jumped over the line of growing fire and into the night air. Once safe, he bent over, gasping. DeMarco laughed.

Chikae shoved his shoulder. "That shit's not funny, man."

"Yes, it is. Especially if you could see your face."

Chikae examined DeMarco and shook his head. He was never going to grow up. "Where's the gas can?"

"Gas can? I left that shit in there."

"Why?"

"It cost three dollars," DeMarco shrugged. "No big deal. Give me the keys."

But it was a big deal. It was, if nothing else, evidence. As Chikae handed over the keys, he wondered how DeMarco couldn't understand that. When the authorities did an investigation into the fire they might find clues out of charred wood and melted plastics. And he had a life, a career; he was going in the right direction and didn't want to be part of this. He'd tried to stop DeMarco. That was why he wanted to know where the goddamn gas can was.

There was no time to contemplate the consequences. While they were safe in the parking lot, the interior of the club was glowing to life as the fire spread. In minutes, the building would be completely ablaze. That would draw attention.

"We need to leave," Chikae said.

But DeMarco leaned against the hood of the car, crossing his arms, his eyes fixed on the growing flames. "No man, I want to watch this."

Someone, anyone, might stumble by on a late-night drive. Cops must still patrol this area periodically. They might come across them at any minute. He didn't need that mess. He wasn't some stupid teenager without a care in the world.

And the flames were growing. Wood popped. Even this far away, Chikae felt its warm breath. With the deterioration of the structure, Chikae thought it would be too damp to catch. He was wrong. Flames danced larger and larger. Something crashed inside the building. The club was going to burn to the ground.

"Fuck this, DeMarco," Chikae said. "Give me the keys. I'm leaving. You can join me or —"

A scream soared above the dull rumble of the blooming fire. It came from inside the club.

Chikae froze. "What was that?"

DeMarco, too, had stopped and turned back toward the building at the unexpected sound. "I am sure ... I'm sure it was nothing."

Inside the club, flames popped up over the bottom of the windowsills, across the span of the building. Heat blew toward them, a warmth that chilled his soul.

"Just hearing things," DeMarco said and began walking back toward the car, moving toward the driver side. "It's intense, right?" He laughed, but it was unconvincing.

Chikae had heard something. It wasn't an after effect of the fire. It wasn't background noise from one of the abandoned industrial buildings. If he heard something, then

DeMarco did too. DeMarco had reacted to the scream. Chikae saw him.

"We can't leave, man."

"Why not?"

Chikae jabbed a finger back toward the building. The flames crackled. "Someone screamed in there."

"I didn't hear anything." DeMarco yanked open the car door and collapsed into the driver seat, starting the car. He leaned his head toward the passenger side window, "Are you coming?"

Was he serious? They needed to help whoever that was inside the club before it was too late. They couldn't just—

DeMarco rolled forward, turning toward the parking lot exit. Chikae took one more look at the club before returning his gaze to the car. The passenger side window was still down. DeMarco leaned across the middle console again. His eyes begged Chikae to give up. "We've got to go, man," DeMarco shouted, a slight quiver in his voice.

Chikae understood. A million thoughts raced through his mind in that instant, no one thought clearer than any other. Behind him, glass exploded. The entire building surged into old age as the fire spread, consuming more and more. Maybe it wasn't a scream after all. Chemicals made weird noises when they burned. Fire destroyed in the most chaotic of ways. It could've been anything, Chikae convinced himself. And in that moment of panicked clarity, he ran to the car. Something collapsed inside the building behind his retreat.

It's just the building. Just a stupid, old building no one cares about.

Chikae's hand was on the door, ready to pull it open when he heard the scream again. It definitely came from inside the building and it was definitely a voice. Not chemicals. Not a weird death call from some inanimate building material. This howl filled the world, reverberated inside his head. A human howl.

A howl of excruciating pain.

"Get the fuck in, man, or I'm leaving you here!" There was no mistaking DeMarco's intentions. Whatever was happening inside that building, DeMarco would leave it to carve out its own fate.

Through the open doorway that was now ablaze with the roaring fire, something moved. It wasn't the musty drapes catching fire and breaking loose of the rods, drifting into his field of vision. It wasn't a partial wall collapsing, sending support beams scattering across the open maw.

Something walked toward the door.

"Get in, man!" DeMarco's voice was muffled in Chikae's ears.

A form. A human form, stumbled through the fire, out of the fire, toward the front door. Neither male nor female, the form was immense.

And it was on fire.

"Jesus Christ."

"Chikae, I'm going to leave you!" Muffled no longer, DeMarco's voice cleaved the night.

"We can't," Chikae screamed. "There's someone in there. They're hurt."

The figure stumbled, its fiery arms swaying to catch its balance. It approached the door, close now. Flames licked at the person's clothes. A man, a large man. Between the fire raging in the background and the dark night, it was difficult to make out much detail about him beyond tattered strips of clothing burning and floating up and away from the burning man.

The man who was burning alive.

"We've got to help!" Chikae pleaded through the open car window.

DeMarco put the car in gear. "Last chance. I'm not fucking around." His icy voice was an appropriate contradiction to the burning world.

Face-first, the burning man fell out of the doorway.

"Oh, fuck!"

Flames licked at his clothes, spread across his back, down his legs, and across his thick arms. They danced on his head. Chikae, frozen, watched this slow, excruciating death. The man didn't move. Gruesome. The unmoving form on the ground faded from the living world even as flames danced to life into the night sky above him.

Tires crunched across the loose rock and trash that polluted the desolate parking lot. DeMarco pulled away.

"Wait!" Chikae screamed in a moment of madness, grabbing for the car door. DeMarco obeyed and Chikae jumped in.

Without another word, DeMarco pulled away. They rode in silence. There was nothing to talk about. There was nothing to say about the man they'd left back in the parking lot.

Because the burning man was already dead.

***

Chikae's cell phone buzzed. He picked it up, looking at the unknown number, then hung up.

"Who is that?" Sonia, his wife, asked.

Chikae shrugged. "It doesn't matter. It's Christmas. Family time. Whoever it was, it can wait."

She smiled as she bounced Kendrick on her knee.

Chikae slunk off the chair and joined his family on the floor, kissing both of them on the forehead. Christmas in Southern California was strange with no chill in the air to remind him that it was a special time of year. But the job that brought them here was one he couldn't pass up. They moved across the country, thousands of miles from their families and their past, for it.

They didn't know many people yet, so this Christmas it would be just the three of them for the holidays. And that was completely fine with Chikae. He wanted to focus on these two; the job was demanding, taking a lot out of him. One day he'd be up to speed, but right now he was still proving himself to his peers and boss. That required sacrifice.

The phone buzzed again. Chikae sighed, reaching behind him and snagging it off the end table. It was another unknown number. "Jesus," he pressed the END button.

"Maybe you should take that," Sonia said, her eyebrows raised as a look of concern passed over her face.

Chikae shook his head. A telemarketer or a wrong number; either way, it wasn't anyone he wanted to speak with. "It's Christmas, babe." He said as if that explained everything. He switched the phone over to silent mode, preferring to enjoy their traditional inside picnic on the living room floor as they watched the classic Christmas movie.

The perfect night.

When they laid Kendrick down, a feat in itself because he was excited about a visit from Santa, night unwound on the balcony. They shared a bottle of wine and the distant view of the ocean, the riches of this new life. Sonia was quiet. Chikae leaned on the railing, twirling her hair around his finger as he thought. This was their fifth Christmas together. Five years!

She wore a permanent smile, the kind of expression content people wore. He got that. The last year had been chaotic, but each challenge was necessary. Being a world away from family and friends was hard. But the huge promotion and related pay raise allowed them to buy a home they could only dream of just a few years ago. And they were living the Southern California lifestyle, something Sonia dreamed about since she was young. He did too. And then there was Kendrick, a healthy, happy toddler.

Life was good.

The sun was setting beyond the reach of the world. A beautiful sight, the way the orange light danced across the open surface of the Pacific.

They sat in reflective silence, enjoying each other's company, even after the orange glow faded to black in the distance.

Sonia bit her lip and tapped the railing. "I need to get Kendrick's presents out and get to bed. We've got an early morning."

"I'll help."

After they finished, Sonia went to bed, accompanied only by her wine-induced headache. Chikae stayed awake, sitting in front of the fire and wrapping the last of Kendrick's presents Sonia didn't know about. He bought them today, against her wishes. She thought Kendrick had enough, but

Chikae figured a couple more small presents wouldn't hurt. Kendrick had everything he needed, but it felt good to give him more of the life Chikae had missed out on as a child.

It wasn't until much later, then, that Chikae noticed he had 14 missed phone calls. "What the hell?" he cycled through the call log, checking each of them. All of them were from an unknown number.

Before he set the phone down, the screen blinked to life, showing an incoming call. It didn't matter that it was Christmas, someone was getting an ass-chewing. "What?" he set the tone for this annoying call from the beginning.

"Is this Chikae Hicks?" a fragile female voice asked.

Chikae's guard lowered with that single question. The woman sounded elderly, sad. "How can I help you?"

There was sniffling in the background of her end of the call. "You were friends with DeMarco, right?"

DeMarco? Chikae thought. When was the last time he heard that name? Not since ...

"DeMarco Morales?"

More sniffling. "I'm his aunt, Gwen. I don't think I've seen you since you boys were ... I don't know, fifteen. Maybe?" Her voice trailed off.

The fire had changed everything. The night Chikae tried to forget, tried to repress, was the line in the sand for their relationship. DeMarco killed a homeless man in the fire, according to local news outlets. DeMarco wasn't charged because authorities never conducted much of an investigation from what Chikae could tell. The, now, sole owner of the property didn't pursue charges because the fire allowed him to remove an eyesore from the world for free. Everyone soon forgot about the dead homeless man.

Except Chikae.

He couldn't forget, no matter how hard he tried. How did you erase the sight of a man lying on the ground, burning to death? Nor did he forget his own failure to stop DeMarco from starting the fire in the first place or helping the man in the fallout of madness. It laid a heavy blanket of guilt and remorse on his mind even all these years later.

Chikae shook his head. The homeless man's final moments were etched into his memory forever. But DeMarco hadn't been. After that night, Chikae did everything he could to forget about DeMarco completely.

And he had.

Until this call.

He should have never picked up the phone.

DeMarco's aunt wouldn't call a dozen times on Christmas Eve to check in for the first time in twenty years. "Is everything okay?"

At the question, Aunt Gwen broke down. Chikae held the phone away from his ear as she wailed. Her reaction confirming something was wrong. He was ready to hear it. Over the years since the club fire, he'd followed everyone else's lead and distanced himself from DeMarco. But it wasn't without guilt.

When DeMarco's aunt stopped crying, her tiny voice responded, "No. He's dead."

Chikae expected that much. There was no other reasonable explanation for calling someone on Christmas Eve from across the country. "Oh," he stammered, not knowing what to say, "I'm sorry to hear that."

A few seconds of awkward sniffling from the other end. "I was wondering ... if-if you knew anything about it?"

There. That was the real reason for the phone call. A drug deal gone bad? Some ridiculous turf war over who got to sell molly on which block? In the end, someone finally made him pay. "No. No," he repeated, softer the second time. Then, morbid curiosity made him ask, "I haven't spoken to DeMarco in years. Do you mind me asking what happened?"

"He was killed," Aunt Gwen answered. "The police ... they don't have a lot of answers right now, but ... the family, we're reaching out to ... to ... anyone who knew him, to see if they have any information."

"About what?"

"About what was going on in his life," she answered. "It was ... his death was pretty gruesome."

Chikae didn't want to ask. He didn't want the details and didn't want to get wrapped back up in DeMarco's mess, but the question was on his lips before he could even process it. "How was it gruesome?"

A few deep breaths answered him. "He was tied up." She began to cry, unable to calm herself. A pause and a number of deep breaths later, the words tumbled out. "They tied him to a tree in a nearby greenbelt and burned him alive. He was ... Burned. Alive!"

Aunt Gwen howled. Chikae didn't know what to say. He felt for the woman and DeMarco's family, but it was difficult to feel anything for his old friend. DeMarco was the only person in the world who made him approach feeling hatred, even over the stabbing panic in the middle of his chest. DeMarco's fate birthed the reality of karma. "I'm sorry to hear that. And I'm sorry for your loss. My thoughts are with you and your family."

It sounded so robotic, so scripted. Chikae wasn't sure what the woman wanted from him, but he knew what he wanted. He wanted off this phone call and to return to a life that did not include the memory of DeMarco. She was the only thing keeping him from that.

Aunt Gwen rotated between whimpered whispers and cries of anguish. It was so typical of DeMarco to hurt everyone in his life and around him. Even in death.

Muffled voices consorted on the other end of the phone line. Chikae couldn't make out what was happening until a man spoke. His tone was stern. "You DeMarco's friend?"

The combative nature, even in mourning, didn't sit well with Chikae. He had no idea who the man was and if he was associated with DeMarco, Chikae was less ready to give him the benefit of the doubt. "A lifetime ago."

There was a tight laugh as if his response humored this man. "Good, DeMarco was nothing but trouble."

Chikae's shoulders loosened.

"I'm Robert, Gwen's husband," the man introduced himself. "Listen, I won't trouble you long. I know it's Christmas Eve and all. I don't know what happened between you and

DeMarco, that boy was messed up in the head. We just wanted to reach out and let you know about his death."

"I'm sorry for your loss."

Robert *tsked*. "It's fine. Thank you for saying so. Listen, we wanted to reach out to you because DeMarco talked about you up until his death. Seems someone was troubling him and he was worried that you might be in trouble too."

Chikae's heart jumped. DeMarco ran with the wrong crowds. It wasn't beyond reason to think his friend had pissed off the worst of Maryland's worst. That didn't explain why anyone in DeMarco's circles would care about him. DeMarco ran with drugs and petty crime, Chikae didn't. They lived in two different worlds, members of two distinct clubs of life, and had been for years now. The distance he kept from DeMarco should have broken all associations with his childhood friend.

"I'm sorry," he began, "but I have no idea what you're talking about. If DeMarco was in some kind of trouble, he—"

"You know how that boy was, always getting himself in the trouble, running with the wrong crowd. Grown ass man, acting like a teen. It was bound to happen." More wailing in the background. Another covered phone receiver. After a few seconds, Robert came back. "But whatever it was, whoever it was, DeMarco was sure they were gunning for you too."

Chikae wiped away a stream of perspiration. It had to be drugs. It had to be. The family was kind to call with their concerns, but they were mistaken.

He tried to lighten the mood, to relieve DeMarco's family of feeling they had any responsibility for this or to him. "Well, I appreciate the phone call, I really do. But whatever DeMarco got himself into, I can assure you I had no association with it. I'm a family man, professional."

It was a strange response and solicited an appropriate reaction from Robert. He was quiet on the other end of the phone line. Chikae was worried he'd offended the man who called to fulfill the family's unselfish motivations in their moment of loss. He felt like an ass.

"That's good for you," Robert finally answered, "but be on your guard. Whoever was bothering DeMarco seemed pretty damned determined. This wasn't an isolated thing. The last, hell, I don't know, the last year or so of his life was a wreck. The man was always on edge. Paranoid. Seeing monsters and shadows where there were none. We actually tried to have him evaluated once and the sonofabitch ran away. We figured he was at that drug house on another month-long high or something. But he came back, swore he was clean and the family took him in. They always rescued him ... right up until the end. But that last year? He acted strangely, I'll tell you that much. Whoever wanted him dead really wanted him dead. And," the voices in the background faded as if Robert was stepping into another room, "whoever it was fucked him up, son. Really fucked him up."

Chikae used the crock of his elbow to wipe forehead, running it over the top of his skull. The house felt like it was 1000°. He was being ridiculous. DeMarco got what he deserved in the end for a lifetime of abusing others. Though they were suffering, he couldn't help them, the most recent victims of DeMarco's narcissistic personality. Anger boiled inside him. Not at them, not even at the situation, but at DeMarco.

"What you mean?"

"They skinned him, son. Skinned and burned."

Robert's comment was a punch in the gut. An accidental "fuck" slipped.

"My thoughts exactly," Robert laughed on the other end of the phone. It was an appropriate laugh, not too humored, not completely sad. The tone was gone. Robert was serious again. "We're sorry about this, sorry about troubling you. Sorry about ruining your Christmas Eve. Gwen felt it was important for you to know because ... you know ..."

"Sir, did DeMarco ever mention anyone? You know, who he was afraid of?"

Robert scoffed. "Crazy talk, son. Nothing but crazy talk from that kid."

Chikae swallowed hard. A sweat bead slunk its way down his spine toward the crack of his ass. "What did he say?"

A big sigh from Robert before the moment of madness. "He always talked about 'the burning man', son. He said the burning man was after him." An awkward pause followed the statement. "Told you, it was crazy talk."

But Chikae didn't hear much of anything. The world was a blur, all sounds snuffed out beneath the cover of trauma.

The burning man.

He wanted nothing more than to hang up this phone call and pretend it never happened and wake up on Christmas morning with Sonia and Kendrick.

"Thank you, I appreciate that." It was all he could mutter.

With that, they wished each other a merry holiday and hung up.

Chikae set the phone down on the coffee table and leaned back, letting himself go into deep thought. Typical, fucking DeMarco.

Even a world away, years removed from each other's lives and beyond the grave, he still haunted Chikae.

He stood and shut off the fireplace. It was hot as hell in the house, so Chikae slid open the balcony door to allow the cool night breeze in. Looking out over the eternal blackness of the Pacific at night, Chikae reflected on his life, grateful for how far he'd come. He thought about DeMarco and the sad life he'd led. But he also thought, reveled, at the fact that he'd overcome that same environment. He'd broken away and not fallen into the traps DeMarco had.

He thought all these things, deeply.

So deeply that he didn't notice the crackling of the fire until it was too late.

And then Chikae remembered.

He remembered DeMarco's addiction to setting the world ablaze.

And he remembered the club.

His throat constricted. The sudden, choked breaths didn't allow him to sob as he remembered doing nothing for the homeless man as he tried to fight his way out of the burning building, dying at the foot of the world.

The same burning man who stood in his living room.

Somewhere in his mind of madness, Chikae saw the burning man's face, set ablaze by a fire that never died. The hulking presence filled the path between Chikae and his only escape.

From his toes to the top of his head, the burning man raged with the flames of the eternal fire. He took a step toward Chikae and small sparks floated off his body. His footfall thundered on the floor, leaving scorch marks with each step.

Chikae backed up, but there was nowhere else to go. The balcony and the drop to the ground was all that sat behind him.

The burning man stepped closer.

"Please," Chikae begged. "Please. I didn't do anything."

The burning man stepped again. Closer. Reaching out. His fingers glowed yellow. Hot flames arced up, releasing sparks that floated in a slight, slow dance.

Step.

The wall of his balcony pressed against his back. Sonia and Kendrick were in the bedrooms, behind the burning man. Chikae needed to get to them. But the large form of the burning man blocked his path, filling the balcony door. A monstrosity of rage and pain.

There was nowhere to go, nowhere to run.

The burning man's fiery hand grabbed Chikae's throat, fire licked his face, searing his cheeks. He wanted to scream but couldn't. His scorched throat was no longer able to open or close as he was silenced forever.

Before Chikae died, the burning man reached for his face. The sizzle of skin, the smell of burnt flesh, filled Chikae's nose and ears.

The burning man's fiery fingers melted into his cheek. Grabbing hold of skin, the burning man began to peel.

END

Slayride

Winter in the foothills of Colorado can be warmer and drier than expected, Sam Bollinger knew that. He'd grown up here. Even so, when the plane landed, he wasn't sure the airline took him to the correct destination.

December in Colorado and no snow? Glancing out the airplane window, Denver looked more like Destin.

This was his first trip back to this part of the world in ... *years?* College took him away, job opportunities and love kept him away. Even the East Coast's tightly-packed communities hadn't pushed him back west. The coast was the center of his world now. Cluttered roads, filthy sidewalks, and people with nasty attitudes were the attributes of the place where his heart converged with the physical world. What he saw outside this small airplane window was a foreign land to him in more ways than one.

Everything was different now.

The trip to Denver was dropped into his life from the other end of a voice message. Two days ago, he ignored an unknown number and let it go to voicemail. On the coast you learned giving people more of yourself than they gave in return was a recipe for abuse. On the coast, even friends were held at an arm's length.

Sam leaned his head back as the plane taxied to the gate, thinking about that call. It came from his mother. That in itself was surprising. He hadn't heard from her in nearly three years. The last time they spoke she let him know how unhappy his choices made her—jobs, lifestyle, lovers. She spent more time arguing than listening. The desire to heal a broken family was her motivation, but he refused to tolerate it then and struggled to forgive her even now. Damn her insistence on having a reunified family. Deep down, his mother understood his motivations for staying out east, even if she kept them to herself to shield her husband. Their selfishness was to blame for the fractured family, nothing else.

That was the last time they spoke. Until she called to break his world.

His father was dead.

Sam closed his eyes, replaying the phone call in his head as his fellow travelers disembarked.

"Sam, this is your mom," the voicemail had filled his small New York apartment from the phone speaker. Her shaking voice told Sam everything he needed to know in an instant. This wasn't the hard voice who'd scolded him for 'breaking her heart' all those years ago. This voice belonged to a woman who'd aged overnight, balancing on the cusp of quitting life. "Your father ... your father is dead. You need to come home. I need you to come home."

And Sam did. All the harsh words, all the proclamations of betrayal, all the toxicity in their relationship was gone before he listened to the end of that short voice message. His father. Dead.

"Sir, is everything okay?" a soft, yet direct, voice pulled him out of his memories. A stewardess leaned across the open seat, annoyed concern peeking through her practiced smile. *It's time to get off my plane,* her eyes screamed. Sam complied with her not-so-subtle demand. He hadn't been thinking about getting up until the aisle cleared of the human cattle call. But the aisle was empty. Everyone was off the plane, except him.

As soon as he entered the gangway, Sam's skin cracked in protest against the dehydrated air. Troubled thoughts prevented even a brief smile at the impact of the brown earth of the Mile High City. Living at sea level had its advantages— not walking around feeling like rice paper all day long was one of them.

Moving away from the clump of humanity at baggage claim, Sam called his mother. "Hey Mom, it's me," Sam said when she answered, keeping an eye out for his single bag. It wasn't going to be a long stay, a few days at most, and then he needed to get back to New York. Back to his life. "I'm waiting on my bag, then I'll pick up the rental car. I'll be on my way soon, okay?"

"Okay Sam," his mother replied. "Drive carefully."

It was all she said.

Facing her was going to be laborious. That's what happened when you disappointed those you loved.

"I will." He hung up and headed toward the rental car desk. It was a long drive to Silver Plume, especially rush hour traffic. Denver, like most metropolitan areas, was a nightmare to navigate at times. A nightmare he didn't feel like dealing with. Traveling always took a toll on him and being back West wasn't helping. He'd already had a long couple of days, and he was hungry and needed a damn shower. Northern Denver did everything it could to slow his progress and frustrate him. Getting out beyond Lakeside was a feat of epic proportions and it was almost an hour and a half later when he finally made it through Applewood and gained elevation into the Rocky Mountains. By the time he reached Idaho Springs, the sun was setting behind the towering peaks.

The loss of daylight sapped his remaining energy. Interstate or not, he had to be careful on these winding roads. The highway that cut across Colorado was wide, but his exhaustion cut down on his mental sharpness. *I should have taken an earlier flight.*

But there was so much he was involved in, so many projects at work. Plus, his best friend, Ricardo, was getting married to Bobbie in two weeks. Sam intended on working on the speech on the flight since he didn't seem to be able to get around to it any other time. But that didn't happen either. And none of these distractions helped ease his trepidation about seeing his mother. Sleep was what he wanted, but comfort was what she needed.

And she needed to come first, for now.

It was going to be a long night.

He got off exit 226 and sighed as Silver Plume greeted him. Small town America was so soul-crushing.

The town wasn't any different than the last time he saw it. But places like this never changed, tucked away in corners of the world, insulated against the way of life for the rest of humanity. Life here remained untouched. Unsoiled. And her people thought they were better for it. Sam shook his head as he turned onto Woodward Street, glad he escaped this place and her obsolete people.

"Oh, Sam," his mother fell into his arms as soon as she saw him on the porch. The house was stale. She was alone, which was unexpected. Sam thought her friends would be keeping watch over her. Even his father's ghost abandoned her.

Sam wrapped his arms around his mother. She felt smaller and smelled like decay. "Hi, Mom. How are you doing?"

Bethany Bollinger backed away, holding her son at arm's length. New creases seemed to spring up under her eyes as they held each other. When was the last time she showed any emotion except sorrow? This time, David had fallen to Goliath. A wave of guilt hammered him. Life had beaten down this poor woman. And all he'd thought about the entire way here was how he wasn't ready to deal with her complaining.

"I'm surviving." Her words were soft, her touch lingered. "The town has been good to me. The ladies have been great, of course. Taking turns coming over, bringing food that I didn't eat. You remember the ladies, don't you? You know how they can be."

He bit his comment off short. *I know how they can be,* he thought. "Yeah, that's cool of them."

The ladies were Rhonda, Cecilia, and Jane, three busybodies who spent more time worrying about how others lived their lives than how to improve their own. Even back in high school, he found their intervention annoying and, sometimes, upsetting. The ladies had caused arguments between his parents, almost every time they interjected themselves into a situation. Their meddling was behind a lot of the unpleasant voice messages his mother left him when she found out that her son was never going to bring home a 'nice, young lady'. They were the types of friends who changed people, even people like his mother. One thing Sam and his father saw eye-to-eye on was how this "Council of Ladies" changed Bethany, and not in a good way. Sam doubted the three were any less vexatious now.

Bethany pulled away, turning back and heading into the kitchen, "Go put your things away and join me for coffee. You look like you need it."

He wasn't about to argue.

As with the rest of the homes around the town of Silver Plume, his old room looked as it had all those years ago. Only the absence of music posters, replaced by pieces of Americana art, indicated life had moved on without him. Knick-knacks, ranging from the gaudy to the horrendous, cluttered the room. This was a shrine of anything and everything Western themed. The room was an offense to God.

Sam collapsed on the bed, promising himself he would get up in a minute and join his mother for coffee.

But he didn't. He fell asleep and didn't wake up until the sun cut off the mountain tops.

"Good morning, honey," Bethany smiled when he walked into the kitchen. Eggs crackled on the stove top.

"I'm sorry about falling asleep on you," Sam apologized, scratching his head.

Bethany's face scrunched, "No need for that. You were exhausted from the flight. And you're a busy boy."

Her expression betrayed her words. Sam came around the counter and gave Bethany a kiss on the cheek. He felt like shit. "I'll take some of that coffee though."

Bethany pointed to the cupboard behind her. "I moved the cups over there. You know where everything else is. This isn't one of your fancy New York diners or anything, so you'll have to fend for yourself. That's how —"

"We do it out here," Sam finished the oft-repeated sentiment with a sly smile. His father, Roger, was a champion of traditional values and often bemoaned that the rest of the country could learn something from 'times before.' There were a lot of outdated and ugly sentiments buried in his ambiguity. That's probably what kept him in this crevice of the world, Sam figured. And resisting that mindset was exactly what got Sam out of Silver Plume.

Soft whimpering drew his attention away from thoughts of this dead town and his dead father. Bethany leaned on the counter, the smell of burnt eggs filling the kitchen, sobbing into her shoulder. Embarrassed.

Sam put an arm around her, squeezing her to him. "I'm here, Mom."

Bethany wiped her tears on her blouse and shook her head without meeting his eyes. "Don't mind me. I'm being silly."

"No you're not, stop that."

She collapsed. "I can't believe he's gone," she bawled. "It's Christmas. How am I going to get through Christmas without him?"

Sam had no answer. The holidays were always a special time for her. She loved decorating, hosting friends—mostly the 'council of ladies,' a nickname his father gave to her tight-knit group of three women who spent more time with each other than their own families—for dinners, gift exchanges, and leading the church's music ministry caroling events. Roger had always been there with her, complaining the entire time, but always by her side. Now she was going to have to do it alone.

She did nothing alone.

"I know. I can't either." It was all Sam could think to say. How else could he deal with the fact that his mother was out here alone and that his father was gone? The suddenness stripped the situation of sense. Sam never planned on coming back to Silver Plume ... or even seeing his father again. But he couldn't find it within himself to miss a man who'd been so hard, so cruel. *So callous.* Even now, holding his grieving mother, he found it difficult to mourn. A character flaw or part of being a human, finding the motivation to miss someone who rejected him at every opportunity was useless.

Still, something wasn't sitting right.

Bethany continued sobbing into his chest. "I just—I wish you two had made peace. He wanted that. Now he'll never get it." Sobbing racked her body and she sagged against him. Sam walked her over to a chair, pulling it out without dropping her.

He squatted. "It's okay. We had some talks from time to time, and everything turned out okay." Sam squeezed her hand and gave her a tight-lipped smile to hide his lie.

Bethany's head shot up, her eyes growing large as she tried to blink away the tears. "You did? But ... he never said anything."

Sam patted her leg. "You know how he could be." All good lies are grounded in truth.

His mother nodded, wiping away a tear with a fat knuckle. "His pride was strong, throughout his life. He better work on that before I see him again," she cry-laughed, a bubble of mucus expanding from her nostril. Sam fetched the tissue box. "I'm so glad you two talked. Who—how? What happened, Sam? Please tell me."

Sam gave her hand one more squeeze. "I will, just not now." He nodded toward the crispy eggs in the pan sitting on the stove top. "I need to rescue those eggs from their suffering and get you some breakfast."

Bethany coughed a second laugh. This one weaker. Sam's chest swelled, the blizzard of guilt subsiding slightly. *A few days of support,* he thought. *That's all she needs. Then I can head home.*

The scrambled eggs were as hard as shotgun pellets. Sam tossed them in the garbage and made French toast instead. French toast cured everything, from adolescent skinned knees to high school broken hearts. It was the family's staple comfort food. The pair ate in relative silence, interrupted only by a smattering of conversation about how things were going in New York. Sam couldn't resist the feeling that she was actually interested in his life in the big city. Before long he was sharing more than he thought he would. Was this the new world without his father? Freer? All the resistance to his other life dissipated now that it wasn't anchored in his father's aversion to it? The breakfast chat quickly became the deepest conversation they'd had in years. Sam shared details of his life he never thought he would—what he did for fun, the work at the charity; even his love life. And he did so without fear of condemnation from a man who didn't want to understand it in the first place.

It was good to connect with her like this again. Very good. He should have written and called more often.

But doing that would've put her in a difficult position. It didn't matter if she'd been braver and accepted who he was, because Roger never would have, even if he'd outlived everyone. And Roger's word was law. Judge. Jury. And executioner. How much verbal poison had Sam willfully swallowed to avoid putting his mother in an unenviable position between the two men she loved? But only one of those men had been around, day-in and day-out. And that was why he vented to friends in New York while avoiding being vulnerable with his mother in Colorado.

For the first time in his life, he was being real with the woman who believed she knew him better than anyone in the world. He didn't have to hide anything, except the sudden joy he felt at their growth. His father was taken in a car accident and he sat at that man's table, bursting at the seams to tell the world that he was finally free.

"Well, this was wonderful, Sam," Bethany reached out and touched the back of his hand. "I'm very, very happy for you."

Sam squeezed her hand in return. He could feel it coming, the cloud of guilt, returning. His chest clutched, squeezed with the urgency of need. What if she became ill a month from now? Colorado winters were harsh. What if she was taken in the blink of an eye like his father? And what if he never had the opportunity to be completely honest with her? Would he be able to face himself again? His father? He wasn't relevant anymore; undeserving of the honesty Sam wanted to share with his mother. "I'm sorry I didn't come home more. It's just that ... that ..."

Bethany squeezed his hand even tighter with surprising strength as if she didn't want him to explain because explaining would strip the innocence from their conversation. "I know he wasn't easy on you and I'm not going to make excuses for him; not anymore. I'm very happy for you and I understand you did what you felt you needed to do. No mother would ever fault her son for that."

For the first time during this visit, Sam fell tears burning his eyes. "Thanks, Mom." Mechanical, Sam had to force his gratitude through a constricted throat to stay strong for her.

Bethany stood, moving on from the tender moment he thought she longed for and straightened her blouse. "What do you say we get cleaned up? The ladies will be by in a short while and I don't want them to see the kitchen like this. They'd think I'm incapable of cleaning up after myself. Then I will never get them out of the house."

Sam laughed. "Deal. I actually wanted to go out for a little bit anyway."

Bethany stopped what she was doing. "Oh ... to see your friends?"

Sam didn't have friends in the area. He lost contact with most of them as soon as he came out. *I didn't lose them,* he reminded himself. *They chose to ostracize me.* They couldn't abandon him fast enough. God, he hated Silver Plume. "No, I ..." he drew a slow breath, "... I want to run out to where it happened, Mom. I need to see it."

I just don't want to tell you why.

Bethany's bottom lip quivered. For a second Sam thought that all the hard work they'd done to give her a reprieve from her mourning had unraveled. But his mother stopped, biting down on her bottom lip and blinking away tears. She was a rock, pain corralled once again. "Okay. Don't be gone for too long."

On second thought, should he stay? What if she felt abandoned again?

"I won't," he said, cleaning up the table and kitchen. "Why don't you sit out front? It's a beautiful morning and you deserve to relax. I can bring your coffee out to you."

If she was outside when her 'council of ladies' showed up, he might avoid having to deal with them. This entire situation was miserable enough; he didn't need those old hags teaming up against him, reminding him of his duties to his mother.

Before he could even finish cleaning the dishes, a Chrysler whipped into the driveway, kicking up a small cloud of brown dust behind it.

The ladies were already here. Like clockwork. Jumping in the shower would be a great way to avoid them, but Bethany would find that rude. They weren't going to deny him a visit to the accident site; he needed it. Rudeness be damned. Sam needed to process everything. These ladies were capable of marathon visits when he was younger, and the way the three of them bounced out of the Chrysler indicated they hadn't lost any of their spryness.

Right now he needed this to be about him and his own style of mourning.

"Are you taking care of your mother?" Rhonda, a woman two sizes too large for good health, professed in full sorrowful spirit. No greeting. No pleasantries. An actress on a stage. She crossed her arms, almost challenging Sam to defy her.

But he wasn't interested. The three of them were exhausting. He never understood what his mother got out of this circle of friendship but, whatever it was, he wanted no part of it. They could piss off back over to Georgetown for all he cared.

But his mother needed these ladies more than ever now. They were there for her when he wasn't, and they were going to need to be over the next few months as she mourned. Sam tried to not focus on the attraction to drama this group of women had. That would get them deeper into his business, and that wasn't going to happen anymore.

Mom needs them. That's all that matters.

Coming back home wasn't in the cards, and she would need someone until he could convince her that her future was on the East Coast. For the sake of their relationship, to support her, he was curt without being rude. "Listen, I'm sorry, but I have a few things I need to take care of. Do you mind hanging with Mom until I get back?"

That would appeal to their small-world self-importance. Providing them with a sense of purpose they'd already determined for themselves would give him a chance to break away.

Rhonda scowled. Jane and Cecilia mirrored her expression as if an invisible puppet master controlled all three. The light of judgment loomed large. After a moment of uncomfortable examination, the three ladies nodded in unison. "Of course," Rhonda's face jiggled. Her dark eyes didn't waver. Sam clutched his jacket closed. "You be careful. Your mother needs you now, more than ever before. Don't forget that."

Cecilia and Jane nodded in rapacious rhythm from their support positions behind Rhonda.

Sam accepted Rhonda's stern guidance without much thought, grateful to be away from them. As soon as he closed the rental car's door and started the engine the weight pressing down on him dissipated. Without waiting for Rhonda to move her car, Sam navigated around it, backing out of the driveway.

It wasn't until he was already heading out of town that he realized he hadn't kissed his mother goodbye. That was going to hurt her. Even though he'd be back in an hour or so. Dumbass.

Too late now, he thought as he got off the interstate and weaved through the square neighborhoods of Georgetown, heading out towards Guanella Pass Road. He'd make it up to her when he got home. He sure as hell wasn't going back there to face their scrutiny after he'd just confirmed his selfishness to her visitors.

Rolling hills rose up to meet soft mountain peaks on both sides of the road. Everything became trickier here. The mountain pass was littered with sharp switchbacks. Even natives were careful with them, especially in the middle of the winter.

Which was why his father's accident didn't make sense. Roger was a life-long resident of Silver Plume, as native as any Coloradoan of European descent could be. Sam rode along with him enough to know that switchbacks weren't an issue, not when he was drunk and not even on icy roads.

The day before the accident was unseasonably warm, according to the report. Sunlight heated the surrounding snowpack, which melted onto the road and froze overnight. Sam's father took the turn too fast, the sheet of ice sending him and his truck careening down the mountainside.

His father fished every weekend. Over his life, he must have driven the s-curve thousands of times, half of them while he was blitzed out of his mind. As bad as he handled Sam's sexuality, Roger knew how to handle these roads.

The accident shouldn't have happened.

But his truck had careened off the switchback straight off the edge of the world, diving and tumbling over boulders, through the ponderosa pine trees, and back down to the pass.

Sam was careful to park as far onto the shoulder as he could so that anyone whipping around this hairpin turn didn't take out his car and leave him stranded. Standing at his father's death site, the scars of the accident were plain to see. Two parallel black lines traced the trail off the road. Chipped and cracked boulders would now serve as eternal markers of Roger's memory. Below, a dozen ponderosa pines showed their scars, the victims of a vehicle propelled too fast into them. The wreckage was gone but the wounds it inflicted on the world wouldn't be so easily erased.

The mountain peaks watched over him as he contemplated the last moments of his father's life. Griffith Mountain and its partner, Alpine peak, side-by-side, fellowshipped with him in the serene loss. Off to the northwest, Silver Blue Mountain beckoned him home. A few miles west, Grace Peak, unseen but omnipresent, an anchor to his origins, watched him. This was home, the foundation upon which his mother built him into the man he was. The irony was, her efforts were what allowed him to leave this area and chase a life he'd always dreamed of living.

Could he do it? Could he take her away from this place that served as her universe? Could he be that selfish to take his own mother away from everything she knew and needed?

That wasn't true. She needed him and in a few days he would return to New York and leave her to fend for herself. He wasn't taking her away; he was walking away. Sam was sick to his stomach, not at the memory of a father lost, but of the mother he was about to lose.

But this was his chance to convince her that a new start might be exactly what she needed. Maybe his only chance. Once she fell back into her routine she would never leave Silver Plume. It was now or never.

From below, Sam could hear the roar of a car engine as it strained to make the climb up the pass. He shook his head. Probably someone from Denver screwing around. People from the city often considered the Rockies to be their personal playground. They never showed concern for the people who actually lived in the small towns that dotted the ranges and valleys. The car was speeding. If they didn't slow down they were going to be in a world of hurt. The approaching switchback would be a pointed reminder why city people needed a dose of humility when they came out here.

Sam judged the roar of the engine, the speed at which the car approached from below. It approached too quickly to decelerate in time unless it was a very experienced and skilled driver. But they would have to be familiar with this pass, they would have to know the danger they were putting themselves in. Natives didn't drive the passes like that. They knew the inherent danger.

But so did Dad.

The noise of the engine screamed its way up.

Up.

Up.

Then faded behind the face of the mountainside below. There was no turnoff, no option for the driver between their location and Sam. Within a minute they would be zipping up the pass. Where he parked, the rental car was at risk, thanks to the juvenile approaching from below.

"Jesus Christ!" Sam stomped back toward the car, slowly at first, then picking up his pace as the roaring engine echoed up the narrow valley. The speeding car had made the first switchback, where the two lanes acted like a coiling snake, pulling back on itself. Good. Sam didn't feel like walking up on an accident scene. His CPR certification expired years ago and he'd never quite made it back around to re-certifying. Besides, he was trying to process his father's death. This atavistic driver's thrill-seeking was screwing up his ability to do that.

Fucking teens!

An old model Chrysler 300 barreling up the road was not what Sam expected to see. That wasn't a teenager's car. That was a luxury vehicle, dated as it was. And if this punk was joyriding in his parent's car Sam fully intended on getting the license plate number, tracking down the parents, and ruining this little asshole's day. The car's headlights locked on him. No, only older people drove these ships with wheels.

But old people didn't race through mountain passes.

"Slow the fuck down, you idiot," Sam snarled, hurrying toward the rental car now. He wasn't sure he would make it.

As if complying with his command, the Chrysler slowed, approaching the hairpin turn. He'd run out of time. Avoiding an accident was now down to the skill of the driver. Sam hoped they would be able to navigate the turn without clipping his rental. Hell, clipping the car might be the best-case scenario at the speed they were going. Moving it now would mean putting himself at risk.

It's just a rental car, he reminded himself. *I won't be at fault. It'll suck to have to try to find a ride out of here, but it's not worth it.*

Car tires chirped. The Chrysler lurched to the left, making an adjustment. It was crazy; the switchback turned to the left. Why in the world was the driver cutting the angle even tighter? They were putting themselves and any passengers in danger. His heart thumped. This was going to end badly for someone. Without thinking, Sam took tentative steps backward. This car was going to share the same fate if the driver didn't act and he wanted to be far out of the way.

I'm going to see someone die, the dark thought bounced around in his head as he retreated.

The driver downshifted. The Chrysler's engine roared in orgasmic joy at the forced thrust of torque.

The car jerked again, this time correcting to the right. Sam felt a brief moment of relief, thinking the driver realized his predicament and was trying to rescue the situation.

But then it all became real. Sam stood in shock.

The Chrysler was close enough to see inside the window.

To see enough detail.

The operator was old enough to know better than to drive like this.

The driver was someone he knew.

That was why the car looked familiar. He'd just seen it.

At his mother's house.

Mind and body scrambled. Survival instinct encouraged him away from danger.

Rhonda was behind the wheel, and Sam swore she was grinning as if she were enjoying this youthful irresponsibility. Shadows of two other heads accompanied her.

He swallowed, stepping back further. Why was Rhonda racing through the mountains like this?

Why was she careening in a straight line that would take them straight past him, off the road to certain death?

But they weren't going to careen past him. They were going to run *into* him.

Sam lunged as the Chrysler 300 slammed on its brakes, leaving the surface road and sliding into the gravel bank where he stood. Seizing pain exploded in his hips at the moment fiberglass and steel met flesh. His legs were no longer his own, unfeeling and useless. The world tumbled.

Sky.

White earth.

Clouds.

Brown boulders poking out of the snow.

His legs flopped, arcing over his downward-pointed head.

Then he landed. The world punched him in the face. Rocks of all sizes, small and tiny, cut into his back, his arms, his face. Sam tumbled over and over before finally crashing into a lawnmower-sized boulder. Radiating warmth in his hip was the only thing that convinced him that he still might actually be alive.

Oh my God! I can't move!

Searing, scorching pain detonated in his shoulders as he tried to push himself up. He collapsed back into the blood-red gravel.

His blood.

Through cloudy eyes, Sam looked down at his useless legs and noticed the pool forming from his hip down to his feet.

Somewhere in the fog of the accident, three car doors closed. Rhythmic, crunching footsteps approached, wafting into his clouded mind. He opened his eyes. Even that hurt. Three shapes angled over him. Indistinct, but known.

"Rhonda?" he croaked.

The council of ladies stood over him. Rhonda was in the forefront, her large frame blocked out most of the remaining sunlight poking through the clouds. She stood with her legs angled apart, her fists planted on her hips. Even through squinted eyes, Sam saw a face twisted in rage.

"You won't leave her," Rhonda spat.

"What?" Forming words was difficult, requiring more energy than he had to give. The icy chill of the boulders began to subside as his body transferred heat into them. Cold. So cold.

"You think you can disappear for years at a time and not check in on her? Not care about her?" Rhonda snarled. "You think it's okay to swing into town like some fancy big shot, pretend like you're worried about her, and then disappear again? Do you know what she's done for you?

Rhonda's voice bounced off the surrounding mountains. Even the world wanted nothing to do with her rage. She was shouting herself hoarse. *She's losing her fucking mind.* "I—I want to bring her home with me."

Rhonda's cackle exploded from her thick frame. Loose skin jiggled everywhere on her face, threatening to detach in clumps. "And take her away from here? Take her away from her home? Oh no, you little bastard, you won't be doing any of that. You're going to be staying here. With her. You will not abandon her again!"

Sam groaned and tried to roll over, tried to roll away. Useless legs refused to participate. Their mercy would now determine his fate. Cecilia and Jane circled him. Rhonda supervised, her eyes never leaving his. She snickered like she was trying to cough up phlegm. "Your father tried that too. Did you know that? Dipping his willie into that slut over in Georgetown. Living his life only for himself. He thought he was so clever, so smart. But we taught him. We taught him good. Taught him the Lord's justice for fornicators."

Cecilia and Jane heaved together, lifting him off the ground. They were so strong. His shoulder exploded in fiery pain. Sam screamed, hoping against hope that someone would hear him. By the time breath came, they were placing him in the trunk. Sobbing, Sam realized his useless legs couldn't even prevent them from closing it. If he could resist them he'd have a chance to crawl to freedom. But he couldn't do anything except succumb to their whims in his condition. He had to fight. What other option did he have? Giving up now would seal his fate. If that trunk closed he'd lose the chance to escape.

But he couldn't. Even as he thrust his good arm up to stop it, the trunk lid slammed down. His elbow took the brunt of the force, sending stinging jolts up into his shoulder. He cried sobs on top of sobs.

And the world went dark.

***

With no idea how much time had passed, Sam came to at the sound of voices. The inside lid of the trunk greeted him when he cracked his eyes open.

Rhonda. The others belonged to Cecelia and Jane. The Council was gathered.

This time, though, there was another voice he recognized. His bones became as rigid as steel. The fight was over. Hope scattered.

"Did he survive?" his mother asked.

"Yes." Even muffled, Rhonda's voice dripped pride. "We took care of his rental car too. Took us a while to drive out to the ravine."

"We opened the door and pushed it over the side," Cecilia bragged.

"It burned," Jane said, her voice devoid of emotion.

Sam was about to pound on the trunk lid, to cry out to his mother for help and warn her that she was in the company of madwomen. But the words froze in his throat.

"Good. Thank you, ladies. Thank you for always being there for me and taking care of me. Thank you for bringing my son home."

"You're welcome, dear," Rhonda replied. "We're happy you'll never be lonely again."

"Never again." Jane and Cecilia mimicked.

"Never again," his mother laughed.

"It will be a long time before he's ambulatory again," Rhonda prophesied.

"That's fine," Bethany giggled. "It'll be nice to have someone to take care of again."

The sound of someone tapping on the trunk was the last thing he heard before the world shattered.

"Honey, that's how we do things around here," Bethany whispered just above the closed trunk.

The council of ladies howled their approval.

END

The Most Terrifying Time of the Year

"Are you sure?" Kilo Harkness asked, leaning sideways toward the window to read the note in the dying daylight.

"Fuck if I know, man," Damien Pierce responded, his eyes focused on the road. The unrelenting snow whited out the lines long ago. Even the signposts were starting to disappear in this fierce display of natural power. "I just want to get us somewhere safe. Even if it's a motel."

Kilo dropped his hands into his lap, no longer paying attention to the note he held. "You don't plan on getting to Shelley's tonight?"

There was a hint of despair in his tone. Damien didn't blame him. He felt it too. A lifelong city boy, Damien wasn't accustomed to snow like this. Or unplowed roads for that matter. He wasn't accustomed to a world without man-made markers to help with navigation.

"I'm not sure we're going to make it." It was an honest answer, the only type of answer he could give. They'd started late out of Seattle on their way to Quincy. Night was falling fast, catching them halfway to their destination. Damien couldn't believe it. They weren't even near Ellensburg yet and this blizzard slowed their progress to a near crawl. He didn't want to admit it to Kilo, but they might be in trouble.

"What do you mean you aren't sure we're going to make it?" Kilo's voice shook.

"I don't know, man, it's pretty bad," Damien leaned forward, trying to make out as much of the road as he could. They'd taken the interstate out of Seattle but halfway through Cle Elum there'd been an accident, backing everything up for miles. And in one of the poorer decisions he'd made in a long time, Damien chose to leave the interstate for the less traveled route 10, a road devoid of signs of life.

Daylight quickened its absence. Kilo shared his unsolicited thoughts. "Man, it's creepy out here when it gets dark."

"I'll bet it's creepy out here even in daylight. You just know there aren't any brothers out here," Damien laughed, feeling disingenuous at the gesture. He hoped it would lighten his mood. The pressure of responsibility for their safety was exhausting.

It didn't work.

Kilo held out his cell phone, aiming it toward the windshield. "Shit," he exclaimed.

"What?"

"I can't get a goddamn cell signal," Kilo explained.

Damien shrugged. "I lost mine miles ago, back in the mountains. That's why Shelley gave us old school directions, isn't it?"

Kilo turned the paper back to the window, using his flashlight app to read it. Seconds later he turned it off.

"Why do you keep doing that?"

"I need to save my battery," Kilo answered. "My phone is almost dead."

A charged phone wouldn't do them any good if they couldn't get within range of a cell tower, but they weren't going to do that without getting their GPS back. And reading Shelley's directions were the only hope they had of finding their way. "Mine is dead."

"I can't believe you forgot your charging cable."

Damien sneered. "Yeah, well I'm driving." It was as good of a response as he had right now. He needed to focus on keeping them on the road, not winning petty squabbles. "Just keep looking for anything that looks like something she wrote down."

Damien regretted not buying a map before leaving Seattle. They didn't check the weather either because, in Seattle, the weather was perpetually gray and wet. He didn't expect it to be such a different world ninety minutes east of the city. It wasn't like he never left Seattle, he had. But his travels only took him north to Vancouver, or south to Portland.

Heading west would get him wet and there was no reason to go east. Until now.

And now Damien almost wished he hadn't.

This was also his first experience with being off the grid. Not having a cell signal was weird at first. Now it was absolutely frightening. Seattle had people; the east side of the Cascades did, he saw some of them before the snow started blowing. But where they were now was anyone's guess.

As blackness deepened, his trepidation grew. They were getting more lost with each mile.

"Yeah, that's a good idea," Kilo said after a moment. "I thought it was a bad joke, you know? Writing directions based on landmarks. Who knew it was a real thing?"

The pair rode in silence, Damien concentrating on keeping the vehicle on the road while Kilo examined their surroundings, trying to pick out anything that might help them find their way.

After a while, Kilo sighed. "Man, I can't see a damn thing."

Damien laughed. It was bitter, born of frustration and growing despair. "That's been the last two hours of my life. I don't know what we're going to do."

"Me either."

So they continued driving into the white evening. The shadow of the earth's curvature passed over them. Damien stared into the eternal void of the universe. Out here, away from the lights of Seattle, the night was blacker than he imagined it could be. The headlights of the car exposed the white landscape and the blinding, curling bombardment of snow, but little else. Only feet beyond those headlights, a black curtain hid the rest of the world. Damien risked a glance at his speedometer. They were going 15 miles an hour.

"We need to find a place to stay," he decided.

"Yeah."

Damien was scared, and Kilo didn't look much better. Neither hid it from the other. That's how bad this was getting.

Pulling over for the night was the only option. But where? Beyond the whitening world, Damien couldn't see a single home or business. Not even a gas station. Time was running out for finding a solution.

Silence became an unwelcome passenger.

Weaved into the quiet, Kilo fell asleep. Damien tightened his grip on the steering wheel. If he wasn't petrified of ending upside down in a ditch he'd crank the speakers. Kilo deserved at least that right now. Who the fuck fell asleep on their friend, leaving them alone to deal with the stress of these conditions? Hours of driving through this unrelenting snow at a speed that would embarrass a sloth had exhausted him. He struggled to keep his eyes open and needed Kilo's help, even as hopeless as the situation seemed.

Especially because the situation seemed hopeless.

What he didn't need was to have to babysit someone.

Damien reached over, grabbing Kilo's jacket. "Wake the fuck up."

Kilo mumbled something and turned away.

Damien shoved him. But doing so unbalanced him in a situation where there was no margin for error. The wheel jerked in Damien's hands. His heart stopped. Snagging the wheel, Damien steered in the opposite direction out of instinct. The back end of the car kicked out, sending them into a disorienting spin.

Someone screamed. Damien was pretty sure it was his own voice.

Kilo bolted upright, "What the fuck?"

The car spun, whipping Damien's head against the window. Stars exploded in his vision. The whirling snow compounded his disorientation. Seconds of eternity passed before the car jolted as it slammed into something.

Unable to loosen his hands from the steering wheel when the car came to a rest, Damien reminded himself to breathe. Snow bombarded the windshield faster than the windshield wipers could clear it, enclosing them in their protective shell.

"Shit."

"Yeah," Damien groaned, holding his head. "We need to check to see if everything's okay."

Kilo looked at him as if he'd spontaneously developed a second set of ears. "I'm not going out there."

Damien pointed out the windshield. "In case you haven't noticed, we're in the middle of nowhere. Let's check the car because, if we're broke down, we're fucked."

"We're probably already fucked," Kilo complained even as he reached to grab his jacket from the back seat. "I didn't bring any fucking gloves."

"Neither did I."

As soon as he stepped out of the car, millions of flakes of snow assaulted Damien. They were heavy with Pacific Ocean water, too far inland to make sense. The car windshield was already covered and the hood, still warm from the drive, couldn't melt the snow faster than it was being buried under it. Scanning the night, Damien looked for anything that might indicate some replica of civilization was close. Nothing. The cold fear made swallowing difficult.

"Fuck!" Kilo went down, his feet kicked up in the air.

Damien raced around the front of the car to see his friend flat on his back. Kilo laughed at himself and decided then was an excellent opportunity to make a snow angel. The moment of levity released hours of tension as Damien watched his friend act like a fool. Laughing hurt his head.

"You're going to be drenched now," Damien advised.

"Yeah, well, it was worth it," Kilo said, still arcing his arms and spreading his legs to carve out the shape. "I've never made a snow angel. Plus, I can change when we get to Shelley's."

"Never?"

Kilo sat up, clapping his hands together to knock off the snow. When he stood, he took a moment to admire his work. "I'm Hawaiian, dumb ass."

"Good point," Damien smirked. "I guess we should—"

A muted scream cut under the storm. Damien spun.

"What the fuck was that?" Kilo's eyes were large ovals. He didn't blink.

Damien shook his head. "No idea."

They listened for a few more seconds but all he could hear was the wind. The night grew colder. Kilo was shivering.

It was only going to get worse. They needed to get moving.

"Let's see if we can get out of here," Damien said. "You check that side and I'll check the side."

This time Kilo didn't argue, going around to the passenger side. He made it all the way to the rear tire before groaning. "Aw, man."

"What?"

Kilo clasped his hands on the top of his head, his face drained of all the humor it held only seconds ago. "The tire, man. It's bent."

Bent? How is that possible?

Damien circled the rear of the vehicle, shielding his face by cinching down his hood drawstring. He winced. The top of the rear wheel leaned into the wheel well.

"Shit." It wasn't eloquent, but his panic drove the crude comment. "We're fucked."

Two brown men stranded in the middle of nowhere in a driving snowstorm? No cell phones. No map. No winter gear besides the jackets they wore.

Damien couldn't fake hopefulness. They had to face the situation as it was. "We've got to start walking."

"What?" Kilo's response was as harsh as it was immediate. "Into this? Man, I'm not walking around in a snowstorm at night. We can sit in the car and wait for someone to come by."

"It's not the middle of the night," Damien reminded him. "It's the fucking middle of winter; it gets dark by 4 o'clock. We'd be sitting here for twelve hours, at least. We don't have the gas to run the engine that long, so unless you plan on freezing your ass off waiting to be rescued, you might want to reconsider that."

Kilo hesitated. "Someone is going to come along. We don't need to wait all night. Just until we can catch a ride."

The longer they stayed out here in the weather, the more trouble they were in. Damien didn't want to spend the entire night discussing this. "I'm going to start walking. No one's coming around. Look around you," he urged, jabbing a finger at the blinding storm. "Do you see anything out here? It's a damn blizzard, man. Even the locals are going to stay inside. Plus, it's Christmas. No one's going to be out. You can stay here, but I'm not."

Damien shoved his hands into his jacket pockets, tucking his chin down into the zipped collar, and started around the car.

From behind him, Kilo called out, "Wait! Where are you going?"

Over his shoulder, Damien responded, "There was a light off the road, about a half mile back. That's where that noise came from too. I'm going there."

"Why? It could be dangerous."

"Because," Damien responded with irritation, "it has to be a house or a barn. Something. Anything is going to be warmer than sitting out in the car until we can get help. And if it is a house, they'll help us."

"You don't know that for sure," Kilo said, running up beside him. "And that scream?"

Damien shrugged. "It could have been anything. It's the only real option we have. I'm heading toward that light."

Kilo didn't say a word as Damien ducked into the car and turned it off. He didn't even laugh when Damien made sure that it was locked. The pair started back down the road in silence, following the tire tracks in the direction they came.

The blistering cold was unforgiving. Damien couldn't remember ever being this miserable. With each passing moment, he was convinced this was the coldest he'd ever been, only to find himself thinking that very thing in the moment that followed.

The distance to the light never seemed to shorten. Damien's feet felt like lead blocks, impossible to lift and set down. It was only a half mile, but it may as well have been a universe away. Damien focused on the tiny point of light. It was the only hope he had. They had to get to it. Focusing on his thick feet wasn't going to motivate him. Only salvation was.

Kilo remained quiet throughout the trek. They were struggling to survive, wasting energy on chatter wasn't helpful.

Step after torturous step, the world grew colder and more isolated. But the light enlarged as they neared it. Damien stopped questioning his decision and began feeling hope. The light poked out from a structure he couldn't make out yet. "Little bit further. Almost there."

Damien chanced a glance. Kilo's head was down against the night, not even looking up to see how close they were.

Damien understood.

Wind whipped, howling in protest at their defiance. The snow bit, thousands of tiny claws digging at exposed skin. Damien's feet now burned.

The light called them.

Then, flowing in the valleys of the storm when the wind quieted to remind them where they were, Damien heard something. Something melodic. Human.

Music.

Christmas music.

"Do you hear that?" He spun so quickly that Kilo jumped.

Kilo's eyes widened, recognizing the sound. "Th—that's people singing."

"Damn right it is! Let's go."

Even the spiking pain in his feet didn't stop Damien from running toward the light. The volume of that singing meant a group of people were together.

A group of humans meant warmth and food.

And help.

***

The music grew louder as they approached the building with the single light hanging above the double entry door. The light's power radiated in a halo glow as thousands of flakes of snow passed through and around it, casting hope at the pair trudging toward the building. The song drifting out was a classic Christmas song, its upbeat tempo lifting each of Damien's feet when he could no longer. He looked over at Kilo as they approached the building. Resembling a barn, the building didn't look like anything that would house a Christmas concert. But this was the country and white people did weird things in the country.

"You ready?"

Kilo shivered uncontrollably. The half-mile hike in wet clothes took a hard toll on his Hawaiian blood. Seattle living hadn't made Damien an outdoorsman by any measure, but he was handling the storm better than his friend who shielded his chest with his arms. "Yeah, I need to get out of the cold," his voice quaked. "But —"

"What?"

The night sky had stripped itself of all color, making it feel as if a lid covered the world. There was nothing around them except for this single structure. Kilo's teeth chattered as he examined their surroundings. "Do you ... do you think it's weird that we don't see any cars?"

Damien hadn't even thought of that. His mind had been focused on getting someplace warm, with cover, to protect them until they could get help. He hadn't expected to walk up on a Christmas party in the middle of nowhere with a hundred of his newest friends. That was dumb luck. The last thing on his mind was the lack of vehicles. It was difficult to see through the storm. These party attendees could have parked fifty yards away and neither one of them would've noticed.

"It's no big deal," he said. "I'm sure they're around here somewhere. Let's get inside. I'm starving. Maybe they'll feed us too."

"*If* they let us in," Kilo tried to smile but his frozen lips resisted forming the new angle. "The white people out here aren't the white people you hang out with in Seattle."

They'd gone to the university together and Damien was well aware of what Kilo thought about a lot of the people of central and eastern Washington. He couldn't say he felt differently. So Damien simply nodded; he didn't want to think about that right now. Plus, Shelley's family lived out here and she was a progressive person. Even the middle of nowhere had to have good people, right?

"Do you think they'll feed us?" Kilo stepped next to him, staring up at the light.

Damien didn't know much about what was happening in that building, but he did know it sounded like a holiday party. And holiday parties meant food. He smiled. "Let's go."

They knocked on the door, a dull sound to his burning ears. They waited, Damien was unsure they could be heard over the din. He knocked again, this time harder. The door rattled under the forceful strike.

"No need to piss them off, man." Kilo bounced from foot to foot in an attempt to keep himself warm.

"I'd rather have them be a little upset than freeze to death on the doorstep of salvation," Damien answered.

When no one answered the second time, he reached out for the handle, relieved when he heard the bolt unlatch on the other side of the door. The towering door swayed open. With the barrier breached, the music flowed through the opening. Unrestrained joy lifted the festive song into the air. A sliver of warm air hit him in the face and Damien bounced on the balls of his feet, half in excitement and hope, and half to keep himself awake. It was so cold.

Whoever opened the door wasn't standing by it. Damien peeked around the door, seeing the group inside the building but not the person who opened it for them. Without checking with Kilo, Damien stepped inside. His stomach applauded him.

Kilo followed behind.

The music was so loud inside that no one in the packed cavern turned around when they pulled the door closed against the storm. The two new people stood, taking in the sight before them. The structure appeared larger inside. The ceiling was thirty feet, angling to a sharp peak. The building was barren, exposed beams the only decoration. Hundreds of plastic, white lawn chairs were neatly set up in wide rows on each side of the central path dividing them. The interior was bright, a warm, tanned glow seemed to warm the air. Hundreds of people faced a meager altar at the far end. A man stood on it, one hand raised. As he danced to the song, he clutched a microphone to his heart. The man was a decent dancer, for a white guy, moving with a charisma of unabashed joy. Behind him, a choir, all dressed in the same robes, swayed back and forth, clapping their hands as they sang. To the side of the stage, a small ensemble provided the music.

These people were happy people. These people were Christians. He and Kilo were going to be safe.

Kilo said something, Damion could see his lips moving but couldn't make out any words. Leaning closer, Kilo shouted, "What do we do?"

Damien shrugged. He had no idea. It wasn't like they could interrupt the proceedings just because they were cold and hungry. He looked around, hoping to make eye contact that would draw someone over to them. Someone in charge of the food. A small kitchen was tucked in the corner nearest them, but even the women standing near that door were transfixed by the music, seemingly unaware of their new guests. They would have to hang in the back of the room and wait out this festive concert. Though the more he thought about it the less he liked that position. The music had been going nonstop since they'd walked from the car and didn't show any signs of stopping. These people were probably planning on going all night. His aunt was very religious; she got into her worship music like normal people enjoyed real concerts, just without all the pot. He knew how religious people could be about their worship through song.

As it turned out, they didn't need to interrupt anyone. The man on the stage looked at them and held up both hands. The music died in an instant and a hum fell over the crowd. "Brothers and sisters, we have guests in our midst. Let us welcome them."

Damien and Kilo glanced at each other. Awkward. The man on the stage stepped to the floor and made his way toward them. He was tall, his full, black hair groomed to perfection. When he smiled, his cheekbones rose, becoming fuller. He was a handsome man who carried confidence with ease. When he shook Damien's hand it felt like a vice, one applied with caution as if he was aware of his own strength. "Well, brothers," he radiated. "You look like the devil has shaken your souls."

Damien tried to smile but, with hundreds of pairs of eyes locked on them, he froze. For some reason, he didn't want to misstep. "Thanks. Our car broke down a little way up the road." It wasn't the absolute truth, but it wouldn't hurt.

The man nodded. "Well, no need for you to be out in the storm. I'm Pastor Richards and this" he said, turning to the congregation, "is the congregation of Heaven's Light."

In trance-like unison, the congregation shouted, "Welcome, brothers!"

Damien resisted the urge to run. He'd seen shit like this on TV, weird religious people, the unblinking masses. But he kept his opinions to himself. These people had a warm building, a hot building, in fact. Damien was already beginning to sweat. They also had food. A delicious smell hung in the air.

As if reading his mind, Pastor Richards nodded once and then tilted his head to the side, indicating the direction the smell was coming from. "You're almost in time for the feast," he said. "The grace of God, delivering you from the binds of hell, to our doorstep, so that you may serve Him. Glory!"

Damien wasn't sure about that, but he did know that he was starving and whatever they were preparing was making him swallow buckets of his own saliva. Plus, the tingling in his toes informed him that his blood was finally beginning to unfreeze. He'd play along with any of their games if it kept him warm until help came.

The faces of the congregation were a sea of smiles, of gleeful anticipation, as if they were welcoming home family members they hadn't seen in years. His aunt looked like that once when he went through his own Jesus phase. It was creepy.

Warmth and food, Damien reminded himself. *That's all I'm here for.*

As soon as someone could give them a ride to Ellensburg or they could call a tow truck, they were out of here.

Pastor Richards reached out, taking a hand from each of them. His grip was uncomfortably warm. "We're blessed to have you in our midst," he said, his voice filling the room. The congregation shouted an *amen* in response. "God is good, very good. He brought you out of the tumult and into our embrace, witnesses to the rebirth."

"Amen!"

Suddenly Pastor Richards dropped their hands and spun, stalking down the wide aisle. Like all charlatans, he was a performer and this was his stage, the congregation his willful and obedient audience. The microphone was back at the pastor's mouth.

Leave it up to a preacher to take anything in life and profess it the work of God as long as it suits their needs, Damien thought.

Pastor Richards was halfway down the long aisle now. "Man is weak," he shouted, "for he cannot sustain without the church. Look no further than our two new friends." The entire congregation turned their gazes to follow him down the aisle, leaving Damien and Kilo standing alone at the back of this strange church.

Damien contemplated. If he could get into the kitchen and grab some food and someone's car keys, he would do it in a heartbeat. He'd return the car in the morning, he silently promised. If they had a landline, he'd call Shelley. Maybe her family's truck could get through the road. He was already weighing the benefits of shelter and a hot meal against walking his way to another town.

"The Lord works in mysterious ways," Pastor Richards approached the stage, "and we are not to know them, for we are imperfect. Only He determines our fate. Because He knows our path. He knew about us when we were in the womb."

Another *amen* from the congregation.

"And when He sets the path, He does so with the love of the father," Pastor Richards boomed. "He does not force us to take the path, for then we would be nothing more than slaves to His desire. No! His love for us is much too deep for that."

"Too deep!" the congregation sang.

"We must choose our path," the pastor was on the stage now, pacing back and forth to engage each side of his flock. "We make the choice to take a right or wrong, eternal life or a life of sin. We choose what type of life to live and lead. Do we set the example for the church and live righteously so that others will follow? Or do we take a path of selfish indulgence, betraying our brothers and sisters in Christ, leading them away from His embrace?"

"Righteous!" The entirety of the congregation raised fists into the air as one. It looked like a military salute in those old war films Damien's father used to watch. This shit was getting weird. Maybe he wasn't as cold and hungry as he thought.

Pastor Richards was sweating now, even from this distance Damien could make out the glean on his forehead. "There are those who will lead you astray, brothers and sisters."

"No!"

The pastor buried the microphone in his lips. "Yes," he said, waving a hand in the air before dropping it, his shoulders slumping. The pastor stopped moving, turned to the side of the stage. Damien felt the edge coming, saw congregants lean forward. Spellbound. Then, the pastor's hoarse voice lowered, barely audible above the thick blanket of quiet. He groaned, "Even amongst us. Even within the family of Heaven's Light."

A woman began to sob from somewhere in the sea of believers.

Pastor Richards made his way back to the center of the stage. The microphone still attached to his lips, distorting his voice, he extended an arm toward Damien and Kilo. "Brothers," Damien realized the pastor never asked for their names "come down, join me. The family will make room for you in the front row."

That was the last thing in the world Damien wanted to do. But at least the pastor hadn't called them out as violators of some imagined code of ethics. He didn't even want to be in this building anymore. He'd take his chances out there, where he understood the risks. But Kilo dawdled toward the stage, passed rows of chairs filled with unblinking congregants. He shot that goofy smile at everyone. Damien knew Kilo was desperate to avoid going back in the storm—so was he—but he wouldn't do anything to stay away from the world outside. Kilo would. Kilo was weak.

Now he was the odd man out. Person by person, row by row, the congregants turned to look at him. Unreadable expressions. This was a group that expected compliance, valued law and order. A group who praised unyielding structure. They wouldn't react well to defiance.

Taking the first step was the hardest, but Damien began to move forward, to join Kilo at the front of the room. The pastor's stoic mask warmed when Damien complied.

Pastor Richards moved across the stage again. Back and forth. Stomping. Stalking. "Our new brothers will be witnesses to the devotion of Heaven's Light. Let them understand that He is not of us, we are of Him! We are Him! We are Him and we are here, together, in His house with His family!"

"Amen!" The congregation shouted. One woman fainted, falling into the aisle behind Damien. He spun to check on her but was blocked by more and more congregants filling the open space, none of them bothering to assist the fallen woman. He looked toward the front door-toward escape. Panic seized his throat. The aisle was now completely filled with congregants. They raised their fists, shouting back at the preacher, lifting the message to the heavens. The air popped. He was trapped in the middle of a horde of zealous white people with no way to call for help. If this got weirder, he would be in serious trouble.

"And the Lord works through us, for we are His vessels on this plane of existence!" The rhythmic annunciation made the air crackle. A man standing near Damien roared, his eyes wide with something that bordered on rage but most definitely wasn't the spirit of a benign maker.

Yet Damien walked on. What else could he do in a room of hundreds of religious freaks?

Ahead, Kilo came to a sudden stop. The pastor looked down from above. "Don't fear, brother," Pastor Richards' his voice dropped its heat, becoming softer, gentle. "Have a seat."

Kilo paused as Damien marched on.

"Not everyone understands the work we're here to do," Pastor Richard said in a pained voice. "Not everyone will appreciate it. But we must still do it. The Lord demands it."

This time, the congregants echoed a soft, "Amen."

Damien glanced at them, unsure what was happening. He wanted to stride to catch Kilo but couldn't. Too many bodies pressed in around and behind him, closing in as more and more mesmerized people spilled out into the aisle. Something hard was pressed into the middle of his back but Damien couldn't even turn in this surge of humanity to see what it was. He heart galloped as free room disappeared in the swelling mass of humanity. Suffocating.

The crowd began to sway, many holding a hand toward the ceiling, their eyes closed. As Kilo rounded the aisle to take his seat he raised his hands in the air. Kilo wasn't a religious person by any stretch of the imagination. But he also wasn't much of a thinker. He would follow along with almost anything if someone was convincing. Hell, that was how they ended up riding out to the middle of nowhere together on Christmas. Shelley batted her eyelashes, swayed her ass, and Kilo agreed to cross the Cascade Mountains to spend the holiday with her. Damien tagged along because he didn't want to spend Christmas by himself.

Even now, he wished he had stayed in Seattle. Damien felt very alone.

The church body pushed him forward. He was almost at the front now.

Food and warmth. Was it worth all this?

The pastor's hoarse voice filled the room again, building in temperature until it reached a crescendo. He held a Bible aloft. "But if the thing is true, and the evidence of virginity are not found for the young woman, then they shall bring out the young woman to the door of her father's house, and the men of her city shall stone her to death with stones, because she has done a disgraceful thing in Israel, to play the harlot in her father's house. So you shall put away the evil from among you!" Pastor Richards was now panting.

What the fuck is he talking about?

Atop the stage, the pastor jabbed a finger toward the back corner, toward a part of the stage Damien hadn't been able to see. He'd been so transfixed by the congregation, by their automatic responses, and every word the pastor had said that he hadn't noticed the display. Now he could.

The pastor's mannerisms had captivated him. The charming looks and his commanding demeanor and charisma had made Damien ignorant, inattentive. But the facade began falling as his body warmed and his desperate need to escape the storm diminished. Damien now understood the full complexity of the situation they'd stumbled into.

In the corner of the stage, away from the choir and the band, was a woman. Completely naked, her arms were tied above her head, lifting her breasts that did not need any assistance to remain firm and perky. Her smooth legs spread at a wide angle. She was tied to something that looked like a cross that had tipped over. Damien stopped, taking in the sight. She was gorgeous, stunning. Her body was the stuff of magazines, perfectly proportioned. Her manicured pubic hair demanded his attention. Yet his sense of right and wrong overrode those carnal observations. Whatever weird things this congregation was into, this woman with not a willing participant. Her red eyes were swollen. Her disheveled hair gave her a wild appearance. The divot between where her collarbones met was as red as the small area above her breasts, which heaved as she gasped for breath.

The woman's eyes met Damien's and his soul dwindled. He was staring into the pit of madness.

"What the fuck is going on?" He couldn't contain himself anymore. He couldn't acquiesce to their righteous demands and interpretation of civility and morality. The woman on the stage had been tortured. Red blotches dotted her beautiful skin. Cigarettes. Cigars. Car lighters, maybe? It didn't matter. Hundreds of small circles peppered every part of her. With revulsion and a sliver of guilt, Damien noticed her inner thighs suffered the same fate.

"Heretic," someone snarled behind him.

"Filthy sinner," another voice snapped to the other side.

"Satan!"

"Devil spawn!"

More and more voices raised in protest against him. Word began to filter to the back of the congregation about his defiance. The ecstatic praise for the heavenly turned to vitriolic hatred. A large man shook a fist at him. He was holding something.

On the stage, Pastor Richards raised a hand and the crowd immediately quieted. "Brothers and sisters, forgive him, for he knows not what he does."

"He's a sinner! Take him to the rock!" a disgruntled congregation member shouted.

"Take him to the rock!" The other hundred voices joined in concerted urging.

"Take him to the rock! Take him to the rock! Take him to the rock! Take him to the rock!"

The congregation repeated the mantra over and over, growing louder with each turn. Even Kilo shook his fist. How could he fall for this madness?

Pastor Richards allowed this to go on for a time before holding up his hands and urging, demanding, quiet. "In time, brothers and sisters. In time. We still have work to do."

A frustrated groan fell over the mob. The music ministry struck up Judy Garland's *Have Yourself a Merry Little Christmas*, accompanied by the choir. Their voices rose into a controlled crescendo along with the melody of the band. Pastor Richards stepped to the edge of the stage. Hundreds of zealots around Damien swayed back and forth, now silent. Satiated.

"Felicity has wronged her community," Pastor Richards began in a passionate voice. "She wronged her parents. She wronged her church. And she wronged her God."

With each proclamation from the pastor, the congregation thrust fists into the air. They held stones. Damien hadn't noticed them before. Why were they carrying them?

"She has failed to control her lust, her animal desires," Pastor Richards spat. "And she must be purified. Purified in the ways of our forefathers, the ways the world is too weak to adhere to any longer. But we of Heaven's Light will not capitulate to contemporary demands. We will not fail our Lord, our Savior, not today. Not ever!"

Electricity raced through the barn that was a church. The mob moved together, a swarm of purified rage. The man next to him grunted like an animal in heat. One woman fell on the ground, convulsing like a fish thrown into a boat. The grunting, the groaning, the growling among the congregation grew in volume and veracity. It could be contained no more.

"Take her to the rock!" The pastor said and stepped down from the stage. A flood of humanity surged forward. Congregation members jumped up onto the platform and those who lacked the physical ability to do so did whatever they could to pull themselves up. As one body, they approached the woman in the corner, stopping only when they were a few feet from her. Damien could no longer see her, could no longer hear her.

Pastor Richards stood shoulder to shoulder with Damien now, wrapping Damien's hand in his. He didn't ask for permission. The pastor's hand was strong, warm. "Watch, my child. Watch as we redeem her on the rock."

There was nothing to watch, nothing to see. The crowd overwhelmed the stage. But Damien didn't want to see what was about to happen. There was nothing he could do to change the fate of the poor woman as the mob raised their fists, rocks aloft, and one by one began hurling them at her.

Their rage screams drowned out her death yell.

Damien's stomach churned. He was grateful that he didn't have to hear the thudding of the rocks off the poor woman's arms. Off her chest. Against her skull. He didn't have to hear the breaking of her bones or the collapsing of her lungs. He didn't have to hear her ribs break, piercing vital internal organs. And he didn't have to hear the moment one of the larger men hurled his rock as if it were a baseball, striking her in the head and collapsing the side of her face.

Not until the end. By then only a handful of armed congregates remained. Everyone else moved off the stage, beyond their seats, toward the kitchen.

Kilo was amongst them. Kilo was smiling.

As Pastor Richards held Damien's hand, the music ministry continued on playing. This time it was a joyous song of revelation and rejoicing.

He began to understand. Understand everything. He was in the mouth of madness with no escape.

Pastor Richards gave his hand a quick squeeze, still examining the collapsed pile of skin and bones that once was a very beautiful young woman. "We'll feast now," the pastor said. "Her lover was an older man, in his 30s, and a prominent member of our community. Married, sadly. But as he failed to serve his Lord in life, he will serve us in death. Come, join us at the feast so that you too can become one of Heaven's Light."

Damien wouldn't become part of this madness, but he was aware he was being watched. He was also aware that large men blocked the front door. They held identical machetes in their humongous hands.

Pastor Richards tugged him one more time. Something told Damien that this was no longer a request. "Come, child. Serve your Lord and his flock."

The pastor pulled Damien toward the kitchen. Somewhere in that mass of humanity, in a room filled with thousands of utensils which could maim and kill, Damien heard a scream. A scream from a familiar voice. And he knew.

The pastor sighed, shaking his head. "I'd hoped he would be stronger. Disappointing. Surely you won't let us down as your friend has."

Utter madness. Insanity.

"What the fuck have you done to him?" Damien tried to pull himself away and was immediately surrounded by a horde of congregates, all larger than him. There was no way out of this. No escape.

Pastor Richards smiled over his shoulder, releasing his grip now that Damien was being escorted into the kitchen by the band of believers. "Felicity's lover was only the entrée. An entrée must have side dishes, lest it be unfulfilling. And no meal is complete without a desert."

Damien was in the kitchen now, populated only by the women cooking. Without the crowd to block his view, he saw it. There, on a large stainless steel table, lay Kilo, his chest ripped open. Three women fished out his organs, separating them into large bowls.

Damien's stomach evacuated itself.

The pastor stood over him, shaking his head. "We'll have to get that cleaned up," he said. "Such a shame. So weak, a sure sign you are without the Lord. I knew it the moment my scouts told me of your predicament out there. Sinners, the pair of you. Even if the sign of your impure skin wasn't enough, your actions have convinced my flock. Oh well, you will still serve His purpose."

On his hands and knees, Damien looked up, tears streaming down his cheeks. "What are you going to do?"

A few women laughed.

But the pastor didn't. He wore a ravenous expression. "I told you. You will serve the Lord," Pastor Richards wiped the trail of saliva from his chin. "You will be the dessert."

Damien was set upon by the large men before he could even scramble to his feet. Chopped and diced, he was prepared for the festive meal.

END

Dear Savior Born

A King of Many Names.
The King of Kings.
Set upon a mound of corpses.
His throne.

The gathered throng, attendees to the Feast of Minds, reluctantly lift their glasses in salute. They regurgitate the official toast to the young king who led them away from the edge of eternal despair. For it was him, born of fate and fury, who set the world right by setting it alight. And all, even the most skeptical, understood the power he wielded. It was an easy display, the day he conquered the world; his power evident to even the casual observer, the ignorant and the uninitiated.

His was a reign of terror and blood.

The man-still-a-boy simply known as Marr leaned over the side of his throne, reaching down. Thana watched his every move.

It was her job.

It was her fate.

Then the King of Rage sat upright, holding the tiny arm he'd severed from a young peasant boy just a few hours ago. Thana had been present to witness the 'justice' of the ritual. The boy had been no more than eight, fragile and weak from a lifetime of malnutrition under Marr's reign. He painted a pathetic picture—a representative of the victims of madness. The boy's crime? Stealing a loaf of bread from a vendor at the market. The vendor hadn't requested justice because he understood the child's plight. So many people did. But he was still brought to justice, his arm severed at the shoulder in the Hall of Witnesses in front of his mother, father, and siblings, lest they think to repeat the violation against the king. Marr refused to let the mother hold him as he died, instead displaying his interpretation of kindness by allowing the family to return home after the boy bled to death on the floor.

The Council proclaimed his kindness. Publicly and loudly. Even the day he ordered his motorcade to run down a group of elderly protesters trying to prevent Marr from using chemical weapons to oust native people from a sliver of land he claimed was his.

There was nothing Thana could do for the boy or his family. There was nothing anyone could do. In the 15 years of Marr's reign, hundreds of thousands had died in his pursuit of justice. Marr always raved that overpopulation of the planet bred profane tendencies in the human species, that the battle for territory and resources was intensifying beyond anyone's capability to contain it. History taught him that, he claimed, citing the deaths of billions during the earlier part of the twenty-second century. According to Marr, humankind committed atrocities against one another in the fatal game of survival and what Marr was doing, he did for the people. His visions showed him a future devoid of hope and prosperity unless he led them. And the people believed. Marr was a master of instilling fear in the populace.

He and those who maneuvered him into power built his impunity on the back of perniciousness.

From the beginning, there were signs for those who watched, for those who analyzed the behaviors of the King of Fear. But what was one to do in a world balancing on the precipice between the rational and irrational, driven by hatred, prejudice, and fear of others? Significant progress drove the regression that was the rise to power for the King of Kings and he was only too happy to snatch the crown when it was laid upon his head, the great child hope of a people. Fear was his platform and religion was the vehicle. Thana was young, only a few years older than Marr, but even she saw the moral purity he claimed as his own was nothing more than a façade to appease the self-professed righteous.

But it worked. A simple, effective strategy. With Marr, people understood again, comprehending a changing world, a world that made them uneasy. A world that made them fearful they were fading into obscurity. And Marr's charismatic proclamations reminded them of a time before, a time of relevancy. And the people embraced him.

Many did, even now. Even at this time of year, when families would celebrate the holiday season in generations past, the holiday season Marr had erased from the calendar. Even after the mutilations and annihilations of enemies, near and far. Even after every unfair policy, every self-serving action; many of those who put him on the throne still reveled at his majesty, even as they suffered as a direct consequence of his machinations.

Marr held the child's severed arm aloft in front of his face, quizzically examining it. Blood dripped onto his lap, but it didn't seem to bother him. To his Council, this was who Marr was. They tolerated his proclivities because he'd made them rich. The people of the kingdom of Aether put the King of Fear upon his throne, allowing him to wield madness like a scythe, and they accepted his temperament because it was too late to stop him. Marr was far too powerful now.

But Marr was mad. The entire Council knew that. The entire country knew that. Looking back, it was easy to see that Marr was mad from the very beginning. He and his trusted assembly simply constructed a persona around his charisma, hiding Marr's greatest weakness. But the shadow taught Thana about the true nature of the King of Kings and the demons who haunted him. It taught her, in hopes that she would free the king from his psychopathy.

Her entire world existed under the umbrella of his reign, like everyone less than twenty years old. She didn't remember what normality felt like, but she heard the stories about what the world was like before Marr sat on that throne. People spoke of a time of progress when the world was learning to be better. They said there was hope then, for everyone. Thana tried to imagine that, but couldn't. This life under Marr was one of survival. Nothing more. His presence demanded it and his madness drove it.

In the shadows, secrets moved. Those without power gravitated toward one another until the day came when they formalized a plan. Plotted. The day would come, they knew, when Marr's madness would realize the finite nature of all things. With Marr astride his throne surrounded by hundreds of corpses, it was obvious even to a young woman who knew nothing more than a mad world, that someone had to serve as the catalyst.

The plans of the shadow were about to be realized.

Marr needed to die.

And Thana was his assassin.

Marr waved the child's arm. The small hand flapped uselessly, bringing a rare smile to his face. "Look," he laughed. "He's saying bye-bye to everyone." The sound of madness filled the chamber. Attendees played their part, some laughing, some faking smiles while others, the brave, sat stone-faced. Marr wouldn't notice which of his attendees were guilty of not responding to him; the King of Kings was oblivious to the world.

Thana was among the few who didn't react. She'd seen such cruelty more times than she cared to admit. Nothing shocked her anymore. At times she wondered how she was ever going to be able to process the last few years of her life serving under Marr. How could she forgive herself for being a passive bystander to the deaths of so many innocent people? The shadow reminded her that her duty was to them, to the country, before herself. That was the duty of the mother of fate. But they had the convenience of ignorance. She existed for this one task, they reminded her. They were never in this chamber to watch Marr call time on the lives of thousands. They hadn't attended his strategic sessions where Marr planned war and genocide with dull frigidness. They never spent a minute in the Hall of Witnesses watching without hope as Marr condemned thousands to excruciating sentences of justice.

She envied them that.

But tonight she didn't have to fake a smile at Marr's actions, she didn't have to assemble the veil to hide her disgust and rage. No longer.

When the laughter died down Marr tossed the arm to the side, bored. "What further business do we have?"

James Karger, Marr's closest advisor, stood with his hands clasped in front of his groin, as was proper. "Nothing, my Lord," James reported, using the title Marr preferred since the day he erased the country's constitution from its history.

Marr set his chin in his palm as he leaned sideways. Thana's heart skipped a beat. It was a sure sign that Marr was done for the evening. The king would likely spend the rest of his night getting drunk and abusing one of the unfortunate women from the city. *Unless they brought him someone from another town*, Thana reminded herself of Marr's preference for what he called 'exotic' women. Anyone outside the city was a foreigner in Marr's eyes. There wasn't a person on the Council who hadn't heard the king in his personal chambers, grunting as he satisfied himself at the expense of another nameless woman to fulfill his own lust. Sometimes Marr required more than a few women attend to him because his appetite was insatiable, for sex and death.

Tonight she was going to free those women from their life sentence.

"Good. I'm retiring for the evening," Marr announced, standing and climbing down the pile of corpses. The way the bodies slid over top one another as he descended made Thana's stomach churn. Those sightless eyes begging the question why she allowed this to happen.

I'm going to be haunted forever.

A smaller council of three of Marr's longest-serving advisors fell in behind him as he left the chamber, escorted by a pair of bodyguards so massive their girth would serve as a hindrance to stopping her.

But the shadow had taught her the one vulnerability of a tyrant was in their conceited belief that they were impervious. Marr had that in droves from his decade and a half of ruthless rule. Conceit filled the king's mind. His council was comfortable. And his security team grew bored years ago.

Tonight he would die.

"What are your plans this evening?" Henry Henriksen asked, collecting the last of his papers he prepared for every meeting—papers he never briefed. Thana wondered if the man put any effort into his reports anymore. She couldn't fault Henry if he didn't; she hadn't for her own reports in a long time. As a financial analyst with doctored credentials, she was responsible for a program that Marr had no concern for. To him, budgets were irrelevant and the status of the tax base equally undeserving of his time. Money was always there when he demanded it. Reporting on it was futile, her job, expendable. In reality, she was only here because frothing old men dominated Marr's perverse council. She was a visual stimulant Marr had grown bored with years ago but whom most of the rest of the Council still enjoyed ogling. It was only through favor and the machinations of the shadow that she reached this level of access to the King of Despair. It was only due to extreme fitness and the lust of old men that she was able to maintain it.

"Sleep," she laughed. "It's been a long few weeks."

"It has, indeed," Henry stood and wished her a good evening.

It will be, she thought.

All members departed soon after, everyone quick to remove themselves. Thana wondered how many of them were sneaking home to their waiting families, to join in secret and illegal festivities. Marr may have outlawed celebrations of the old holidays, but not everyone complied with his edicts.

Thana stopped to speak with a few counterparts on her way out of the chamber building. To establish a solid alibi, she needed to be seen by a number of people. Those conversations put her behind schedule, so she was forced to hurry along to the breach in the wall. It was where the shadow said it would be, a side wall with a temporary plaster facade she slid out of place and returned once she was inside the building, covering the vulnerability.

Thana sprinted down the passageway and across the only open hallway. It was the only time she was going to be exposed. Sweating, she breathed a quick sigh of relief, checking her watch. She was on schedule again. Marr's guards walked to take up their station for the evening. The secured observation booth gave them a site line of the hall leading to Marr's chambers. Her window to cross the vulnerability was closing. Once the guards locked themselves inside the bulletproof booth she wouldn't be able to cross the hall without them seeing her. They would be able to sound the alarm before she could kill them.

As the two guards reached the booth, Thana sprinted across the threshold, her footsteps light. Silent. Tucking herself into the cove across the hall, she peeked around the corner to make sure the guards hadn't noticed. They busied themselves unlocking the booth door. Neither saw her.

She was cleared to kill now.

Depressing the door handle, Thana slipped into Marr's antechamber. Without even a wisp of a sound, she secured the door with a titanium brace. No one was going to get in now.

The antechamber was silent. At the far end, tucked in a corner, two oak doors stood prominently together. Marr's sleeping chamber.

But the king wouldn't be sleeping. Not yet.

His subjects held firm beliefs that he spent his evenings consorting with the devil. The rumor had gone unsubstantiated for years. But the truth was as relative as it was true in this world. Thana didn't believe in angels or demons, gods or devils, but she did believe the King of Kings was mad. The shadow did its best to confirm Marr's tendencies. Those reports were consistent. Marr spent a good number of evenings alone in his chamber before being attended to by his choice of women. Reports obtained by the shadow confirmed that the king's madness was rampant in privacy. Each night he locked himself away and could be overheard speaking with another. The identity of the mysterious person remained a secret, but rumors persisted that the visitor wasn't of this world. Witness testimony spoke of demons, or even Satan himself, of strange occurrences in the chambers, and of an overpowering scent of sulfur. As difficult as the reports were to believe, they were consistent. The shadow had prepared Thana for any eventuality.

The shadow had prepared her to kill. It told her she was born of this fate, to free the world of the King of Despair and plot its new course. For all they had done for her, plucking her from hopeless obscurity and training her to be a killing machine, she owed them this. She owed them the kingdom.

Thana approached his door, her calculated footfalls too soft for the untrained ear to pick up. Even if those lumbering bodyguards knew she was here, they couldn't stop her from finishing her task.

Leaning close, she pressed her ear to the door, listening for Marr's whereabouts. She could hear him shuffling across the room. Knowing his location was imperative; the moment she stepped into his private chambers he would sound the alarm and she would have less than two minutes to kill him and escape with her life.

The shuffling stopped. Thana held her breath, not wanting to give away her presence.

On the other side of the door, something thudded. She listened for any indication that Marr was approaching. When he resumed his movements, she breathed again.

Then his muffled voice floated through the door separating them.

"Yes, my Lord, it's in the works."

So, the rumors were true? Someone was in the room with the king. That was going to complicate the operation.

But Thana hadn't observed his entire walk to his chambers. During the transition, it was possible that one of his advisors joined him. It was feasible. *Dammit*. The shadow had scouted this mission for years. Marr was most vulnerable in his personal chambers. For someone else to join him now was the most inconvenient of circumstances, for both the shadow's mission and for the unlucky person who fate chose to die alongside their king.

Marr whined. "I live to serve, finding faith in his favor. You know this."

Thana put a hand on the door handle. He wasn't close, approximately 15 feet away. That would give him plenty of time to sound the alarm if her sudden appearance didn't shock him. She held the attack, for now, preferring to listen for further assessment.

"Yes my Lord, I'm grateful he is pleased. Has he noticed my ruthless vengeance of late?" the King of Madness said to his unknown company. Thana imagined the influencer on the other side of the door. How powerful did a person have to be for Marr to sound so docile?

Thana strained to make out the other voice. Her ability to distinguish voice and range was one of the things that made her a prized asset, yet even she couldn't make out any other noise coming from the Marr's chamber. If he were with someone, she would hear that person. But she couldn't. Why?

Because he's alone and mad.

"Yes, the plans are all set," the king sounded lucid. His madness cycled quickly. It was strange, almost as if the man she had observed for the past three years was an actor. This was his true self. "The Council has moved. My Chiefs of Staff have positioned the military assets. Everything is ready. Everything."

Ready for what?

Still no second voice. The king truly was mad. So mad as to convene with himself? The only demons here were the ones in Marr's mind, unfounded rumors be damned.

"By this time next week, the world will know pain. The world will know His justice."

She could strike now but even Marr's murder might not preclude the rain of death he was about to release on the world. She needed to hear more detail so she could report back to the shadow. It would know what to do.

"You've done well, my child," a deep voice suddenly answered from nowhere, and everywhere, at the same time.

Piercing pain. Thana jerked her ear away from the door. The inflection was rich. Mesmerizing. Even the physical barrier didn't deter its luminosity.

It sounded from within her.

Thana shook her head, blinking away the stupor. She wouldn't put it beyond Marr to put up some fantastic pretense exclusively for his entertainment. The shadow had said there were no video cameras in here, Marr wouldn't allow them, but she still doubted. His madness was boundless. This was a trick of some sort.

"Thank you, my Lord," said Marr, muffled, so unlike the ethereal voice that arched through her.

"Your reward will come in time, my child," the other voice thrust into her mind.

Thana stumbled backward, pressing a hand against her ear. What sort of trick was this? The shadow hadn't prepared her for this level of manipulation. How was Marr doing this? He was much more powerful than the shadow thought.

Thana spun, sure she had missed something, some clue, a presence that would threaten her. Kill her. The sound was too clear, too distinct. The closed chamber doors didn't inhibit it in the least. No, it had to be coming from within this antechamber.

But the room was empty. She was all alone in the vast space. This was madness. Was she becoming mad like the king himself? Was his influence so great?

"Will He take me then?" The King of Pain asked the intangible voice.

Thana leaned closer to the door, risking discovery, to hear the answer. She wanted to. She needed to. The answer to everything lay in the response.

"Your time is near, my child," the deep voice boomed in her head, disorienting her again. "Very near."

Thana winced, tears of pain obscuring her vision. Was this all part of a ploy, a game for the King of Sadness? Was she nothing more than his latest victim of manipulation? Was she about to fall prey to his whims and demands, charmed by his magnetism to do things unholy, things her morality objected to, but things she would do just the same? Was this some trick of illusion? That was explainable. *Security cameras.* The shadow must have missed them during the scouting missions. *Yes!* They missed them and now Marr knew she was here, invading his personal space. And this was all a game to him. To torture before he killed. That was Marr's way.

Marr's justice.

The shadow!

She was here to execute the shadow's mission.

But she was losing control of her thoughts. Slipping.

Thoughts, anew.

Why was she here? Who was she, really? Who sent her and what did they need?

The shadow began to fade. A presence of something greater than it or even the King of Madness himself pressed on her, began to penetrate her. It hurt. It pierced. A virgin, by decree of the shadow, Thana had no idea if what she was feeling was the same as the first experiences of sex her friends described to her all those years ago. Her friends had taken joy in her growing discomfort at their explicit descriptions of the carnal act. This mimicked their stories.

She felt vulnerable, open.

Madness seeped in.

Further delay would be to risk everything. She had to act now. Now, before it was too late.

Thana shoved the door open. A wall of sulfur assaulted her.

"Now, child!" The voice boomed in her head, urging her forward. Its will was her own. Its desires, hers.

The Lunatic King whirled around, jumping to his feet as Thana surged into the room. She knew exactly where he was, exactly where he would be kneeling. She could tell by the volume and level of his voice. The position she found him in was exactly the position she anticipated. All her training, all of her sacrifices, had been for this one moment.

And she executed with perfection.

Before the target could defend himself or sound the alarm, Thana pulled the blade from her belt and jabbed it into his throat, through to its handle.

"Yes, child. Yes!" the voice vibrated in her head, reverberating around the empty room.

Thana moaned. She was pleasing him. She was fulfilling her destiny.

Penetration.

Filling her.

The King of Death coughed, gurgling on the blood filling his throat. His hands went to hers in an attempt to pull the blade free. It didn't matter now; he was as good as dead. Her strike had been true. The lengthy blade passed through and exited his throat on iconic display, piercing his larynx and shredding his esophageal muscles. Marr could do no more than release a small death choke. Thana released her grip on the blade. Marr's eyes widened, blood flooded from his mouth, down the immaculate silk robe he wore. His bedrobe. The robe that served as a last vestige of dignity each time he raped one of the local women. And it would now serve as his death garb.

Marr fell to his knees again, his mouth opening and closing rapidly in silent questioning. Then he tilted to one side and collapsed. Thana stood, watching as the man-who-would-always-be-a-boy died.

"You've done well, my child," it vibrated through her, stimulated her. "Your Lord is pleased."

Thana arched. Her wetness a sign of approval as the presence filled her. Inside, she warmed. He searched. Through her. I, into her. Becoming one with her.

She swelled, the heat of his importunate desires made her face flush.

"And you are awarded," the loving voice teased.

Thana tingled everywhere at once.

Warmth, His warmth, spread through her. Life sprung up inside her.

"You will bear him."

Thana unbuttoned the bottom of her tunic with shaking fingers to allow her swelling stomach freedom to breathe. It rose. Swelled. Perfectly symmetrical.

Perfectly perfect.

She placed a light hand over her belly. Love and pride, pride and love. The honor was all hers.

"You are the carrier, but you are also the protector."

She nodded, sobbing as she caressed her swelling belly. The baby kicked. She felt its first touch. The first contact establishing the eternal connection.

The shadow had been right.

She was the mother of fate.

"You will see our dear Savior born," the voice ordered.

And Thana knew she would.

END

The Three Wives' Men

Kelvin Wright never heard of the Pishon Valley. He wasn't from this area. Born and bred in Portland, he'd only come up this way for a weekend getaway from life. He spent his entire life avoiding things. As a teenager, he avoided responsibility with all the ease his angst provided. Instead of running off to college after high school, he spent a year exploring the world. And even when he finally went to the university, Kelvin neither applied nor challenged himself to any great degree or extent. His aversion to confrontation and challenges, personal or external, put him behind in life. That started with an abusive father but didn't fade when he did. But life wasn't about meeting some fabricated and universally-accepted goals. To him, life was about the moment he was in and living it for what it was worth.

There was no good or bad, life just 'was'.

So when the marketing firm he worked for closed its offices without warning, Kelvin found himself unemployed and unmotivated to plot out the next step in his journey. Whereas his now ex-coworkers scrambled to figure out how they were going to provide for their families, Kelvin simply kept living, understanding that this moment was the only one he could guarantee himself.

And that principle brought him here, to this part of the Pacific Northwest which he would have otherwise avoided. Places like this were places black men usually didn't spend a lot of time, for their own safety.

A place like this was definitely not somewhere to get lost.

Kelvin Wright was now lost.

Strange things happened in the valley between the Pishon River and that of the Gihon. Things wicked and disturbing. Located in a valley, in the dip of the plane of the earth, where life fell away from reaching for the stars and sought the toxic depths of hell.

Where life has rotted.

The rivers run green with toxic algae. Trees droop, their branches reaching toward the earth as if capitulating to existence, reaching for the Mother, the eternal bond. Even the people of the valley lost the will to live, their gray reality a manifestation of the hopelessness and despair they were born into and incessantly pass along to subsequent generations.

Of lost hope.

Even now, during the holiest of the holy periods, joy found no home here.

Locals stayed away from some parts of the valley. Rumors bespoke of mysterious disappearances. The valley was mysterious to them. Many perpetuated the myth of a local bogeyman to frighten their children into subservience. There are parts of the valley, they said, where only ghosts roam.

One area, in particular, was the devil's home, they said. Those who knew of the location never ventured near but even more spent their entire lives only miles from it, never learning of its existence. Those who registered the narrow road leading to this part of the valley forgot it soon after passing the cutoff. Bordered by western yellow pines whose branches stretched across the dirt path that carved through the undergrowth, it was easy to miss. Though many braggarts swore they had, none ever traversed the full extent of the path and lived to tell about it.

To find this part of the valley, one must want to find it.

Or one must be unlucky.

Kelvin never had any luck.

He sat on the shoulder of the road, angling his cell phone in a creative variety of ways required by his current circumstances. He hadn't seen another car in a half hour and each turn took him to more and more remote parts of the region. The highway wasn't where he thought it would be. There hadn't been a sign for it in hours. Farms and houses gave way to empty nature. Foreboding nature. Kelvin cursed himself for not stopping and asking for directions when he had the opportunity. But it wasn't that easy for him to do, to put that kind of trust in people who didn't like him, even if they gave him the time of day.

Now he wished he had. As he sat on the shoulder of the road, undisturbed by traffic in either direction, Kelvin held up his phone and prayed for cell phone reception he would never get. Soft snowflakes danced across his windshield.

"Great," he groaned. It was the last thing he needed, not remembering the last time he'd driven in the snow.

Kelvin looked down the road. The graying sky deepened to slate in the distance. Shadows elongated before fading completely as the thick clouds rolled in, delivering fatter snowflakes as it approached. The snow was building up. Unless he wanted to get stuck, alone and without a single blanket to keep warm, Kelvin was going to have to do something besides searching for enough of a cell signal to pull up his GPS. Staying here meant freezing to death. But continuing to drive was a lottery. There could be a small town around the bend half a mile up the road. It could also be another turn in a series of hundreds he'd convinced himself to take in pursuit of the chance to come across other life. Was it worth the risk?

In all the time he'd tried to get a signal and figure out what he was going to do, Kelvin hadn't seen a single sign of life. So the decision was easy; he put his phone back in its cradle, put the car in drive, and began moving forward again.

The only thing that interrupted the constant drone of tires turning over was the occasional thump of uneven blacktop. With each passing mile, the road became rougher. He wasn't surprised civilization had given up on this part of the state.

A few miles later he longed for the droning of tires, now snuffed out by the snow-covered road. He drove into the storm, not away from it, and the snow was accumulating faster than he could reason a better course of action. Miles passed without sight of a town or village; he hadn't even stumbled across a solitary farm.

Kelvin was on his own.

Why should this be any different than the rest of his life though? Isn't this how everything played out? From his job to his love life, and even his family, people around him didn't seem to remain around him. He was a globetrotter, but he also had the emotional intelligence to understand why many saw him as nothing more than a vagabond.

A lone wolf.

The relative silence helped him concentrate on the road, a challenge that was becoming more difficult with each mile. Hills rose up and away from the road on each side. Pines provided a partial canopy for the shoulder, its defined boundaries serving as the only thing that now kept him on the road. The snow had become thicker over the past 20 minutes as it fell faster, blotting out the road. For the first time in his life, he was afraid for his capabilities to get himself out of a situation. All he needed was—

—twenty yards down the road he saw it. His lungs expanded with the breath of hope. Two slight parallel impressions carved through the snow, appearing from a side road.

Tire tracks.

The surge of adrenaline made keeping his speed down difficult. Tire tracks meant life, someone who could help.

His tires spun, kicking the back end of the car toward the shoulder. He countered and let off the gas, allowing the tires to grab purchase on whatever road surface they could find. No street lights illuminated this world and dusk dominated the sky. Only his headlights helped him follow those tire tracks once he regained control. Every few seconds, they disappeared behind a blown cloud of smoky white snow.

The night grew black. Underneath that expansive cover, the trees stood tall and proud, like menacing sentinels, ushering Kelvin in the direction they wanted him to go. Still, he drove. He'd be happy tripping across a cheap motel. Right now he'd take a homeowner with the carport.

The white blanket on the road deepened. Snow filled the once distinct set of tracks, fading them into obscurity. Hope waned. His sports coupe wasn't built for these conditions and a glance at the fuel level indicated the impossibility of waiting out the storm in a warm car. Even if he could, there was no promise of getting help before he froze to death in this winter wonderland.

Why were white people so crazy about the snow? He'd never understand that.

Then the tire tracks left the road. Kelvin's heart thumped as he slowed to a stop, idling in the middle of the road—or where he guessed the middle was. Ahead was an unadulterated field of white. The road disappeared.

"Fuck," Kelvin put the car in park and got out. Fat, wet snow assaulted him. He shielded his eyes and tried to make out the tire tracks. They hadn't disappeared. The tracks turned off the road, making a hard right through a gap in the trees onto a side road he would have never noticed. The gap was narrow, wide enough for a single vehicle. But the tree cover helped the tracks appear more pronounced.

Kelvin contemplated. If nothing else, it would get him out of the storm and possibly provide enough protection from the wind that he could stay warm even if he didn't run the car all night. Or maybe he'd find the owner of those tracks.

And even a warm bed for the night.

He got back into his car, crammed it in gear, and turned to follow the tracks.

***

It was a bumpy ride, one he had to take at a crawl as his car struggled through and over more bumps and potholes than were healthy for a sports coupe. At a few points, Kelvin had to give a wide birth to tree limbs that had broken off and fallen onto the path, once almost getting stuck on the soft shoulder. The night grew darker and he imagined the storm raging somewhere behind him. But underneath this umbrella of green, Kelvin was safe. Without the snowfall to blind him, Kelvin could see as far as his headlights projected. And all he could see was an endless row of trees jutting up into the blackness overhead.

The soft orange low fuel indicator popped on with a pleasant bell. Kelvin grimaced. He was running out of time and fuel.

"Shit," he slapped the steering wheel. Rocking back and forth, he peered into the darkness, searching for anything that might serve as shelter for the night.

But this straight path rolled on. The car creaked and groaned in protest as Kelvin picked the shallowest potholes in the way. But, a few miles into the forest, there was nothing smooth about the surface. Every part of the path was rugged, every option, undesirable. The neglected road looked uncared for in a few lifetimes. Only the fresh tire tracks on top of the dusting of snow kept him moving forward. Otherwise, he was sure he was driving off the edge of the world. Turning back wasn't an option. Ahead, he had the hope of the owner of those tire tracks.

Then it happened. One particularly bad section of the road, covered from side to side in divots and potholes, bumps and troughs, was impassable. He stopped, getting out of the car to assess the risk, and decided to give it a try. He couldn't sit in the car all night and he definitely couldn't search out the owner of that vehicle on foot.

Inching forward, the road gave away and the car collapsed into the pothole. An excruciating *crunch* informed him that he'd bottomed out. Under its own willpower, the car rocked back and forth a few times, even as he depressed the brake.

"Shit, shit, shit," Kelvin slapped the steering wheel again. He got out and rounded the car, groaning as he saw the undercarriage resting into the dirt, having carved a neat niche for itself.

Stuck.

He stood in front of his car, illuminated by its headlights and wondered what to do next. Only two choices existed and one of them mocked him, challenging him to select it. Either he could start walking or try to survive the night in the car.

Kelvin began walking.

Bundled against the night, as under-dressed and unprepared as he was, he trudged on. Misery descended into painful awareness that his body was shutting down. The shivering started almost immediately. When he started losing full sensation in his toes, when each step was more painful than the last, Kelvin recognized that he was beginning to die. His teeth clunked against each other, and each breath became harder to draw. The night faded in and out as the urge to sleep beckoned him. He thought about the few people in his life, like his mother, who would never know about his fate. They would never learn of this last aimless adventure that finally jettisoned him over the brink, just like they'd warned him about his entire life.

Out here, he would finally prove them right.

Then, off the road, back through row after incalculable row of tree trunks, an orange pinprick of light blinked in the darkness. Kelvin's head snapped up. Light meant life.

The owner of the truck.

He had hope and a destination now.

If his body could get him there.

Each footfall sent jarring stabs of pain coursing up through him, but he plunged ahead. Renewed. The orange light seemed to drift as he walked, teasing him toward an unachievable goal. But it underestimated his desperation and determination. Soon, he came across another side path, this one much narrower than the road he got stuck on. He bent, feeling for the tire tracks. They were wet and soft. Fresh.

Kelvin followed the new path that forced him to walk into the face of the wind. It was bitter cold, raking at his face. The single prick of light in the blackness expanded, revealing three more aligned lights. Structures. Kelvin's steps lightened, the stabbing pain eroded. Before long, he was walking up to a neat row of small wooden houses. Each of them projected light into the cold world. Each house's chimney spewed white clouds of warmth into the frigid night air.

Life, Kelvin smiled.

The world swayed as the cold crept through him. As he drew closer it became apparent he'd been wrong. A handful of small gray houses didn't spot this hidden world; there were more than twenty houses here. All were identical, rectangular homes. Each entryway was located in the same exact spot on each house as if a master designer who would later inspire cookie-cutter construction had tested his skills here. The houses weren't larger than a few hundred square feet. Kelvin didn't question any of it. He didn't care.

He was going to be safe. He was going to survive the night. That's what mattered.

The tracks he'd followed stretched out into the darkness toward a larger structure in the back of this village. A faint clinging noise came from back there. Kelvin headed for it, approaching cautiously so as not to surprise anyone and get himself shot before he had a chance to ask for help.

There were no walls on this structure, just an expansive roof that sheltered everything stored below it. Thick beams held up the large expanse of a ceiling, some thirty feet above the earth. This place wouldn't provide shelter, but the life underneath that overhang might. A man leaned into a truck, an old Chevrolet. As Kelvin approached, the headlights went out, pitching Kelvin's view into murky confusion.

Lanterns hanging on the wall cast enough light that Kelvin could still see the man, just not well enough to determine if he was armed or not. The man backed out of the vehicle and stood to his full height. He was a mountain of flesh, nearly seven feet tall. Burly and thick, he filled the gap between the truck and another vehicle, an ancient Cadillac de Ville Kelvin couldn't put a year to. The man rotated, facing him, but if Kelvin's sudden presence surprised him, the man didn't show it.

"Hi," Kelvin said, swallowing the urge to crumble at the immensity of the man. "M-my car is stuck, and I'm lost. I was hoping someone could help me."

The man stared at Kelvin for a few uncomfortable seconds and then glanced away, toward one of the houses. Kelvin took the chance to look around the area underneath the overhang. It was filled with a variety of farming equipment besides the two vehicles. A tractor sat in one corner. A hoe, its faded wood handle and rusted head betraying its age, sat next to a contemporary replacement. Gardening hoes, hammers, sickles, and other farming tools leaned haphazardly in a hand-made rack near the center of the dirt floor as if that was the only way this small community could protect its equipment from the weather. Whatever this place was, agriculture was the way they sustained themselves. That made sense all the way out here, so far away from any other life.

The silent giant moved toward Kelvin. There wasn't a lot of space between the two of them due to the packed confines. Kelvin stepped aside, hoping the man was taking him to food and warmth instead of throttling him for invading this home. He finally let loose his breath when the stranger passed him.

Without a word, the man walked toward a clump of houses off to the side of the opening. They passed a well, around which were a number of wooden benches. They trudged through the deepening snow, by dozens of picnic tables. Kelvin distracted himself from thinking about the size of parties that required all those tables by trying to keep up with the big man's stride.

The man didn't protest against Kelvin following him or even look over his shoulder to track the visitor. The lack of cordial company gave Kelvin a chance to look around. It was neat and organized. Desolate and remote, the tiny village looked cared for. The houses weren't made of the contemporary residential housing materials. Some looked like a series of patchwork repairs had dominated their recent past. This was a strange place, but it wasn't one of those places dying of neglect. These residents cared.

A good sign.

"I-I really appreciate your help," Kelvin said to the man's back, hoping some friendly chatter might warm the giant and make him more willing to help. Most of the houses had gone dark during his short time here, telling him that not everyone was willing to help a stranded stranger.

The mountain of a man loped toward a house that stood apart from the others. Larger than anything except for the open structure storing the farm equipment, the house projected significance. The home of a mayor, or whatever this community would call that person? Its siding looked newer than the other homes. A tall, wide deck wrapped around the front and sides, almost as if it were an observation platform.

The man ascended the stairs, his thudding footsteps announcing their arrival to dozens of nearby homes. Kelvin followed, taking the steps slowly to create space between them in case the situation changed. He had no idea what he was being led into and he wasn't interested in surviving the storm only to end up as a plaything for some twisted mountain people.

The man stopped at the door, thudding a massive fist twice. Kelvin waited out the awkward silence. The door creaked open, casting an orange glow onto the foot of the deck. Kelvin stepped back as the light illuminated the man he'd followed, revealing him. Scars zigzagged across his cheeks and forehead, etching his appearance with past trauma. His greasy hair was thin, only partially covered the back of his head. It was as if half of his scalp was incapable of growing anything under the scars. An accident? Kelvin collected himself, resetting his face so as to not offend. The giant man leaned down into the slit of the open door. From only a few feet away, Kelvin couldn't hear what he whispered. Taking a subtle sidestep, he tried to get a better view of the proceedings. When the man straightened up Kelvin saw a thin woman, in her 40s, with long, blond hair that lost all its vibrancy a decade earlier. The skin under her eyes sagged, painted with a tired shade of gray.

"Your name, stranger?" the woman said.

"Kelvin," he answered and repeated what he told the man a few minutes ago. "I also don't have any cell service and I was hoping to find a hotel for the night because I don't have enough gas to keep driving. The snow, it got bad, and I don't think I can make it through the roads to the next town."

The tired woman's smile disappeared as quickly as she showed it. Then she stepped away from the doorway. "Come inside. It's a bitter night. I don't want to leave the door open. We don't want to upset my sisters by letting cold in." The scarred man moved to the side, allowing Kelvin to pass.

The inside of the home was completely open, no walls to partition one room from another. The expanse was only broken by the occasional support pillar, squared logs that jutted into the rafters above. On the far side, a wide hearth dominated the entirety of a wall, where a fire pitched warm light into the home's interior. Three beds lined a far wall and a large wool rug covered the bare floor between. To the opposite side was a kitchen, a simple space with a long counter that would fit more appropriately in a restaurant prep area than here if it, too, weren't made of wood. A large oak table, spotted by swirling knots that darkened its texture, was surrounded with no less than 10 chairs. A massive meeting place that consumed the kitchen area. Everything in this home was a direct descendant of the forest around the village.

No television, no radio, nothing on the countertop that reflected the modernity of the world outside this village. Now that he thought about it, Kelvin hadn't seen a single sign of electricity since his arrival. This place was the definition of isolation. Kelvin had the sudden feeling that he'd stepped back in time, not the most comfortable situation for a black man surrounded by white people.

"That's Dodi and she's Love," the tired woman pointed at the pair of women sitting in chairs near the fire. They too were slim and blond, looking equally tired. Neither turned around to acknowledge him. It wasn't the best welcome he'd ever had but being ignored wasn't anything new. Plus, he wasn't here to make friends; he needed to survive the night and get help in the morning. "I'm Elsa," the woman finished.

"Nice to meet you. I appreciate any help you'd be willing to give me. I don't know what else to do."

Elsa examined him with those tired eyes. Life had beaten her down more than a few times. "George will see to it that you have a bed for the evening," Elsa indicated the large man standing watch outside the door. "We'll talk in the morning."

And with that, Elsa turned away and moved to the empty chair in front of the fire, picking up a tangle of wool. Dismissed, he knew that much. George waited at the door. Giving a timid wave of thanks, Kelvin stepped out into the cold night before his body had a chance to warm. This was especially cruel.

The pair of men were silent as they made their way to a much smaller house across the courtyard. Six mats, four of them currently occupied by sleeping men, were spread across the small interior. It looked like a tiny barracks. George pointed at an empty mat next to the front door before moving to his own. Without a single word, he stripped off his shoes and the rest of his clothes. Kelvin settled himself in, trying not to watch George standing there in outdated long underwear. But George was going to be warm tonight and that mattered more than how ridiculous he appeared. Even in the small confines of this house filled with grown men and their body heat, the air held a menacing chill. George's outfit might look like something out of a Mormon nightmare, but Kelvin bet it helped him sleep through nights like this.

Still, he was forced to stifle a smirk.

***

A few hours of poor sleep later, Kelvin woke. The cold winter weather coupled with the shack's shoddy insulation made the evening uncomfortable at the best of times. The single wool blanket they gave him didn't hinder the constant creep of cold. The only heat was the heat his body created by shivering all night. In the morning, Kelvin woke feeling like a gang of red-tailed chipmunks had given him a violent pillow party throughout the night.

He bolted upright when he noticed he was alone, and for a second, he wondered if it had all been a dream. His

211

unfamiliar surroundings reminded him that it wasn't. At least he'd survived the nightmare of the cold.

Noise drifted in from outside, signs of life and labor. Kelvin folded the wool blanket and set it at the end of the mat. Everything hurt.

He opened the door to a sunny morning, wincing as the brightness stabbed at his eyes and the immediate chill that gripped his bones. Sun bounced off billions of snow crystals covering the village courtyard. He panicked, wondering what the snow depth meant for the possibilities of getting his car out. Maybe he could use George's truck to get it free? The man was quiet, but he had been helpful last night. So maybe he'd be willing to help Kelvin out of his desperate situation with the car?

Men, at least eleven that he could see, milled around the open area. Some sawed or chopped wood, others worked on repairs or improvements on some of the homes. Metal clanking on metal rang out from underneath the large overhang. A pair of young girls, no more than eight, dressed in long dresses complete with wool hats and gloves, giggled as they raced in front of the small house, throwing snow at each other. How were they not frozen?

It was nice to hear the laughter of children. As strange as this village was, at least it felt normal and he didn't feel so desperate. George was nowhere.

A small boy in ragged clothes ran up to him, offering a thin-lipped smile.

"Good morning," Kelvin said.

The boy tugged at the bottom of Kelvin's jacket and then raced up away, waving for Kelvin to join him. He followed.

The boy raced across the courtyard in the direction of a large fire pit, spanning at least 20 feet across. Picnic tables, broad and rough, encircled it. A thick column of faint white drifted into the air above. Children filled the benches, accompanied by the occasional man spotted in between. Probably to keep peace amongst the boys and giggling girls.

The boy ran back to Kelvin, wearing that same smile, and grabbed his hand, pulling him toward the fire. He didn't resist, even from this distance the heat cast off by the fire welcomed him. Plus, the smell of roasting meat made Kelvin's mouth water.

As they neared a picnic table the boy gestured for Kelvin to sit. He did.

"Good morning," Kelvin said to the gaggle of boys and girls seated at the table. The boys didn't respond, and the girls giggled, some of them whispering in the ears of others. Strange children in a strange village.

But these children were the last thing on his mind. The thin-lipped boy set a plate, piled high with bacon and potatoes, in front of him. Kelvin's mouth watered taking in the sight. He'd never seen such thick slabs of bacon. He wasn't sure he'd even be able to bite through it. Distraction from the trauma of the previous night ebbed away. Kelvin was ravenous, the night's drama forgotten. The potatoes were firm, requiring Kelvin to use his molars to break them down. He didn't care. There was a sharp seasoning. Sage? And the bacon? When was bacon not good? Sitting outside at a picnic table filled with weird kids, eating a heavy breakfast off a plate that wore its battle scars proudly, Kelvin couldn't remember a better dining experience. Was this what desperation did? Changed your view about everything?

Kelvin couldn't help himself. He ate second and third helpings. The girls giggled each time he asked for a little more. The men at the other tables watched him. It was odd that none of them had come to greet him, but he wasn't shocked. A stranger, a *black* stranger, invading their remote home wasn't going to get the red carpet treatment.

Not surprised. Disappointed.

But none of that mattered. As soon as George could help him get his car out he'd leave these strange people and their village behind with a promise to immediately forget about it the minute he reached the civilized world.

"Are you feeling better?" A raspy, female voice asked. Kelvin turned around to see Elsa standing with her arms folded across her chest.

"Yes, yes I am," he said, brushing food from his lap and standing out of respect.

Elsa said nothing but gave a quick nod. Even if these men couldn't show him decency, he could still give it. If nothing else, he could serve as a model for these children.

The girls at his table giggled again and Elsa shot them a sharp glance, immediately silencing them. "My apologies for the children, they can be rambunctious at times," she said.

These were some of the most well-behaved children he'd ever seen in his life. "Oh, they're no worry at all. They've been great," he said in half-apology, hoping he wasn't responsible for giving Elsa the impression the children bothered him.

"Be that as it may, we expect more out of them," Elsa answered. She dropped her arms to her side. "Come. Love and Dodi wish to hold counsel. Before we do, we'd like to speak with you."

"Okay," Kelvin stammered, dropping in behind Elsa as she made her way through a trough carved in the deep snow.

They didn't speak as they crossed the courtyard, passing dozens of men working themselves into a sweat even in this cold world. Children raced here and there, the girls playing all sorts of imaginary games. A good number of boys of all ages assisted the village's men with various tasks.

As if reading his thoughts, Elsa spoke over her shoulder. "We're a small village, quite a ways from other towns. So we depend on the skills of the community to survive. We have to. I'm sure you've noticed that. We teach them young."

"It must be difficult."

"What?"

Kelvin looked around. "Surviving out here. So far away from everything."

"We like it."

"I'm sorry, I didn't mean—"

Elsa ascended the steps of the large house. "Most people would never understand why we do what we do. But most people couldn't survive out here either. We're not interested in their opinions." With that, she stepped inside. Kelvin followed.

Love and Dodi sat at the kitchen table. "Close the door behind you," Elsa ordered over her shoulder.

"Come, sit," Love patted the chair next to her. In the daylight, her resemblance to Elsa was even more striking. She was striking. By far the more beautiful of the three. He'd been wrong, Kelvin realized; the shades of exhaustion didn't dampen her skin as it had the other two women.

Dodi also now looked like true blood to Elsa, but far shy of Love's attractiveness. Two of them got the short end of the genetic stick. Dodi watched him with an unwavering stare.

Kelvin smiled as he sat. Something told him that these women were who saved him last night. Without their approval, he would be the blackest snowman this part of the world had ever seen. "Thank you again for what you did for me. I don't think I would've made it if you hadn't been so kind."

"You wouldn't have," Dodi shook her head. "Storm would've taken you in the night, for sure as we sit here."

"This part of the world can be challenging," Elsa said. Kelvin didn't have time to translate her cryptic statement. "We don't usually open our home to outsiders. I hope you appreciate what we've done for you."

Kelvin nodded. "I do. I do. I'm extremely grateful."

"Good," came Dodi's curt response. "What we've done, we've done from the goodness of our hearts, as our Lord would have us do."

"We're God-fearing people," Love's soft voice fluttered into the conversation. "All we do, we do in His name. There are no strangers in Christ."

"You will respect that," Elsa leaned forward on an elbow. "This is our home. We provide shelter, structure, and love for the community and we won't risk that." Kelvin wasn't sure what she was implying. The last thing he wanted from this situation was to be seen as a troublemaker. He wanted to get as far away from these hill people as he could, as soon as he could.

"I get that," he replied, hoping that would satiate the women. Was this a squeeze play for money? But what would a community like this need money for?

"Men can be fickle about what they choose to understand," Dodi leaned back in her chair, arms crossed.

"Full of empty promises," Love sighed.

"Thinking they can charm you into capitulation," Elsa sneered.

In an instant, the conversation darkened. Kelvin was confused. Had he done something to offend them? What could he have said? He'd just joined them at their request.

Before he could defend his entire gender, Dodi leaned forward, thrusting a finger at him. "We won't allow you to bring sin into our home," she accused him.

Kelvin leaned backward out of instinct, the urge to defend himself biting at his conscience. "Well, I don't know what—"

"We haven't asked for your counsel," Love's soft voice held a steely edge even as her eyes flirted. "When we do, you'll know."

"Until then, you remain silent. You listen. When you listen, you'll learn," Dodi barked.

Elsa reached over and patted the woman's hand.

"Learn what?" The question was out. Kelvin wasn't trying to be antagonistic, but he also had no idea what was happening here.

"God's will," Love stated, the corner of her mouth sneaked upward in a half-smile. Kelvin caught her gaze moving to his chest.

He was about to respond when the distinct sounds of an approaching engine stopped him. The weirdness of this conversation had him on edge, but the familiar sounds of civilization raised his spirit in an instant. Someone had found their way into the village. Whoever they were, they could give him a ride back to his car and maybe get him unstuck. He wouldn't need help from George or this weird clique. He would take a ride into the next town if that was all this new arrival could offer.

Still, no reason to fan the flames. Kelvin stood. "Look, I'm sorry if I offended you. I don't mean to be a bother and I definitely don't mean to disrespect any of you or your beliefs, so I'll see myself out."

He hadn't taken two steps before Elsa spoke. "And where do you think you'll go?"

The comfortable cockiness in her words flared his anger. Kelvin spun. He'd been patient enough, but this was undeserving. White people routinely treated him like an inconvenience, like garbage. He didn't deserve this. "I'm leaving. I'll head into town."

"And how will you get there?" Elsa teased.

Kelvin cocked a thumb at the front door. "I'll get a ride from whoever pulled up."

The three women at the table smiled.

"You'll be disappointed," Elsa smirked.

Kelvin squashed the urged to slap that expression from her face. He wasn't that kind of man, no matter how tempting it was. "What are you talking about?"

Dodi flicked her wrist at him. "Go look."

Kelvin did. They were too confident. Something was wrong. He needed time to process this and think of a way out if salvation hadn't come in the form of a visitor. Then he saw it. It wasn't a stranger or new arrival. It was George, in his truck, towing Kelvin's wrecked car. The entire front end was smashed as if something heavy had been dropped on it. The front tires were gone, fully exposing the bent rims. Someone punched out the windows too.

Something—rage?—stirred in his gut.

"What the fuck?"

"Sinner!" Dodi snapped.

Love whimpered.

"What happened to my car? What the fuck is going on here?" Spittle flew from his lips.

Elsa and Dodi shared a look. "The rage of man is his greatest weakness," Dodi said, her voice dropping the temperature of the large room even as it flamed his temper.

"In his belly rages the fire of hell," Love shook her head.

Elsa stood, smoothing her heavy slacks, which looked identical to the pair he'd seen on the boy earlier. The same as all the children wore. And all three women. Everyone dressed in those same heavy, wool slacks. How had he only noticed this now?

Kelvin stepped back, ignoring the sudden shaking in his legs. This village wasn't just isolated, it was a completely different world. He wondered if these people had even seen the outside world. That would explain the silent treatment he got from almost everyone. It wasn't lost on him that the only people who'd spoken to him since his arrival last night where these three women.

A vehicle door banged, followed by thick footsteps on the stairs. George had arrived.

The door creaked open and the monster-man filled the opening. "Thank you, George," Elsa said with a warmth that bordered on intimacy while her icy gaze mocked Kelvin. "You won't be needing your car."

Fire burned inside him. Fury. His throat tightened with tension and boiling rancor. His arms shook with the fire of a man shoved too many times by the world. "The hell I don't. I don't know what kind of sick game you all are playing, but I'm not hanging around for it. I needed your help. And this is how you treat people in need? This is some sick shit."

Love giggled, receiving a swift slap on the hand from Dodi. Then she covered her mouth behind the reddening hand.

Elsa didn't seem to notice. "You will be staying. You are our guest. Plus," she swept her arm in a half circle, gesturing toward the world outside the house, "we need help around here."

"We need a man like you," Love giggled again, twirling a loose strand of hair around a finger before shooting a quick glance at Dodi. The other woman returned it with a stoic glare.

Kelvin backed away a step. Stress made moving his shaking joints difficult. His throat constricted. Tightened. Itched. Could he take on George? The monstrosity blocked the door, but his size meant he would be slow. If Kelvin could get George to move into open space he would be able to evade those gargantuan hands and give himself a fighting chance.

But then what? How far could he run? There was nothing but mile after mile of winter horror land separating him from the civilized world. Plus, they had at least two vehicles, one of which could make it through the snow with ease. They could run him down before he got a couple hundred yards.

What other choice did he have?

"In time, sister," Elsa turned to Love, responding to the woman's salacious comment.

"I'm ... not ... staying," Kelvin croaked. The scratching in his throat now burned. Without a thought, he reached for the small divot underneath his Adam's apple but yanked his hand away when he became aware that the three women recognized what he was doing. Why were they watching him as if they were tracking his actions? Something was wrong. It hurt to swallow. "What ... did ... you ..."

Love wrung her hands. Elsa stepped closer. Not a threatening gesture; a domineering one. The movements of someone in full control. "The mercury won't take full effect for a little while," Elsa smiled, clasping her hands in front of her.

Kelvin panicked. Was she saying what he thought she was?

Love closed the space between them, running a hand down his trembling arm. She examined him as she stroked him. "A fine man," she said in a dreamy voice. "A fine, fine man. Even if he is a little nervous."

It wasn't nerves. He couldn't control the tremors. His stomach knotted.

"He'll serve," Dodi said from the table.

"You ... poisoned ... me?" It was a struggle to voice such a simple sentence. He winced, his throat scorched from the contamination. The world lost focus as his eyes watered. Excruciating.

"What else were we to do?" Elsa asked. But she smirked, like a person who had gotten the better of a life-long adversary. "If we didn't strip you of your voice you'd still have one. We can't have that."

The world swam. Kelvin reached out for something to sturdy himself on and missed, collapsing onto the floor. The impact stung but he couldn't even move to ball himself up in comfort. A chair scraped as Dodi finally pushed away from the table and made her way to stand by her sisters. The three women hovered over him. Dodi's expression was ice cold, uncaring. Love's, one of infatuation and passion. And Elsa? Total control.

"He'll serve nicely," Dodi repeated in a voice so flat she could have been describing the meal she was planning for the evening.

"He will," Elsa agreed.

Kelvin grabbed at his throat, tore at it. Breath refused to come. But Kelvin fought back, forcing out the single word. "Why?"

"George, we'll need to sanitize his throat before the mercury wears off," Dodi directed.

The giant nodded.

The three women looked down with pity as George closed in, hoisting Kelvin into the air. His arms and legs didn't cooperate; he couldn't fight back.

The poison. Had they done this to all the men in the village? Was that why none of them said a word to him? The men and the boys alike, each of them as silent as the other. It came together in a sudden flash. The silent men. The quiet boys. The thin-lipped one who took him to breakfast. All as silent as a cold winter day. In all his interactions, only the women and the girls vocalized anything. His mind went back to the boys playing, as silent as a cold, winter day.

How do they get away with it? Where were the other adults, the other mothers? Why hadn't they intervened on behalf of the children, at least? Kelvin opened his mouth to take large gasps of breath.

Dodi shrugged. "This is paradise. Our utopia. You were always meant to serve us."

"Eve's Trinity," Love bounced.

But Elsa took her time. She laid a hand on George's arm just as she had to Kelvin only minutes before. Her other hand ran the course of Kelvin's legs, up past his groin, over it, finally lingering on his chest. The heat in her eyes burned as much as his throat did from the poison they'd served him. Her eyes consumed his body as she spoke. "For 2,000 years men have silenced women. But it's us who are the life givers. Without us, there would be no master race. And for 2,000 years men have demonized us. Blamed, for the fall of man."

"Wicked men," Dodi snapped.

Elsa continued on as if she didn't hear the interruption. Her hands rubbed his stomach, went up under his shirt. "What you see out there is the way the world is meant to be run. We don't have war. We don't have strife. We don't have violence."

Dodi moved forward, rubbing Kelvin's inner thigh. "Here we have peace that only a sisterhood can create."

Love bounced by his head now, lightly tracing the lines of his face with the back of a single finger. "We three, Eve's Trinity, have created this world so that all can rejoice."

Kelvin tried to speak but his throat cracked, he gasped for air.

Love bent down and kissed his forehead. Elsa rested her hand in the middle of his chest. Dodi ran her hand over his cock, lightly at first, firmer as he grew erect against his own desires.

Love's eyes wet even as Kelvin's began to cry. "It will hurt for a while," her mouth turned down as she ran a light thumb over his lips. "And it will pass in time like all things do."

"Well, after we burn your vocal chords, of course," Elsa corrected. "You'll need to sleep."

"Rest," Dodi and Love recited in unison.

Elsa nodded. "Yes, rest. But then you'll join us here, in our community, our homes and—"

"And our beds," Love covered her giggle before bending down to steal another intimate moment.

Dodi rubbed him. "You'll father a nice stock."

221

Elsa was close now, her lips brushing his ears. "When the pain passes you'll see that we can offer you something no one and nothing in the world can. A world of balance, peace, and harmony. Where you are rewarded for hard work, not penalized. Where women, the three of us, determine the course and fate of the people."

"You and the children you'll father will be part of correcting mankind's transgressions ever since he poisoned the word of the Lord," Dodi said with an acidic voice that contradicted the affectionate way she touched him.

That was why there were no other women. These three, this Eve's Trinity, were the mothers of the village, the wives to all those men. One polyandric family. George's hold never wavered. The man was not only a monster, he had the stamina of an ox. Kelvin wondered how many of those children playing in the courtyard were George's.

"Imagine it," Elsa's tongue reached out, glancing his earlobe. "A life where you have everything you need. Women who will love you, children who will adore you, and men who will support you without envy. No greed or lust. No need for money, politics, or any of the ugliness the rest of the world demanded before God delivered you."

"Just the love of the Lord and the enrichment of His bounty," Love leaned over his face, lowering her mouth to his, kissing him. Her tongue thrust deep into him.

Kelvin's body locked in protest and the ravages of the poison they fed him at breakfast. He couldn't stop this violation of his body or his will. Here, in this village in the valley, he was the weaker gender. Here he would have no say. The poison, alone, didn't suffocate him. The promise of lost autonomy was a harbinger of doom even as these three women hovered over him like insatiable carnivores. Elsa rubbed his chest roughly now, up and down, left and right, circular. Gripping. Pinching. Love's tongue invaded the deepest reaches of his mouth, pressed into him again. Cold air assaulted him as Dodi had unzipped his pants and wrapped strong fingers around his throbbing penis.

"The valley is your home now. You'll never leave," Elsa bit his earlobe. For the first time since the poison began to take effect, Kelvin's body reacted. He jerked, a shocked reaction at the sudden pain.

Love slapped him, hard.

Dodi gripped him, squeezing his testicles, threatening to crush them.

Kelvin opened his mouth to scream. Silence.

"He's weak," Dodi seemed disappointed. "We need to test him."

Elsa backed away, examining him for a few seconds before nodding.

Love looked worried. "He won't break, will he?"

"We will have to see," Elsa's firm voice had returned, all the heated intimacy she'd displayed was gone in a wisp. She looked at George. "Take him to the breeding bed. If he survives we'll commence with purifying his throat."

Dodi nodded.

Love bounced on her feet and clapped her hands.

George, for his part, turned in silent compliance and carried Kelvin away to father his fate.

END

Sign up for Paul Sating's newsletter to follow all the news about upcoming novels, like "RIP," and "The Scales." You can also find more information about his audio dramas (fictional podcasts), like his thrillers, *Subject: Found* and *Who Killed Julie?*, his horror, *Diary of a Madman*, or his nonfiction podcast for writers, *Horrible Writing*, by heading over to http://www.paulsating.com.

For even more stories, become a Patron. By supporting Paul Sating's fiction on Patreon, you will have exclusive access to even more horror, dystopia, drama, and fantasy. Go to https://www.patreon.com/paulsating, pick a pledge/reward level that works for you, and start enjoying exclusive fiction each month!

If you enjoyed this book, I would really appreciate getting a review from you.

Reviews not only help other readers find something they might like, but they help me as an author. Your reviews are important to me because they allow me to see what readers like you enjoyed about the book and what I could have done better.

Thank you to each and every one of you who takes the time to leave a review!

Also By Paul Sating

Fiction

Chasing the Demon
The Plant

Nonfiction (Coming, Fall 2018)

Novel Idea to Podcast, How to Sell Books Through Podcasting

About The Author

Paul Sating is an author, audio dramatist, and self-professed coolest dad on the planet, hailing from the Pacific Northwest of the United States. At the end of his military career, he decided to reconnect with his first love (that wouldn't get him in trouble with his wife) and once again picked up the pen. Four years on, he has numerous novels published (or in the works) and hundreds of thousands of downloads of his fiction & nonfiction podcasts.

When he's not working on stories, you can find him talking to himself in his backyard working on failed landscaping projects or hiking around the gorgeous Olympic Peninsula. He is married to the patient and wonderful, Madeline & has two daughters—thus the reason for his follicle challenges.

Acknowledgments

This book was an idea I came up with while decorating our Christmas tree during Thanksgiving weekend in 2017. It started as a game. We have a tradition of playing old Christmas carols while we decorate and, this night, we were being silly, seeing who could come up with the funniest alternative name for each song. Of course, I took the game down a dark avenue, naming the songs with the most horrific titles I could extemporaneously come up with. That was a moment of inspiration and this concept was born. I realized there were enough potential titles to make a horror anthology and I had a year to write one. So it was done. That night, I began outlining the potential titles and story ideas.

Funny how and where inspiration can strike, isn't it?

12 Deaths of Christmas was written in a month and though some of the story titles do give away what is going to happen, for me it was such an enjoyable ride to jump into full-blown horror, complete with monsters of the human and supernatural variety. Honestly, it's been a long time since I've played around in that type of arena and it felt good and helped, I believe, the concept I had for season three of my *Subject: Found* audio drama podcast, which is far more supernatural than the previous two seasons.

I hope you enjoyed reading it as much as I did (or more, honestly) writing it.

This first anthology couldn't have happened without some very special people.

First and foremost, my incredible wife, Madeline, for constantly supporting me and being the best beta reader any writer can ask for. You sacrifice so that the rest of the world doesn't have to slog through garbage stories. Everyone should be grateful, because my early stories are ... an interesting read. Thank you for loving me so much that you read horror—a genre, I know, you wouldn't be sad to see disappear into the annals of human history.

My daughters, Alex and Nikki. We don't get to have Christmas together like we used to, and I miss the 'task' of decorating the tree together. Those nights were always special for me and I'll cherish them forever. This was our last one with Alex, and it's a curious thought to know that a book was born out of silly game during such a significant personal event. Maybe this could be a new tradition, no matter where we are in the world? Hmmmm.

Everyone needs a champion and Kevin Baker is that for me. Writers can be self-deprecating bastards, and I know I'm at the front of that line. But sometimes subtle comments and thoughts tip the balance and we do worse for ourselves than some not-so-good-natured ribbing. Kevin, you've always had impeccable timing with your uplifting comments, saying the right thing, at the right time, to pull my brain back into focus and simply believe in myself again.

Eric Thomas & Jason Evilive, for stepping up to help me adjust these stories well before anyone else saw them, and for helping me make sure that my inner-Clive wasn't taking over. Reading the early versions of these stories couldn't have been easy, especially when I dumped three of them on you in a week. True warriors, the both of you. Your feedback encouraged me to throw myself into this project with abandon.

To my Patrons. Without your constant support I couldn't have done what I did. I wouldn't have believed that people wanted to hear the stories I had to share had you not been there, month after month, sending encouraging messages, getting excited about what I was excited about, and providing the support I needed to be able to do this in the first place. To, Kevin Baker, Elsa Howarth, Sylvia Lynn, Alaina Malack, Dohai, PB Sebastien, James Hill, Ian Troman-Mason, Morgan Barber, Adam Burke, Shelley Perrin, Greg Bowman, Brent Moody, Dan Foytik, Cynthia Waddill, Sandy Smith, Jon Grilz, Genesis Murray, Zane Desjarlais, Glen Collins, Nate Bonilla-Warford, Brian James, Matteo Masiello, Philip Flynt, E. Kirkensgaard, Erin Karper, A. Dragon, Robert Chauncey, Anthony Dallape, Patrick Monroe, Sarah Rhea Werner, Ryan

Beyer, Desdymona, Stacey Holbrook, Tim Niederriter, Cheyenne Bramwell, Raymond Camper, Roseann White, and George Greene. Thank you for your never-ceasing, always-awesome support!

To Mom. Life is a path best explored with the people we love. We may have stubbed our toes on a rock or tripped over a tree root, but we continued walking it together.

To all of the wonderful people who took time out of life to help me proofread the book. I'm never as good as I am until you kindest people on the planet. Thank you for everything give so much of your time. You are some of the you do! Adam Burke, Cheyenne Bramwell, Mel Baxter, Kevin Rowland, Bob Tinsley, Pam Giltner, Stephanie Mikkelsen, Brent Moody, Ann Steward, and Natalie Aked.

And, of course, to the hundreds of thousands of you who have listened to one of my audio dramas. To date, I've released over 100 episodes of fiction podcasts. You've been a part of the growth my author career.

Thank you to each and every one of you, for what you've done, in your own way, to help me find the self-belief I needed to get past the monster of doubt. These holiday horror stories might not exist if it weren't for you and what you've done for me. Thank you!

Chasing the Demon
(Available now)
(Chapter 1)

The stench of old wood and unwashed people didn't surprise Jared Strong.

Stale beer, peanuts, and people. A lot of the hole-in-the-wall type bars in this western corner of the Olympic Peninsula, his home, smelled like this. His current drinking hole of choice was no different, no better. He smothered a handful of nuts between his palm and fingers, squeezing until he heard the satisfying crack of the shells. Picking out the nuts, he tossed them into his mouth, discarding the shells on the floor. It wasn't something he would do at home, especially not when he and Maria were still together. But, in fairness, this place didn't look like anyone had loved it for at least a generation.

That observation made him wonder how much time had passed since Maria had loved him.

Maria.

Best not to think about her right now. There were other problems he needed to face first. Like the reason for the stack of papers sitting in front of him on the sticky bar top.

This was Olympia, the capital of the state. The gem, right? He laughed to himself, glancing down at the shell-covered floor underneath him. What a dump. He shook his head at how quickly his life had gone off track.

"Great place to start chasing a demon," he mumbled to the stack of papers. They didn't answer.

The drunk seated next to him sneered. "Whatch'da say?"

"Huh?" Jared asked, "Uh, nothing. Sorry. Didn't mean to bother you."

"You ain't no bother," the man said, then returned to his beer.

Jared laughed. "Let me know if that changes, will ya?" God knows I've already done that to enough people in my life.

The old man's eyes narrowed as if he was examining Jared's soul. Awkward and uncomfortable, Jared put his attention on the papers, an idle finger tracing their edges.

The drunk squinted at him and laughed, coughing up things that came from deep within his lungs. "Whatcha lookin' at there?"

Nothing. The instinct to protect the knowledge on those pages was strong. It had to be. It was something all hunters of his kind developed early. If they didn't, they didn't stay in the game long. Jared had seen enough of them come and go in his twenty-plus years in the game. He knew what to do and how to do it. And when you hunted the things he did you learned to be careful. "These?" Jared tapped the pile of notes with his finger, looking at them instead of the drunk, "These are my life's work. Child's play to some, but to me ... well, to me they're everything I have."

"Mind if I ask what they're about?"

He smiled absently. "I track wild game, I guess you could say, and these," his fingers wrapped around the stack, feeling the texture, an intimate connection, "these are some of the most important things I've spent my adult life on." There was a time when he cared enough to have the notes bound and protected. But they had come loose during all those lost days since his life was turned upside down, becoming nothing more than a frayed and fragile system of knowledge.

"Wild game, you say?" the man leaned toward him like there was an unspoken secret they shared. "Olympics or Cascades?"

Everywhere. "Olympics mostly. I love the peninsula. Spend a lot of time out there."

The drunk nodded as though satisfied. "There's worse places to be if you ask me. Used to do some hunting myself. Stopped when I couldn't get around so easily. Now? Spend most of my days in this dump, drinking away the last of my brain." The bartender scowled from his spot a few feet away, where he busied himself cleaning a few dirty glasses. The old man tipped his glass in the bar keep's direction. "Oh, come now, Jack, you know I love your fine establishment. Just making conversation with ... whatcha say yer name was?"

"I didn't, but it's Jared."

"I'd shake your hand but ... well, you don't want to know where it's been today, ain't that right, Jack?" The drunk laugh-coughed again. It sounded like water gurgling out from a pipe. Jared wondered how long this man had to live. Would he finish the investigation before this poor soul saw out what was left of his life? Jared wasn't betting on it. "Anyways, nice to meet you, Jared. So, you on your way out to the Olympics for the weekend?"

Jared nodded. "Something like that. I go out for a few days at a time."

"Whatcha do that for?"

What did he do it for? There was nothing to come home to now, not anymore. What was there to stop him from just staying out for a week or two, or until his supplies ran out? It was something he'd never thought about — not until now, and now it seemed so simple. He laughed, "You know, I don't have a good answer. Habit, I guess? Used to come back every few days when I was married but I don't have that obligation now. Just have a dog at home."

The drunk leaned toward his beer as if he was trying to smell it. Jared guessed it was a ploy to distract, that maybe the man had demons of his own — maybe an unfortunate ex-wife story, maybe something worse that hit too close to the heart. "Some of those habits are hard to break, my friend," he finally said when he spoke again. "Don't mind me if I'm prying too much into your life, but I'm imagining she didn't want to be waiting for you any more than she already was? Prolly supported you the best she could until she couldn't any longer? Somethin' like that?"

Something like that. Now it was Jared's turn to look away.

"Well, listen to me, going on and getting in your business," he said. "My apologies. You look like a nice young man. Life's going to throw you enough stress, don't be letting me add to it. Got to ask. Ain't deer season. Never seen a duck hunter, hell, any hunter, collect notes like you got there. Whatcha after?"

Jared's dead eyes never left his notes even as he replied, "a monster."

Published by Paul Sating Productions
P.O. Box 15166
Tumwater, WA 98511
paulsatingproductions@gmail.com

Made in the USA
Las Vegas, NV
27 November 2023

81618411R00142